BAIT

B.A.D. INC BOOK #3

ANGEL DEVLIN
TRACY LORRAINE

BAIT DEFINITION

BAIT
Definition

1.   Put on a hook or in a trap to entice.

2.   Deliberately annoy or taunt (someone).

Once upon a time the fucked-up world claimed a new victim. The only way to survive was to fight back. But the past has a nasty habit of not staying there, and sometimes the good guys have to go B.A.D.
- Anthony Warren.

CHAPTER ONE

Lola

Those hours are forever burned into my brain.

A living nightmare I'll never wake up from.

The worst thing is I can't tell a soul. Because my sister and my mother would die inside if they knew the truth about the hours when I was missing.

Instead, I'll try to put one foot in front of the other each day. Try to go one step further towards living my life. But nightmares threaten to drag me back under as they remind me of my kidnapping and the events that followed.

It's ridiculous, but the man I now know as Ant rescued me from that situation and he rescues me from my nightmares sometimes, bursting into my dreams and taking me away.

But there's no one in real life that can do that.

So I'll wear a mask that looks like I'm doing okay, while inside I'm living in pain.

I have too much time on my hands and my mind likes to fill the empty time by replaying everything over and over. I'm trying to read a book, trying to relax enough to fall asleep, but I'm wasting my time. The only thing that helps me sleep these days is sheer exhaustion and help from alcohol and spliffs.

"Keep in touch!" I shouted at my friend, Kenzie, as I made my way out of uni. We'd just sat our final accountancy exam. I was a free woman. Well, until the results came in, where I'd hopefully passed and could then apply for jobs.

"Yeah, you too, Jade." She shouted back. "Fingers crossed we pass."

Jade.

The fake name I'd now been known as for several years. My mum and I had left our home in New York and moved back to London where she was from when I was younger because of problems with my dad. He was a bastard and when he'd found out my sister, Anna, wasn't his after she had an accident, it wasn't safe for us to stick around NYC. Anna worked for him and despite her not being his biological daughter, she stayed.

I might have been young, but I wasn't stupid. If we'd

had to leave and come to London, then him keeping Anna couldn't have meant anything good.

When she escaped herself, and we all moved in together, she told us he'd used her in frauding businesses. My mother was horrified, but as I looked at the expressions that passed between them, I knew that somehow there'd been an agreement that Anna would stay in NYC to keep me safe. I knew that the dark shadows that lived behind Anna's face were borne of more than fraud, and I wondered exactly what she'd endured for my survival.

I was about to get a clue.

We didn't live in the best area in London. Trying to hide from Thomas De Loughrey meant dark corners and less than salubrious surroundings. And it was from a dark corner that two men came from behind me and bundled me into a car.

I never even got a chance to scream into the streets.

A hand around my mouth, and the shock of being tipped backwards. Thrown into the back seat and away, before I had time to make the noise that might have saved me from what came next. But as my mouth opened and I finally made the sound, I saw who was driving the car.

My father.

And I knew that screaming was a complete waste of time.

The man I called my father is dead. The man who could be my father is dead.

The answer to the question was destroyed in the clean-up operation, but would it make any difference to me anyway?

Once I was Lola De Loughrey. Once I was Jade Hawley. Now I don't know who the fuck I am. My mother fusses around me, glad all her secrets are revealed. My sister confesses what my father did to her. Somehow, I'm supposed to forgive them because they suffered too.

Now my sister is married and pregnant. Mrs. Tyler Ward. She's drawn a line under having ever been Lucia De Loughrey and kept the name Anna. She's happy. She wants me to be happy too, so in the morning I have an interview. As an intern for the accounts department at B.A.D. Inc.

I'll be working with Anthony Warren.

The only person in the world I might be able to trust, is the person who rescued me from that room that day and who cared for me. The one who rescues me from my nightmares.

Anthony Warren will be my new boss.

And I want to get the job.

Not only because it can hopefully occupy my mind and distract me from my fucked-up memories, but because I know when I'm near him I'll feel safe.

Dark-haired, brooding Anthony Warren picked me up like I weighed the same as a dandelion seed floating in the air and reassured me, as he carried me naked and shaking and took me to help, that everything would be all right.

Perhaps I have some kind of messed-up hero worship going on, but I don't think so. I'd like to think I just recognise a good man when I see one. God knows, I've experienced enough of the bad ones.

Finally, with thoughts of Anthony in my mind, my eyes close until my phone alarm wakes me a few hours later.

I make it down my first cup of coffee before my sister is on the phone to me nagging. "Are you ready yet?"

Double checking the clock, I see that there's well over an hour until my interview. "I need to get dressed, but stop flapping, there's loads of time."

"What if there's traffic? We need to get there early so he knows you're there. It shows willing."

I sigh. "It's your husband's company. Ty would get me a job there somewhere if Ant doesn't want me."

"You can't rely on the family connection. Those guys don't work that way. Fuck them off and they'll fuck you over, believe me."

I roll my eyes to myself but forgo the second cup of coffee I was going to have, to go and get myself ready to set off. I dress in the suit Anna insisted on buying for me, a dark navy-blue; add a white blouse and a pair of kitten heels. I feel awkward. I've spent weeks in my pyjamas.

"Car's here." My mum shouts, and I realise I'm about to take a step back towards the real world.

We have drivers everywhere now. I'm used to just getting on a bus. This life is alien to me. Anna doesn't get that. She's fallen into this like she belongs here and she does. The business and the billionaire lifestyle. She wears it as comfortably as her Louboutins.

Well, she might now be Dolce and Gabbana, but I'm New Look and Primark.

As I look in the hallway mirror before I take a step outside, I know that while my outside looks shiny and put together, I'm an inner mess of epic proportions. But I'll do what I do best. Put one foot in front of the other and push my problems out of my mind. Forget the past, focus on the future. Forget those I left behind, forget what happened to me during my time with my daddy.

Tyler Ward has a nickname, 'The Fixer', but he can't fix me. I wouldn't let him. He and Anna are the perfect recipe for love and I'm like salt. Try and press me for my contents and I'd spill out and ruin everything.

Best to keep everything inside.

I'm in the car and on my way. I actually feel nervous and I don't know if it's the thought of having to actually work every day, to act like a normal person, or if it's just the fact of seeing Ant.

Anna's back on the phone to me. "So, you need to

get this on your own merit." Jesus, my sister can witter on. "You need to show him you have brains."

"Anna. Please, for pity's sake, can we talk about the honeymoon you're about to go on? You're making my nerves worse. If you carry on, I'll not be able to get out of the car."

"Sorry, sorry. I'm just trying to help."

"You can. Tell me more about your honeymoon so my nerves can die down a little."

She tells me about the luxury location where they're staying for a whole two weeks. It sounds blissful and I can't help but think it will be blissful for me too. Two weeks without her nagging at me.

Finally, I pull up and I walk through the building where security check why I'm here and then let me up in the lift to the reception where my sister is waiting for me. She rushes over and gives me a hug. Love looks good on her; she's glowing.

"Whoa, you look so good," she says, looking me over.

I raise a brow at her. Then again, every time she's seen me of late, I've been largely unwashed.

"Thank you. You really didn't need to do this, you know?"

"Oh, so you were applying for jobs yourself, were you?" she adds with sarcasm.

I don't meet her eyes. "I was getting there."

"Of course you were, but we'll consider this a head start, shall we?"

She rambles on about us going back in the lift to the

top floor where the Accounts Department resides, but I'm just taking in the luxury appearance of the B.A.D. building. I don't know what I expected, but Christ, this place is really something. Sleek and polished, and that's the staff as well as the building and furnishings.

I can see Anna is staring at me and she's biting her bottom lip. She's nervous for me. This is what I hate. I don't have the energy to constantly reassure her that I'm okay, especially when it would be a lie.

The lift opens and we exit. I follow Anna as she walks up to a couple of women, who again look the epitome of elegance. I feel myself sinking lower with every footstep and it's not due to the thick pile of luxury carpeting that forms part of the decor.

One of the women introduces herself as Rachel, Ant's assistant, and she tells us to go through. She's pretty and I can't help wonder how much she's assisted him with. I can feel myself instantly take a dislike to her because she might have fucked him.

We both come to a stop outside his door when Ant's voice booms through.

"You don't get to just turn up here like this."

I turn and look at Anna, my eyes widening in a 'what the fuck is kicking off here' kind of way. This is the sort of outburst we used to get on the streets Mum and I lived in before, not what I'd expect to hear in the polished, perfect B.A.D. building.

"Why? Don't you want me, Dad?"
Dad?

Anthony has a kid? Anna never mentioned that,

though why would she? She doesn't know I'm crushing on my saviour.

And then his 'kid' bursts through the door, and she's not much of a kid at all. Her appearance is shocking for more reasons though than just her age. She hurtles past but not before I've seen a tear-stained, drained face. Her dark hair is everywhere and she looks like she's been attacked. Her clothes are ripped. And while I think myself New Look, this girl is dressed like a hooker.

Oh my god. Is that it? Is she not his kid at all but a hooker and he's been playing out some bizarre daddy shit that just went wrong? Has my saviour turned out to be damned? Anna said the B.A.D. lot were fucked up, but this is more shades fucked up than the bruises on the girl.

"Ellie, get back here." Ant rushes to the door. His eyes rest on Anna and then me, like he forgot I was even coming. I feel crushed even though it's ridiculous. He clearly has shit going on.

"Fuck," he bellows, before dropping his head into his hands. He turns back to his office and almost slams the door in our faces.

CHAPTER TWO

Ant

I blow out a frustrated breath as a knock on my office door sounds out. I fucking told Rachel to hold all my calls and cancel my meetings. Who the fuck has she allowed through?

I'm not in the fucking mood for this. I haven't been in a good mood since *she* decided to walk back into my life like she fucking belonged there and threw my world into turmoil.

I was quite happy watching everyone else's drama unfold around me. I don't need any of my own.

I know the five of us are a bunch of fuck ups, but with everything going on in their lives, I was beginning to feel like the normal one, like I'd been able to leave my fucking nightmare in the past where it belongs. But then *she* had to show her fucking face and deliver a blow I was not expecting.

"What?" I bark, but before the word even falls from my lips, the door is opening. Whoever it is on the other side clearly decided they didn't feel they needed my permission to enter.

Mistake number one.

This is my fucking office and I'm the one that makes all the rules. Just like with any of my previous assistants or receptionists, things are either done my way, or you find yourself out on your arse with no working security pass to get back in.

The only person I intend on seeing today is Lola, Anna's sister. Anna convinced me to interview her for an intern position seeing as she's just graduated with an accountancy degree and is in need of a distraction from all the shit that went down.

I don't need a new intern, but I could hardly say no. Anna's one of us now. Our little unit of five fucked-up individuals seems to be growing faster than I know how to handle. First Deacon got himself whipped, and then Tyler by some fucking miracle bagged Anna. I'm still not sure how the lucky motherfucker went from demanding she suck my cock to putting a ring on it in a matter of weeks, but I guess that's love for you. Turns you into a motherfucking fool. The exact reason why my interactions with women are about as well planned as my business deals.

The guys say I'm a dictator. I just say I like things done properly. I like order and I like routine. Neither of which I had in my former years, which is why I crave them now that I'm the one in control.

My fingers grip the pen in frustration as whoever is on the other side of the door seems to take forever to step inside.

The second she appears, it snaps. The plastic splintering in my grip. Shards piercing my skin.

My heart races to the point my vision begins to blur. This can't be right. I can't be seeing who I really think I'm seeing.

No. No. No.

This is a joke. What *she* told me was all lies. It has to be. I can't accept it any other way.

"Get the fuck out of my office."

I keep my eyes on the girl, praying this is just another one of *her* sick jokes.

Her dark hair is a mess, her equally as dark eyes red-rimmed and tired. Her make-up is smudged all over her face, but that's not the most obvious thing about her. That would be the swelling, blood, and bruises that seem to cover every inch of her.

Her shirt is ripped, exposing her bra; and her fishnet tights are ruined, her skin grazed and bruised beneath.

Whatever she's been through today has not been enjoyable, of that I'm sure. But she has no place here. She has no place in my organised and streamlined life.

I've no reason to believe any of the words that come from *her* mouth, although I can't deny that the timings would probably be right. My stomach turns over at the thought.

I avoid thinking about that time of my life at all costs, but it's not all that easy when it keeps appearing in front of my face.

A bitter laugh falls from the girl as a sinister smile curls at her lips.

"Not until I get what I came for."

"You don't get to just turn up here like this," I bark. My fear about who she is and what she wants gets the better of me.

"Why? Don't you want me, Dad?"

Dad?

Fuck. Fuck. *Fuck.*

I stand, my palms resting on the desk as my lips purse.

Taking a step towards her, she jumps backs in fright and pulls the door open before running as fast as she can.

"Ellie, get back here," I bellow, not needing her running around the offices looking like a beaten up fucking call girl.

I storm through the door, praying that no one is out here to witness this, but to my horror, when I step outside my office, I find Anna staring at me with wide eyes, her lips parted in shock. Lola, her sister, stares off in the direction Ellie just ran.

This is not the ideal start to her interview.

"Fuck," I shout, dropping my head into my hands

and marching back into my room, slamming the door behind me.

I can't deal with this.

It was bad enough *she* showed up and started attempting to blackmail me. But for her to send the girl who's supposedly my daughter here, to my office. Christ

This is seriously fucked-up.

I walk straight to my liquor cabinet and pull out the bottle of whiskey sitting at the back that I'd been saving for a special occasion. I'm sure meeting your long-lost daughter again and having her look like a cheap, beaten fucking hooker classes as such, right?

I twist the top and forgoing the glasses sitting on the side, I lift the bottle to my lips.

The alcohol burns, but it's not a match to the pain radiating from my chest.

I gave my life—almost— for that little girl. I had no idea she was mine. No fucking reason to suspect— exactly as *she* planned it— and even when she told me 'the truth' I didn't believe her. I couldn't. How could I have fathered a child when... I shudder even thinking about it.

Everything about that time in my life is so wrong, so surreal, that even I have trouble believing that it really happened some days. That is until I wake in the middle of the night, covered in sweat and feeling exactly like I did back then.

My stomach turns over and for a second I think I'm

going to puke right there on my pristine ivory-coloured carpet.

Thankfully, the feeling subsides as my head continues to spin out of control.

I've got the bottle to my lips once again when the sound of my door opening hits my ears.

"Get the fuck out. I swear to fucking God I'll—"

My words are cut off when I find Lola closing the door behind me.

She looks different to the last time I saw her. For a start she's fully dressed and put together. Her long, raven-coloured hair falls in soft waves just below her chin. Flicked black eyeliner and coats of mascara make her grey eyes more defined. She appears older than she did that night I carried her from the dingy hotel room with her wrapped in nothing but a sheet.

Although she looks older, she's certainly not old enough to capture my attention. I prefer my women to be a little more... worldly, shall we say?

Lola is too young. Too innocent. Too much of a similar age to my newly discovered daughter.

My past resurfaces and my stomach turns over once again.

"A- are you okay?"

"Who said you could come in?" I bark, not happy about anyone seeing me like this, let alone a girl I was about to interview for a job.

"U- um... n- no one. Your assistant went with Anna a- after your..." she trails off. "Is she really your daughter?" she asks, but it's clear she regrets it the second the words are out of her mouth. Either that or she didn't mean to say them aloud. Her eyes go wide with shock and she swallows nervously.

"Fuck knows. I don't know what's the fucking truth anymore." I tip the bottle to my lips once more.

"Do you... um... think that's a good idea?"

"Who the fuck are you, the alcohol police? I'm not sure you're really in any position to judge my life right now," I spit. "The last thing I recall is that your life is the biggest shit show going."

She balks but despite her make-up, you can't miss the shadows she tries to hide under her eyes.

I feel like an arse for bringing up her own past, but she's witnessing something right now that I wouldn't even want my closest friends to see.

"You need to leave."

I take a step toward her in the hope I might look menacing enough that she'll back away. Most women— hell, a lot of men— do almost instantly when I turn on them. But unlike them, she holds her ground.

"No."

"N- no?" I stutter, amazed by the gall of this bitch.

"I came here for an interview. So I expect you to interview me," she sasses.

It's not really necessary, I'd already decided that I was giving her a job. I knew all I needed to know about Lola. At least, I thought I did until she decided to go up against me.

I take another step towards her, staring down at her with my jaw set and my shoulders squared.

I try to keep everything that she just witnessed from my mind, but the anger, the disbelief, and the overriding knowledge that everything *she* told me is true refuses to leave me.

"Can you follow instructions, Lola?"

"Yes. I'm good at following orders."

"Good." I take another step toward her. The sweet floral scent of her perfume hits my nose and my mouth waters. "Are you loyal? Trustworthy? Reliable?"

"I like to think so."

This time when I take a step toward her, she takes one back, only she doesn't realise that she's close to the door she closed, and she bumps up against it. An evil smile curls at my lips. She's not as confident as she thinks she is.

"So you can keep a secret?"

"I've got enough of my own," she says quickly but clearly regrets it. "Shit," she mutters.

I narrow my eyes at her wondering why she seems unable to keep her thoughts in her head. Is it me? Or is this a normal thing for little Lola? Her shock each time she admits something sure points to the former. It makes me wonder what other secrets I could get out of her.

I know she's not talked about that night. Anna has said a couple of times that she's concerned about her bottling it all up.

"Do I intimidate you, Lola?" I ask, changing tack.

She blinks at me for a moment, getting a little whiplash from my sudden change of subject.

"No. You can't hurt me."

"Is that what you really think?" There are only a few inches between us now and I can't deny that the feeling of her body heat seeping into my skin doesn't feel good.

Her eyes have darkened since I first locked on them and there's a blush of colour on her cheeks.

"You rescued me. You're not like them."

A menacing laugh falls from my lips. "Oh, Lola. That is where you are so very, very wrong." I lean in so I can whisper in her ear. Her body tenses before me and her gasp of shock is deafening in the otherwise silent office. "Everything inside these walls is bad; very, very bad. Do you think you belong here, Lola?"

She whimpers beneath me. She's putty in my hands right now. She's the ultimate distraction from my reality and I've no doubt she'd jump in with both feet should I lay a finger on her.

"Am I bad?" she asks, turning to look at me.

I pull back slightly. Our lips are only a whisper apart, our increased breaths mingling.

"I guess that's for you to find out."

CHAPTER THREE

Lola

He's inches away from me. In my personal space and looking down at me, his expression a mix of anger and... hunger? It's my dream fantasies come true and I slowly move myself nearer to him and close the space between us.

I touch my mouth to his. Just rest it against his lips. Because I know his anger is not directed at me. He's just a pan of boiling water threatening to run over the edge, and I know exactly how that feels. I can help him this time.

There's a pause and then his mouth takes mine hungrily. His hand is at the back of my hair, pulling me towards him.

I sink into his embrace and my mind is recording every movement of his skin, his body against mine, because this is no dream, this is reality. Right now,

Anthony Warren is devouring me and it's not in a sweet 'Knight in Shining Armour' dream rescue mission way, it's in a starving man way where I'm his next meal.

His hand pulls my blouse out of my skirt and he smooths his fingers up from my waistband to my bra. He grasps my breast and I gasp against his mouth. I can feel my panties dampening and he's only cupped my breast on the outside of the cup. I thrust my hips towards him. I'm needy. Oh so needy for his touch.

A loud knock on the door has us springing apart.

"Fuuck," he growls, looking at me in... horror? And then he's moving back towards me, trying to help me tuck my blouse back in.

"I can do it. Go see who's at the door." I hiss. I'm annoyed that this got thwarted. I want him. My core is desperate and I'm left craving more of his touch. What would have happened if someone hadn't come to the door?

My sister steps through into the office, completely oblivious to the awkwardness and heavy breathing of the current residents.

"She's gone. We tried to get her to come back, but she took off. Is she really your daughter, Ant?"

Ant scrubs a hand through his hair and then turns and swipes his whisky bottle. It flies off his desk. The glass hits the floor although it doesn't break, liquid falling everywhere. His papers rain down in a storm of A4.

"What do I do?" he yells in frustration to the air around him.

Anna grasps my arm. "I'm going to get Ty. Stay and make sure he's okay." I nod and she leaves the room.

I step towards Ant, my thoughts that of putting my arms around him to calm him, to help... save him like he saved me. Maybe we can save each other?

But when I step towards him, he takes a step away. His voice is a low growl. "I shouldn't have touched you, Lola. I'm so sorry."

I'm about to tell him that it's okay, that he can lose himself in me, but he carries on talking.

"The job is yours of course. If you still want it?"

Of course I want it. The general office is within his view when the blinds to his room are open. I'll be near the man who makes me feel safe and alive. And I'll have a job where I can forget my ordeal for a time but I might also have a chance at freedom. Of getting my own place. Because I need out, but I don't want to do so with a handout from my brother in law. I want to succeed on my own merit, to achieve something as Lola Hawley. I might not know who the fuck I am right now, my name indicative of the halfway place between my past identities, but I can travel a path to arrive somewhere where I feel I belong. That's what I hope anyway.

"Yes, I'd like the job." I accept. "Are you sure you don't want to re-interview me, when things are a little less... chaotic?"

His eyes meet mine and he lets the truth hit them, his guard down. "I don't think either of us does life without chaos. Do you?"

I do a huff come laugh. "Yeah, that's true enough. So, when do I start?"

"What about now? I'd already organised for one of my team to come show you around and get you settled in. We may as well go ahead as planned. No sense in us both being derailed by my unscheduled appointment this morning."

I take a deep inhale. "If you want to talk about it—"

"I don't. Though I'm sure the minute Ty crashes through this doorway he's going to demand answers. Anyway, you have enough secrets of your own, little Pandora."

"Pandora?"

He nods. "Yes, you keep all your secrets within you, but at some point, little Pandora, they'll all spill out, just like mine have this morning."

"I'm fine."

He moves closer and tilts my chin up with his fingertip. "Are you? Because you've yet to tell anyone, haven't you, what happened while you were captive?"

"There's nothing to tell. You saw me. I was just strapped to a chair in a hotel room."

His eyes explore my face as if he can read what happened from the goose bumps marking my skin, but he drops his finger from my chin. "I've spent my whole life guarding my own secrets, little P. Your lies don't wash with me. But I also understand not wanting to face them, to deal with them. Unfortunately, as you've seen this morning though, sometimes they come crashing into your life like a blown tyre on a motorway, threatening your very existence. So take care, little one."

"Stop calling me little." Really. That's all I have in my defence? Way to go, Lola. "I'm not some defenceless little girl. I'm a grown woman. And you know that because your fingers were trailing over my body not so long ago."

He hangs his head. "That was a mistake. I'm sorry. I shouldn't have done that. It's my defence mechanism to sink myself into a body instead of having to deal with shit. But you're way too young for me, Lola, too innocent. I take my women older, much older."

"And how's that worked out for you so far?" I get the courage to speak my mind when I'm around this man.

"It's worked out just fine," he says, walking away from me and moving behind his desk. He presses his intercom button. "Rachel, can you send Rob down." The moment between us is completely severed as the businessman returns in front of my eyes. Face composed, he straightens his tie and gets ready to face the door and this Rob guy.

I can't help feeling disappointed that he didn't say he was still busy and then fuck me across his desk.

I'm not sure what exactly happened between the two of us here this morning, but I know I crave more of it.

I'm pleasantly surprised when Rob walks in and introductions are made. He's around his mid-twenties with wavy, slightly grown out blonde hair, green eyes, and a cheeky grin.

Ant explains how I'll be working under Rob's supervision for the next week while I learn the ropes.

"I promise I don't bite," Rob says and as I smile at him, I can feel Ant's eyes on us. Hmm. He says this morning was a mistake, but he doesn't seem all that happy at Rob's friendly demeanour.

Concentrate on the job now, I tell myself as Rob explains to me what we'll be doing this morning. My mind runs on and on at the best of times and I have problems in stopping its constant inner chatter. Right now, I need to focus so I can grasp this opportunity with both hands. I can't let my almost obsession with Anthony Warren interfere with the chance I have at independence.

"I'm sure you don't." I laugh. "Okay, well, I'm ready when you are. So, let's go."

I can feel Ant's eyes on me and as my gaze hits his, for a moment I see they're narrowed. Within a blink it's gone.

"Thank you for the opportunity, Mr Warren." I reach out my hand. He holds out his own and I shake it. He's not the only one who can bring down a mask and switch his true feelings off.

Rob opens the door for me and I step through. I'm just passing through the reception area when Tyler hurtles past me, my sister hot on his heels. She rolls her eyes at me.

"I'll call you when I get a minute," she shouts as she goes past.

"Looking like a busy morning for the B.A.D. bosses. Any gossip on what's happening?" Rob asks.

"Oh, nothing of any excitement unfortunately. Just an advertiser trying to renegotiate terms." I lie.

With that, I walk away from Ant's office wishing I had a spy camera in the room.

———

Rob's a really nice guy and the fact he's easy on the eyes makes my first day that little bit easier. However, my mind continually wanders back to Ant. He stormed off shortly after Tyler went into his office. My sister sent me a text to say her and Ty were still going on their honeymoon at Ant's insistence. When I asked how Ant was, she just said *wondering how to deal with things* and that was it. Now she'll be on her way to St. Lucia. Two weeks of sun, sand, and sex. I could use a two-week relaxing break, but unfortunately for me, time to myself means time with my thoughts and that isn't a relaxing place to be.

"Thanks, Rob. For making my first day so easy," I tell him. He flicks his blonde fringe out of his eyes.

"My pleasure, Lola. You've picked up everything really quickly, far quicker than I did when I started. I think you'll fit right in here."

I smile. "Do you know, I'm actually looking forward to coming back tomorrow."

ANGEL DEVLIN & TRACY LORRAINE

There's a pause and I hope Rob knows I mean I enjoyed the work. I stand and reach for my bag.

"Right, I'd better get home as I've arranged to have dinner with my mum."

Rob steps back. "Oh, right, okay. Well, I'll see you tomorrow."

"Yeah, bye." I give a little half wave as I leave.

Rob is nice and seems interested in me, and with what he told me about his life, he seems... reliable and uncomplicated.

You could do with someone like that. I tell myself.

But my thoughts just return to the man of mystery who's now my new boss. The one who has decided to nickname me little Pandora when his own secrets are like each brick of the Pyramids. Stacked together and no one knows how they were built.

I walk into our home and the smell of pasta and garlic permeates the air, making my stomach grumble.

"Hey, Lola, baby. How did your first day go?" My mum steps out into the hall, a tea-towel over her shoulder and a spatula in her hand. I'd sent her a text that I'd got the job and was staying at work.

"Good, Mum, thanks. I think I'm going to like it there."

She claps her hands together and a little sauce flies across from the spatula. "That's wonderful news. Right, hurry up and get changed, dinner's nearly ready. I got a bottle of wine to celebrate."

"Thanks, Mum." I dash to my room and change into some grey lounge sweats and an off-the-shoulder oversized t-shirt in the same shade and I join Mum at the dining table.

She's plating up spaghetti carbonara and there are slices of garlic focaccia. My stomach gurgles once more.

Mum pours us a glass of wine each and holds her glass to mine to chink together.

"To you and your new job. To a fresh start."

We chink and take a drink.

"I'm so happy for you, honey. I have a feeling that this is going to be just what you need." She adds.

I nod my head in agreement while inside my stomach knots with frustration. My mum wants a miracle. She wants all the darkness from the past swept under a carpet. She's been like this all my life. We spent years living in New York, before she whisked me to London without truly acknowledging why, other than we couldn't see Dad anymore. Just giving bland reassurances that everything was now fine even though I'd been given a new name and had to keep my mouth shut about the past. My older sister came here and again, there was no true explanation of why, but we were still not talking about things, and I was just told everything was okay.

I pour myself another glass of wine and my mum is too busy being excited about my future to realise that I drink almost the whole bottle to myself.

CHAPTER FOUR

Ant

The second she walks out, trailing behind Rob, I realise that I may have made a mistake. More than one actually, but I really don't need to think about what happened only feet away from where I'm standing next to my empty desk and paperwork all over the floor. The scent of whiskey permeates the air. This day could not have turned out any worse.

Picking up the phone that's amongst the heap on the floor next to my desk, I press the speed dial button that links directly to our PI, William, and sit my arse in my chair even though doing any actual fucking work is looking unlikely today.

It rings and rings before clicking over to voicemail.

Once the beep sounds out, I bark out my message. "Call me, motherfucker." Slamming the handset back on the base, I scream out my frustration at the shit show my life is turning out to be. And just because I need more, only a second later, Tyler comes barrelling through the door quickly followed by Anna.

Fucking brilliant. He's here to try to fix me when he should be heading to the airport for his honeymoon.

"I'm here, what's the emergency?" he falls down on my sofa and rests forward with his elbows on his knees.

"There isn't one. Now fuck off on your honeymoon both of you and get out of my hair." I spin away from them and look out at the city beyond the window.

"I don't think so," Anna says, despite what I just said. Great, now there are two of them. "Ty, did you know Ant has a daughter?"

"Anna, shut the fuck up," I bark, spinning back and finding them both staring at me like I've turned into a fucking alien.

"Don't fucking talk to her like that, dickhead," Tyler demands, like how I speak to his woman right now is the most pressing fucking issue.

"Fine, then how about both of you fuck off and leave me to it?" I wave my hand at both of them and look to the door, more than ready for this day to be over already.

"I don't think so, douchebag." Tyler stretches his legs out before getting comfortable for my enlightening tale. "Start talking."

"Oh here he is, Tyler fucking Ward. Fixer of all issues."

His lips purse in anger. He fucking hates it when I tease him about this. It's one of the main reasons I bring it up so much, but sadly, there's nothing amusing about right now. This has been a long time coming. He's been on my arse since *she* first turned up and flipped my world upside down. He knew the second something was up with me, Jack too. I'm amazed they've let it lie this long to be honest.

When I refuse to say anything, Anna helpfully starts filling in the blanks for him.

"Ant's got a daughter; about Lola's age by the looks of it."

"How is that even possible? He's only thirty-one."

"Three," I mutter. "I'm thirty-three."

"Right, that doesn't make it any more believable though."

I blow out a breath, resting back in my chair and closing my eyes for a second, wishing that when I open them again it turns out that this is all a fucking nightmare and my day can continue on as it was. Without unexpected visitors or a trip down fucking memory lane in order to explain this.

"I know. But it's true. Apparently." I look down at both of them. Their concerned faces piss me off.

"Apparently?" Tyler repeats.

"Don't worry, I'll be sorting a DNA test if I ever find her again. But I'm ninety-nine percent sure that it's unnecessary."

"How old is she, Ant?" Anna asks, speaking again for the first time in ages. I can see her trying to work it all out. Sadly, the situation is so fucked-up that I doubt she'll even get close.

"Eighteen."

I watch the cogs turn as they work that out.

"Fucking hell, Ty. Early starter?" Ty half jokes, trying to lighten up the situation.

"Something like that," I mutter, really not wanting to get into the reality of the situation. The bonus of having four best friends with lives as fucked-up as ours means that if we don't want to talk about something then it's accepted. We've all got parts of our pasts that we keep hidden, and everything from my childhood is one of those things. But as both Tyler's and Anna's eyes drill into mine, I fear my time hiding my past might be coming to an end. I guess that's what happens when ghosts you thought you'd outrun, and surprise children appear unexpectedly.

An uncomfortable silence settles around us. They clearly want details that I really don't want to give.

I might not have seen her for years, but I still remember the burning need I had to protect her all those years ago. I guess her being mine makes sense now. I just thought my need to look after her was because she was so helpless against everything that was forced on her. I'd have done just about anything to stop any child from having to endure the things I did. But the second I saw her run, it returned with a vengeance. If I weren't so fucking shocked, I might have gone after her. Demanded some answers. Discovered if that lying, abusive whore was actually telling the truth or not.

But for now, all I'm capable of is outrunning my issues again.

"This little chat has been fun and all, but I've got shit to be doing," I say, pushing from the chair and straightening my suit.

"Oh no. You can't just leave it like that. We're not leaving this office until you've told us everything."

"Well then you'd better get comfortable because I'm done. Fuck off on your honeymoon. I'll no doubt still be here dealing with this shit when you get back."

"But—"

"No," I bellow, turning on Tyler when he stands to his full height. "I'm fucking done, all right?" I stand toe to toe with him. The prospect of having to talk about the truth of the situation stirs an anger within me that I've not felt for years.

Anna reaches out and places her hand on my forearm. The move has the desired effect because I almost instantly relax and take a step back.

"You need me, you need to talk, you fucking call. You got that?" Tyler asks, poking me in the chest.

"Trust me. I never need to talk about what led to me having a fucking daughter."

"Ant," Anna says softly. "Coming from someone who kept dark shit bottled up for years, please find someone to talk to. It doesn't have to be Tyler, or me, or any of the guys. Just please find someone. I promise you it'll help."

I open my mouth to respond, but I soon find I've no words there to speak. I've only spoken about it once and that was to get the bitch locked up.

"I'll see what I can do," I lie, before spinning on my heels and marching through the door. "Please just go and enjoy your honeymoon. You both deserve it."

Ripping the door open, I bark at Rachel to cancel all my meetings and put off any phone calls other than William, and I'm out of the office as fast as my feet will carry me.

———

Dropping down into my car, I rest my head back for a few seconds and just breathe. I know what I need, and I also know that it's wrong, just like I do every time. But I can't help myself.

Pulling my phone from my pocket, I find her name in my messages.

Ant: Where are you? I need...

My thumb hovers over the screen, not wanting to admit the next part to her, although I have a suspicion that she already knows. *Fuck.*

You.

The message shows as read almost immediately and the little dots start bouncing.

Vivian: At home. I'll be waiting.

Relief floods me and a tingle of excitement runs down my spine. I'm going to be able to forget it all momentarily. Even if only for an hour, everything in my fucked-up life is going to disappear like it's nothing while I act out my regular screwed-up revenge plan on a woman that doesn't deserve it.

Scrubbing my hand down my face and across my rough jaw, I throw the car into reverse and get the hell away from the office.

I try William again as I make my way across the city, but just like before there's no answer.

"What the fuck?" I bark at no one. He never doesn't answer his phone.

Thankfully, the sight of Vivian's building comes into view and I push it all down.

Just go and take what you need. Empty your head for a bit, then come back out and deal with your fucking life.

My fingers wrap around the wheel with an almost painful grip.

I hate doing this. I hate that I need this. But I fucking do. I need it like a fucking junkie needs their next hit. It's my addiction, my escape.

"Fuck," I bark, slamming my hand down on the wheel before forcing the door open and climbing out.

I can tell myself how much I hate it over and over, it's not going to stop me doing it.

The fucked-up part about all of this is that she needs it just as badly, which is fine, each to their own. But if she knew my reasons, the truth behind why I willingly treat her the way I do...

I shudder as a memory of my childhood fills my mind.

Is it wrong to use this willing woman to unleash my frustrations on the bitch that ruined my life? Absolutely, but I've not got the power to stop it.

The second I buzz and announce that I've arrived, I'm allowed inside.

I take the lift to the top floor as excitement, unease, and guilt begin to swirl inside. I've not even touched her and I'm regretting it.

Fucking hell, Warren, this is seriously fucked up.

I don't need to knock. As usual, the door is already temptingly ajar.

Pushing through, I don't say anything, although I know she's heard my arrival when the door clicks shut.

"Where are you, slut?" I call out, cringing slightly as I do and forcing myself to get into character.

As usual, she doesn't respond.

This is a game after all. A game of hide and seek. A game of pain, pleasure, and an escape from fucked-up pasts and even more likely fucked-up futures.

Turning the corner to her bedroom, I immediately find her standing against one of the posts on her four-poster bed. She's clad in a tight leather outfit that I don't think I've seen before, with a collar around her neck, the lead in her hand, and when I look to the bed, she's already laid out exactly what she wants to use this session. Good. The less thinking I have to do the better.

"Well, well, well, it looks like my little slut wants to play." I kick the door closed behind me and shrug off my jacket as I run my eyes down her curvaceous body.

Vivian is exactly what I look for in a woman and she's enough of a reminder of the bitch from my past that I'm able to unleash a dark side of me that no one else ever gets to witness.

Pulling my belt from my waist, I crack the leather as a wicked smile covers her face.

"I've missed you, sir."

CHAPTER FIVE

Lola

Three-quarters of a bottle of white wine is enough to take the edge off when the feeling of ants crawling over my skin comes, but it doesn't make it disappear. And the more I use it, the less effect it has. How can my body harden towards the effects of alcohol, but not what happened to me? Why can I not completely shut it down?

Mum tells me she's arranged to go to the cinema and for a drink with a friend, which explains why she didn't have more than a glass of wine herself. Since Tommy died, she's been a new woman. For her his death meant the end of watching over her shoulder. Now she was free to live her life. I envied her, but then again, I couldn't get in her head and I couldn't know what the years of marriage to him had done.

When she leaves, I go up to my room, switch on the TV and try to find something to distract me, but it doesn't work. I start tapping my fingers on my knee, like some manic lunatic, while the call from inside me for help to stop it all gets louder and louder.

I spring to my feet, my hands on my ears and then I reach for my handbag, taking out my phone and dialling the number I'm trying to resist.

"I knew you'd be back, baby. No matter what you said."

"Johnny, I need it."

"I got you. You home alone?"

"Yes." I gasp. "Yes."

"Thirty minutes."

"Please, be as quick as you can." I'm begging and I hate myself.

Thirty minutes is a lifetime when I'm like this and it's no good. It's too long to wait. I reach into my underwear drawer and I take out the vibrator box. But that's not what I'm looking for. I just know the box is the perfect place to put anything I don't want anyone else to look for. I take a fresh blade from the packet and I strip down to my bra. I'm well practised and I rub an alcohol swab over the blade before I put the edge of it to the top of my left inner arm. There's a beauty in the simplicity of the blade and in the way that as it draws across my pale flesh it cuts a line where a fresh bead of blood pops. It's like strawberries and ice-cream, an irresistible combination. I sigh as my frustration seeps out alongside the blood, lost in the moment.

I've been cutting for years and no one knows. Not even Ant, who wrapped up my naked body and helped me into the bath, saw my scars. Easily hidden by wrapping my arms around myself.

I put everything away and dress again now the ants have stopped their march over my body. I regret phoning Johnny, but as the doorbell goes, I know it's too late.

Johnny Hudson, the older brother of the only real friend I made in Hackney. But where I cut ties with his sister Cherry, I formed new ones with the man I knew could give me what I needed.

His smirk greets me as I open the door. "Come in." I tell him, looking over his shoulder.

"Scared the neighbours are going to see your bit of rough on the doorstep, hey? Ashamed of me now, are you?"

"Never. I remember my years in Hackney and your sister is the reason I survived."

"You told me you were done with this, but yet here I am again." He moves closer to me and tilts my chin up with his fingertips, looking into my eyes.

"Seems the dark side of life can't let me go." I tell him and I watch his brow crease.

"Do you want me to call Cherry? You need someone to talk to?"

"No." I exclaim. "I don't need to talk. I'm not on

suicide watch. All I need is to feel good." I trail my own finger down his face. "And you can help me with that."

The smirk is back. "In oh so many ways, but I'm guessing it's this you want?" He takes out the baggie, "rather than any other comfort I could provide."

I take the bud from his hand. "Let me get my purse."

"Price went up." He tells me.

"Oh?"

He quotes me an amount four times what I used to pay a long time ago in another life.

"Why? It's not any more special than what I always got."

He snorts. "Babe, now your drugs come with a side serving of my silence."

"Of course." I don't blame him. It's a dog eat dog, fight for survival world he frequents and to him I'm a woman who now has everything while he still has relatively nothing.

I reach back in my underwear drawer for the box. His eyes light up until I remove a wad of cash.

"And there I thought it was my lucky night."

"It is. Your customer is paying four times what your merch is worth." I pass the money over.

"Pleasure doing business with you," he says, then his eyes soften. "Look after yourself, Jade." My old name seems strange as the sound hangs in the air. "Cherry missed you, you know."

"I missed her. Still miss her. But my life isn't what it was, and my past and present don't mix." I laugh, but there's no humour in it. "I'm a mess, Johnny, and she's better off living a life without me in it."

He shakes his head. "You need help. Go see someone."

"I'm fine, honestly. Just need to come to terms with a few things and this is going to help." I waved my baggie. "I didn't order a ton of tablets to OD on, so quit being such a pussy."

He put a hand on his dick. "Ain't no chance of me being one of those, doll. Right, I must go. This business does not run itself. I'm a busy man. Take care." He kisses me on the cheek. "And ring us if you need us. New life or not."

I nod and then I see him out. When I get back to my room, I put the baggie in the box and put everything away because the ache from my arm has settled me and I finally feel like I can sleep.

But my nightmares don't leave me for long.

I'm trying to breathe, trying to fight the fear coursing through my body. "Lola, sweetheart. Do you know how much I've been missing you?" My father stares at me through the rear-view mirror. "I can't believe your mother took you away from me and re-named you Jade. Diana, Anna, and Jade Hawley. So very boring at the side of who you really are Dolores 'Lola' De Loughrey, don't you think?"

All I can think is 'where is he taking me?'. I stare out of the window trying to remember signposts in case I manage to escape or he abandons me in the middle of nowhere.

"I'd ask if you'd missed me too, but clearly you haven't or you'd have been in touch."

"What do you want, Dad?" I decide I may as well ask what's bothering me.

"Dad. Hmmm, well that's the question isn't it? That's exactly what I'm here to find out; whether or not you're mine. Only she took you before I had a chance to find out. Left me with the cuckoo that had been hiding in the nest."

"What are you talking about?" He's pissing me off now, because he was never much of a father to me before we left and hid from him. My sister had spoken little of what she'd endured staying in New York with him, but I knew from her haunted features that protecting us had hurt her. She'd spoken of fraud, but I wasn't convinced that was the whole truth. Then again, I was always the last to know everything. All I'd known was that we'd had to leave and hide because he'd threatened Mum.

"Oh, Jesus. Don't tell me that your mother is still protecting you from the truth? Did you know that she'd been cheating on me? Or did she tell you I drove her away?" He was looking at the road now, but I could hear the amusement in his tone.

"Mum wouldn't do that." I stated it clearly as I knew it for the truth. No way had my mum done anything like that. She was the person I set my stall by. Not my negligent father.

"Oh dear, Dolores. Let's get you up to speed, shall we? When you left it was just after Lucia's accident, was it not? The accident where Lulu needed a blood

42

transfusion and I discovered it wasn't possible for me to have fathered her. And then your mother took you away before I had a chance to find out if you're mine or some other bastard's too."

His hands grip the steering wheel so hard that his fingers go white.

"And then I realise, when your sister decides to make a run for it, just exactly who Lulu's father is. A man who's been hiding in plain sight. And now we're going to go see if he's your Daddy too. I have the test kit for us all."

My mind reels. Dad is not Anna's dad? He might not be my dad? The possibility my father might have had some kind of mental break occurs to me as it sounds like the words of a rambling man; but he's cool, calm, and collected, just as I've seen him when he's been dealing with difficult businesspeople.

And if he is telling the truth, then my beautiful mum, who I've always worshipped, is a liar and a cheat.

I wake in a cold sweat. I was still in the car, it was okay. Nothing had happened yet. I try to even out my breathing as advised for panic attacks, but it's hard. I did what I always did these days; to focus on picturing Ant's face, and this time I can actually recall his mouth on mine and his touch because of what had happened in his office yesterday. I make my mind think of every single part of his skin touching mine, from the moment he moved near me to when we sprung apart, and it calms me, my heartbeat returning to a normal rhythm as Ant unwittingly saves me all over again. I manage to fall back asleep until my alarm sounds.

My heart skips a beat at the thought of seeing Ant again. Even if I don't get to be near him, even if it's only snatched sightings of him toing and froing, it's better than my usual days at home. I stash my bud in the bottom of my handbag along with the rest of what I might need, and I head for the kitchen. I'm up early and this time I fix breakfast and coffee so that when my mum comes downstairs looking a little the worse for wear, I can hand her a drink.

"God, thanks, love. You've no idea how much I need that this morning," she states.

"Your face gives me a clue. Good night was it?"

"Yeah." She smiles. "The film was fabulous and then we went for tapas and had cocktails. It was a lot of fun. There was dancing."

"Good. I'm glad to know you had a good time. Right, I'd better be off to my new job," I say smiling.

"It's good to see you looking so happy, Lola. I can already see this job has been exactly what you needed. You look better already."

Nodding, I make my way out and then I place my thumb where I know I cut last night and I press down hard, just so it burns a little. So I don't scream out loud that of course my fucked-up life has just been magically reset because I'm an accountancy intern at B.A.D.

CHAPTER SIX

Ant

I walk away from Vivian's penthouse full of regret, although I can't deny that the tension that was pulling my muscles tight has reduced slightly.

Every time I visit, I tell myself that it'll be my last. That I don't need the relief she can offer in the form of her leather flogger or studded paddle.

My fists clench as I remember having my fingers wrapped around the handle and the punishing slap of the fabric against skin.

"Fuck," I bark, wrenching my car door open and falling down onto the seat.

I shouldn't still need this... this... pain to cover the nightmares of my past, to try to make *her* pay for what she did to me. For what she did to Ellie.

I think of that helpless little baby and the neglect she was forced to endure. At least I could fend for myself. I may have only been a child, but my past meant I had to grow up fast even before I was unlucky enough to be placed with *her*.

If I thought group homes and other foster parents were bad, then I was dropped straight into Hell the day I was left with that bitch.

Scrubbing my hand down my face, I tip my head back, running the events of today through my mind.

I need to go home and wash it all off me in the hope it helps put some of the memories behind me.

Starting the car, I only make it to the end of the street before the sound of my phone ringing fills the space around me.

Looking at the dash, I find Jack's name staring back at me.

I could ignore her, but I'm not sure it's the best idea. She's going to know by now and she won't stop until she knows I'm okay.

"I should have fucking known he'd have sent you to check on me," I bark.

"Ty's just worried. So... secret daughter. Gotta say, Ant, I didn't see that one coming."

"You and me both." I turn left with the intention of heading straight home, but the next words out of her mouth have me changing my mind.

"Meet me at the bar. Something tells me you could do with a drink."

"You got that fucking right. I'm only ten minutes away."

"Okay, I'm getting in a cab right now."

I park around the back of XCluSiv. It's early still, yet the car park is almost full. It seems that things still seem to be going swimmingly even without Ty's uncle or brother in charge.

Unable to resist the allure of a decent glass of whiskey, or six, I push from the car once again and step inside the bar via the back door in the hope I can slip into our usual booth and not be seen by anyone. The last thing I want to do right now is chat fucking small talk with people I don't care about.

Thankfully, when I slide into our booth there's already a familiar face waiting for me, or more importantly, a friendly face with a bottle of the good stuff sitting right in front of her.

"Well aren't you a sight for sore eyes," Jack says when I ignore her and instead go straight for the bottle. The few shots I had in my office earlier have long worn off now and I need this almost as much as I do my next breath.

Assuming she's already heard about everything that's happened today—well probably not everything but the most shocking bit—I go with my most pressing question.

"If you were eighteen and just discovered I was your father, where would you go?" I ask, as she slides a glass toward me.

She thinks for a second, swirling the liquid of her own drink around. "I'd probably go and get drunk."

"Whoa, thanks."

"I didn't mean because of you, just that it would be a shock. Plus, isn't going and getting wasted what most eighteen-year-olds do? They rarely need an excuse to get on it. Hell knows, we all didn't."

"Do we now?" I ask, thinking about how often we all sit and drink.

"I guess not. To your daughter," Jack says, lifting her glass and downing it in one without even wincing.

"So say she's gone to get drunk. This is London, she could be fucking anywhere. How am I meant to find her?"

"I don't think you're meant to, Ant. She's eighteen. She's already proved that she'll do exactly as she pleases. Hell, she got herself into B.A.D. without too much effort. When she's ready, she'll find you."

"What if I don't want to wait?"

"Then pray for a miracle because I know from experience that if a girl doesn't want to be found, then she won't be."

I nod, not wanting to say anything that will drag up Jack's past as well as my own. One of us having a meltdown is enough for one day.

Silence settles between us, but I can feel the weight of her unspoken questions pressing down on my shoulders.

"Talk to me, Ant. How'd you end up with an eighteen-year-old at your age?"

I stare at one of my dearest friends. I know she'd understand if I were to lay it all out for her. Hell, she's experienced enough not to be shocked by most things, but even still, the words won't get past my lips.

"By ending up somewhere really fucked-up."

"She's really yours?"

"I'm pretty sure, yeah. If I ever find her again, I'll attempt to do a DNA test to be sure."

"Jesus, Ant. Have you asked William?"

"Of course I fucking have." He's been looking for her for weeks, since that fucking ghost turned up thinking she could blackmail me. "He's MIA too. His phone just goes to voicemail."

Thankfully, Jack doesn't ask any more questions despite the fact it must almost kill her. Instead, she changes the topic and starts telling me about the band Deacon has secured for a future front cover.

Apparently they're hot shit right now, but seeing as I've been living in my own head the past few weeks, I've barely even looked at social media, let alone the fucking charts.

She chatters on about their success and I think I nod in all the right places.

As glad as I am that things seem to be on the up and up for the magazine after the recent demise of Fully Loaded, our biggest rival, I'm struggling to get excited about it. My head is full of images of my broken daughter, the girl almost her age that I had up against the wall of my office, and then the woman I use to get my kicks from when things get too tough.

This day needs to fucking end, that's all I know right now.

By the time Jack and I head for the exit, I can barely feel my legs. Exactly what I needed.

She's already called for a car for both of us and after pushing me inside the one she's booked to take me home, I almost instantly fall asleep.

The driver ends up throwing something at me to wake me up when we get across the city and to my building.

"Fuck, shit. Sorry, mate," I say, wiping some drool from my face.

I stumble out of the car and toward the front door to my building. I greet the security guard on shift tonight, but none of his words register in my head as I crash into the lift and slam my hand down on the button for my floor.

The next thing I know, I come to, face down on my sofa and still wearing yesterday's clothes.

"Motherfucker," I grunt as the pounding in my head increases as I crack my eyes open.

Rolling over, my stomach complains about the fact the only thing that passed it yesterday was alcohol.

"Fuck." My head spins as I push myself to a seated position with my arm on the cushion to help keep me upright.

After dragging in a few deep breaths, the room slowly stops spinning until I'm able to push myself to stand and make my way down to my bedroom, bouncing off the walls as I go.

I've no clue what the time is, and quite frankly, I really don't give a shit.

Stripping out of my clothes, I leave them in a pile on the floor and dive into bed, hoping that the next time I wake, things will hurt less, although I already know that life won't be any less fucked-up.

I'm woken once again a few hours later by my phone that's ringing somewhere on the floor.

Thankfully, when I push from the bed, the room doesn't tilt, and the pounding at my temples is significantly better than it was a while ago.

Pulling my phone from a pocket of my discarded trousers, I immediately sober up when I find William's name staring back at me.

Swiping across the screen, I put it to my ear.

"Where the fuck have you been?" I snap, less than impressed that Ellie found me before he found her.

"Sorry, I had some issues yesterday."

"Well, you're not the only fucking one. Ellie turned up unexpectedly at the office yesterday. How is it that a fucking eighteen-year-old kid who had no idea who I was, found me before my fucking PI did?"

"I did find her first. How do you think she got your details?"

"I don't fucking know." I fall down on the bed, already confused by this whole conversation.

"I had a tip off for where she was. When I turned up, some guy was laying into her. I recognised the guy immediately—he's one of London's most notorious pimps." Groaning at his words, I don't say anything so he can continue. "I dragged her away from him, trying to protect her. She kicked off, telling me she could fight her own battles.

"Anyway, one thing led to another and she ran while I ended up taking on Wood. I went to call you the second it was over, to tell you that I'd found her and that she wasn't in a good place, but I couldn't. Bitch swiped my phone in the commotion."

"What?" I bark, unsure if I'm horrified by that bit of information or impressed.

"She must have found our conversation or something and come to you."

"Jesus fucking Christ, William." Rubbing at my rough jaw, I reach up and push my hair back from my face, tugging on it until it hurts.

"I know, I know. Not my finest hour. I'll find her okay?"

"You mean if she doesn't find me again first?"

"Trust me."

I laugh at his words, failing miserably to do that right now.

"William, my daughter was being beaten by a pimp. Fucking find her. Now."

He hangs up without even responding, for which I'm grateful because there is nothing he could say to make this any better right now.

"Fuck," I shout into my empty flat.

She was fucking right. She came to me claiming to have information about my daughter—one I didn't know existed—and how much trouble she was in.

Problem was that she wanted money—a lot of fucking money—for the information, money that was going nowhere near her bank account.

She might have been clever enough to figure out that I had money now, but she clearly wasn't clever enough to consider me having other ways to get the information I needed.

She'd fucked me over one too many times in the past and there is no way I'll believe a word that passes her lips ever again.

I'd hoped that when I put her away all those years ago that I would never have to see her again.

I was almost physically sick the second she walked into my office, strutting as if she fucking belonged there after claiming to be someone she wasn't to get a meeting with me.

Manipulative cunt. Seems that prison did fuck all for her.

What she's forgetting is that while I may now have money, I also have power, and I have a hell of a lot more ways to make her go away this time. Prison will have been a walk in the park compared to the hell I can make rain down on her now.

CHAPTER SEVEN

Lola

As I walk out of my front door, guilt floods my body when I recall that not only did I cut myself, but I invited a drug dealer to my home. I'm going to have to go see someone and talk about what happened with me. I need professional help before this gets any worse.

But... I just need them to see in my head. I don't want to talk about any of it. Don't want to launch what happened to me out where I have to think about it in detail. It was too horrific.

Today, I'm wearing a black blouse so should I knock my arm no blood would bloom on a pale blouse. I refuse to dwell on the fact I put a silver hip flask in my bag full of vodka 'just in case'.

The driver I called ahead for greets me outside the main door of our apartment block. My life has been like the revolving doors I just walked through, a discombobulating spin through stinking rich, not having much money, and then back somewhere in between. But there's now no reason why this can't be the life I have going forward. I can finally put down some roots that stay and as I climb inside the back of the car that actually makes a smile emerge on my face.

When I get to the accounts floor, Rob comes straight over to greet me.

"You came back." He claps and I shake my head at him.

"You loon. Of course I came back. I need a job, and this is a good one."

He mock sulks. "And I thought it was because I was the most friendly and helpful colleague ever."

"Are you two going to be doing some work anytime soon?" Growls out from the doorway. I turn to see Ant looking thunderous. He heads past us before I can point out my shift hasn't technically started yet, and I watch as he storms over to a woman sitting in the corner and bawls her out.

"Grab your things and get the fuck out, Terri. If you want to show Wesley Knox your cunt that's your decision, but photos of our investments and giving him inside information is our business. It's our piece of prime pussy we've worked hard to own. You'd better hope he'll help pay your court fees." Picking up her laptop, he hurls it onto the floor where it breaks into pieces.

The woman is hysterical and no matter what she's done, how wrong a move she's made, he's no right to frighten her like that. I run over to her and put my arm around her. "Come on, let's get you to the bathroom, freshen you up and then you can make your way home."

I can feel Ant's eyes on me. "She sold us out, Lola. She doesn't deserve your sympathy. Do you think anyone else here feels sorry for her, given she could have cost some of them their jobs?"

"She's still a human being, Mr Warren." I turn away from him and help Terri grab her bag. Once out of the room she turns around to me, wiping her eyes and sniffling. "Don't jeopardize your job. Not for me. I'm fine now. Well, I'm not, but I will be. Just need to go home and lick some sore wounds." She holds her head up and walks away.

After standing there a moment, I notice Rachel's assessing gaze is on me.

"B.A.D. and the environment we live and work in. It's not for the faint of heart, Lola. You'll see things you don't like here. You can't go around trying to save everyone. Some don't deserve it." She taps onto her iPad and walks over to me. There's a security camera feed which shows the outside of the building. I watch as Terri walks out, clearly on the phone. "Keep watching," she tells me.

A few minutes later a car pulls up at the kerb and Terri gets inside.

"The car will have been sent by Wesley. She's a spy. We've been watching her for weeks. They think they're getting away with it and they get careless. The information she thinks she obtained was false. She'll be surplus to Knox's requirements soon."

"And this happens regularly?" My eyes are wide.

"Within the different departments there is always someone trying to ride the success of B.A.D. Usually we come out on top. You just dangle the bait to them and they take it. Every damn time. Temptation you see. Leads you down a path of ruin sometimes and yet they're willing to take the chance."

"How did you know what she'd do though?" I question. "Do you have her bugged?"

"No, Lola. I used to be her. I was just damn lucky that I had a conscience and went to see Anthony before I'd done any damage." She looks at the floor for a moment, and then back up at me. "He's a fantastic boss. But you can't spend a day here and think you know better than he does. Get back in there, sit down and do your job. Or go home, Lola. You're an intern, here to learn and your first lesson has been a large one. Ant Warren runs this department and you have to trust he knows what he's doing, no matter how it might look on the surface."

"Fuck. I'd better go apologise," I say, just as the man himself comes out of the main office.

"A word please, Lola," he says firmly.

I nod my head. "I was going to ask to speak with you." Following, I wonder if I've just fucked-up my new career before it has even started.

"Sit down," he says sharply as we enter his office.

"I want to apologise." I blurt out before he can scream at me like he did at Terri.

"Lola." He steeples his fingers, his elbows resting on the edge of the desk. He has long slim fingers and I can't help but wonder how they'd feel trailing down my stomach and slipping lower...

"Wh- what?"

"I'm not about to tear you limb from limb, so please stop looking apprehensive in my company. Look, I realise all you've seen of me is when I helped get you out of your situation, but I'm a businessman. A part-owner of an enormous corporation and we have a lot of enemies. I wouldn't have survived here if I wasn't a ruthless, vindictive bastard, but I like to think I'm a fair one. God knows we have Deacon if we just want to go psycho on anyone's arse."

I smile at that.

"But believe me. If you weren't actually someone who I thought could benefit my department, when you did that today, undermined my authority in front of everyone... if you'd just simply been a favour to your sister, you'd have right behind Terri, make no mistake."

"I spoke with Rachel and she made me realise what I did." Taking a deep breath, I look him directly in the eye. "Ant, I've not had a job before. I have no idea what

I'm doing. I really am an intern, in, well everything. I need a Beginners Guide to Life."

"I'm sure you're not a beginner in everything. I'm sure you have expertise in something." He smirks, trying I think to put me at ease.

Instead, I feel myself tense more. "No. I don't think so. Other than having to try to pick up pieces and start again." I huff. "If you ever have a jigsaw, I'm your girl, although I never seem to get the pieces all together before it gets swept onto the floor by an unseen hurricane."

The following silence makes me think it's my cue to leave, so I rise to my feet and smooth out the A-line black skirt with white trim I'd put on this morning. "I won't let you down again, Ant. Or undermine you. I seriously apologise. I just need a chance to prove myself."

He walks me to the door and I remember the last time we were here, when we were interrupted by Rob walking in.

He's close behind me when he says, "When you said you're an intern in everything. A beginner. You didn't mean in...? Shit. Don't answer that, it's not my concern."

"In bed?" I turn around so there are barely inches between our bodies. "I'm a virgin, Ant. I've spent most of my life being watched like a hawk. This is the first time I've ever been free to roam, since *he* died."

"But your kidnap. I assumed they'd... because you were so traumatised."

"They didn't rape me, Ant. I would have taken that any day over what they actually did to me."

His hand trails up the side of my cheek and he whispers. "What did they do to you, little Pandora?"

I shake my head. "No. That's not up for discussion. I'll never say the words."

"Secrets burn you up inside." Ant tells me. "I know because my heart is ash."

I shake my head. "For someone whose heart is burned, you still manage to care about people."

"No, Lola." He tips my chin up. "I care about very few people, and yet somehow, and I don't know why, you're becoming one of them."

Leaning forward, his mouth touches mine and he sweeps me up. My legs wrap around him and he backs me up to the wall. His mouth devours me while his hardness grinds just where I want it, right against my core.

He breaks the kiss, panting. "It's only the fact I believe they're already all dead that stops me from taking out every one of them. If they had taken away your first time..."

"They touched my body and it makes me feel sick to think of it, but when you run your hands down me, it's like you're taking away their touch and replacing it with your own," I confess. Needy for his touch.

"I'm too old for you, Lola."

"But I want you. I want you to be my first." I grab his hand and guide it under my skirt. His fingers dive under the edge of my panties and he finds me slick and wet. I need him so badly. Need his touch, need him to fill me, heart and soul. He pushes a digit inside me.

"Fuuucck. So tight. Not here, Lola. Not here."

"Yes, here, right now. Pleasssse," I beg. I can feel it won't be long until those fingers make me come. He moves me so my feet are back on the floor.

"I'm locking the door. Take your panties off." His mouth meets mine again in another possessive kiss before he breaks off and strides for the door. Just as Jack walks through it. She looks at him and looks at me, her brow rising and then she says.

"We have someone you've been looking for in the security room."

And then it's like he forgets I even exist.

"You don't mean Ellie, do you?"

"Yes, your potential offspring was caught giving Demetri Marlow a blow job in the bathrooms outside of the studio."

I gasp. Demetri is the lead singer of Hendon Street, the band Deacon has secured for the magazine's front cover.

Sighing heavily, Ant grasps the door handle and storms through it, Jack hot on his heel.

I stand there, my panties halfway down my legs, wondering what the fuck I'm doing on only my second day of employment.

CHAPTER EIGHT

Ant

My fists clench and my teeth grind as I follow Jack out of the lift and directly into our main security office.

Inside we find our top three guys and a defiant looking Ellie sitting on a chair in front of them.

"What the fuck is going on?"

"Someone reported—" Gavin, one of the security guys speaks, but I interrupt him.

"Not from you. I want to hear it from her."

I take a step towards Ellie and she lifts her chin, her lips pressed into a thin line.

"Her has a name," she spits. Her tone does nothing for the fury raging within me.

Twice now she's got into this building. Twice she's turned my day on its arse without a second thought.

"Excuse me for ignoring the pleasantries when you've once again broken into my office."

"You really should get better security, you know. Anyone could walk in." Her head tilts to the side like an innocent fucking puppy, but she's not fooling me. She's anything but fucking innocent.

Spinning, I pin Gavin with a look that has him swallowing nervously. You'd think he'd be used to our wrath by now.

"How did she get in here? Again."

"I- I don't know. We're reviewing the security tapes right now."

Jack and I both take a step towards the wall of screens that show almost every part of our offices.

"There," one of the guys says, pointing to the bottom left screen.

"She's just swiped herself in. She's got a fucking pass." *How is that fucking possible?*

A loud bang sounds out behind us, but I don't look, not until I hear Jack's voice.

"Uh... Ant?"

"What?" I bark, getting increasingly pissed off with this situation by the second. I've not even accepted her words for what my daughter was caught doing yet.

"She's gone."

"What do you mean she's fucking—" I follow her stare to find an empty seat.

"For fuck's sake." I turn my furious gaze back on the three guys watching all of this play out. "Find out what the fuck is going on here. She's eighteen and she's running rings around the lot of you. It's pathetic."

Wrenching the door open, I storm out of the office and race toward the reception, but as I expected, it's empty.

It seems my daughter doesn't want to be pinned down. She doesn't know who she's dealing with though, I will get her and I will get the answers I need.

Thoughts of another young woman fill my mind and my cock once again stirs to life.

No one under the age of forty has interested me for... well, a very long time. My sick need for revenge has meant my women have all been of a certain maturity for many, many years, so why Lola makes things within me stir, fuck only knows. All I know right now is that I left her up there dripping fucking wet for me and hell knows I need exactly what she can offer right now.

"But I want you. I want you to be my first." Her words from before we were interrupted come back to me. They should be enough to stop me, to make me turn in the other direction and not look her way again, but my own sick and twisted past leads me to want to make hers special as if that can rewrite my own.

My hand taps against my thigh as the lift seems to take its sweet arse time to get to the top floor. By the time it dings and the door opens, I'm damn near desperate.

I forgo my office, assuming that she's probably not still in there waiting for me. She might want me for some unknown reason, but I doubt she's that desperate. I'm proved right when I turn the corner and find her back at her desk with none other than Rob leaning over her and pointing at something on her screen.

My jaw pops as I take in his closeness to her and it only reminds me that I made a huge mistake asking him to mentor her. I should have chosen Sheila, or Jennifer. They'd both have done a fine job.

Fine. The word taunts me. I don't do fine. I want good. I want perfection.

"Let's go," I bark the second I'm behind her.

Both Lola and Rob spin and take me in with wide eyes, but I don't look at Lola. I keep my glare on Rob, needing him to know that I see what he's doing.

"I... I was just," he stutters, pointing over his shoulder as he starts to back away sheepishly.

It's not until he's at the other side of the office that I drag my eyes from him and to a pissed off looking Lola.

"Let's. Go."

I grab her upper arm and lift her from her seat, not that she attempts to fight me anyway.

"Where are we going?"

"Away from interruptions." Her eyes instantly darken at my words and my cock stirs to life once more.

I reluctantly release her so she can grab her bag before I place my hand in the small of her back and guide her towards the lift.

A few sets of eyes follow us, but I pay them no mind as we pass numerous desks. They can think whatever the fuck they like, they just need to remember who pays their wages.

As the lift doors close, the tension becomes almost unbearable.

Turning to her, I stare down into her lust-filled eyes as she bites nervously into her bottom lip.

"Ant, what are you—"

Her words are cut off when I step into her and run my hand up her thigh. I'm desperate to know if she followed orders earlier or pulled them back up as I left the office.

In a blink I'm at the apex of her thighs once more, her heat seeping into my skin.

She gasps when I cup her.

"I'm disappointed, Lola."

Her cheeks redden as she must realise what I'm talking about.

"Take them off."

"O- okay."

She rushes to do as I demand and in a second she has the small scrap of black lace in her hand. She's just about to drop them into her bag when I reach out and snatch them from her, tucking them into my jacket pocket.

The lift dings on the third floor and frustratingly, the doors open to allow a couple of employees inside. I don't recognise either of them, not that it would stop me if I did.

Standing beside her once more, I reach out and run my fingertips up the back of her thigh.

Her loud gasp fills the enclosed space and one of the guys in front of us looks around to ensure that she's okay.

I can only assume that her face didn't give anything away because he soon turns back to stare at the doors.

The moment I get to her pussy, I part her lips and run my finger through her wetness. Her body trembles from my simple contact and when I glance over, I find her eyes squeezed tight as she tries to fight the need to react.

I'm just about to slide a finger inside her when the lift comes to an abrupt stop and the doors open to the underground garage.

The others step out and I reluctantly pull my hand from Lola's skirt.

"This way," I instruct, leading her to my Mercedes that's parked only a few spaces down from the lift—perk of being one of the bosses.

I pull the door open for her and wait as she gets herself situated before heading for the driver's side.

"What are you doing?" she asks the second we emerge from the garage.

"Finishing what we started."

"And the office wasn't good enough?"

"No," I reply simply.

The journey to my penthouse is short but I swear it's the longest it has ever taken with her sitting beside me with a bare pussy that's ready for the taking.

You shouldn't be doing this, a little voice says in my head, but I push it aside as she takes my hand as I lead her inside.

She's too young for you. She's your employee. She's Anna's little sister.

All the reasons why I should put a stop to this are on repeat in my head, but still, I ignore them.

Instead of sending her away like I should, I stand with my front to her back, crowding her as I walk us into yet another lift. My only relief comes from the knowledge that when we get to the top only my penthouse awaits.

Slamming my hand down on the buttons, I keep my eyes on her as she spins before me.

Her lips part as she takes in the look on my face, but she doesn't get a chance to say anything because my hand slides around to the nape of her neck and I pull her to me.

Our lips connect once again and a low growl rumbles up my throat.

The second our lips connect, every thought I had falls from my head.

All the reasons why this is wrong. Gone.

The unknowns surrounding Ellie. Banished.

Her. My ghost from the past. Non-existent.

All I can think about is her. Lola. All I focus on is how sweet and addictive she tastes, how warm her skin is, how compliant she is when she should be screaming and running in the opposite direction.

Needing more than just her lips, I lean down

slightly and push the fabric of her skirt up her legs before grabbing onto the soft skin of her thighs and lifting her.

I press her back into the wall of the lift and press myself against her. The heat from her pussy burns through the fabric of my trousers, making my cock so fucking hard for her.

I think of her admission earlier that she's a virgin and my mouth waters knowing that I'm going to be the first, the only man to give her this.

The lift dings and I pull her from the wall. She panics and tries to scramble from my arms, but my hold is too tight.

"Too late to change your mind now," I growl as I walk us from the lift and toward my front door.

"I- I'm not... my arse." Her hands drop from my neck in an attempt to cover herself up.

"This is my floor. No one will see you, and more importantly, no one will hear you screaming."

She stills, her eyes locked on mine as I come to a stop at my front door.

Her tongue licks across her bottom lip and I lean forward to suck it into my mouth.

"Fuck," I mutter, releasing it with a pop.

"Don't stop. Not now," Lola says in a rush, clearly getting the wrong idea from that one word.

"Oh... don't worry. There's no chance of that. Not now."

I push through the door and kick it closed behind us before walking straight through my penthouse and to my bedroom. We've no need for any other room right now.

I kick off my shoes the second we're in the room before dropping her onto the bed. I watch for a beat as she bounces before taking her knees in my hands and parting her legs as wide as they'll go.

Her pretty, pink, glistening pussy stares back at me.

"Fuck. I'm going to fucking ruin you."

If she replies, I don't hear it. I drop to my knees, wrap my hands around her hips and pull her to the edge of the bed before latching on to her clit.

She cries out, her back arching as her fingers slide into my hair and she holds so tightly that I worry she might rip it right out before this is over.

Her sweetness explodes on my tongue as I lap at her proving that I was right about just how good she'd taste.

Fuck. I'm fucking addicted already and I've only had one taste.

This is bad. So very fucking bad.

CHAPTER NINE

Lola

Ant is feasting on my pussy and all I can think is, am I dreaming? I thought I was going to end up losing my job today, not my virginity.

There is no anxiety, no fear about what's ahead as his tongue seeks entrance inside me, just sensations I've never experienced before. Ant is my new addiction. If I can have this every single day I'd have no need for the substances I rely on or the temptation of the blade I'm sure.

He breaks off and looks up at me, his eyes dark with lust and sin. "Let's get naked." He smirks.

My body tenses.

"Relax. I'll be taking extremely good care of you."

He doesn't realise that my panic is because of the

fresh cut on my inner arm and the scars that mar my skin.

"My fantasy is that you can't wait to get inside me," I tell him. "You can't even wait to get my clothes off. You tear open my blouse and then you're pushing into me."

"Then that's what we do," he says. Moving, he pulls my skirt off and dumps it on the floor. Then reaching up, he grabs my blouse and rips it open; the sound of tearing fills the room. He pulls the cups of my bra down, releasing my breasts over the lacy material and runs his tongue over the swell of each, before moving lower, trailing that hot, wet tongue over my breasts, capturing my nipples in his mouth in turn and sucking and biting slightly.

My breathing comes in faster pants because what this man is doing to me is driving me to the point of insanity. I need him inside me. My pussy is dripping wet and begging for him.

"Ant, please," I beg.

And then he moves away from me and tears well at my lower lashes as I think he's rejecting me. But instead he reaches for his bedside table getting a condom and relief blooms in my chest.

His face is filled with worry when he returns and sees me. "Lola, what is it? Do you want to stop? We don't have to do this."

I shake my head. "When you left. I thought you were rejecting me."

"Lola, it would take a tsunami to separate me from

you right now." He strips off his own clothes and I take in his perfect abs, the dark trail of hair that runs down into his boxers and then his massive cock as he lowers them to the floor. He grasps himself and runs a hand up and down his girth. "Do I look like I don't want you?"

Now I'm a little nervous because the reality that we're doing this hits me. That we're going to fuck is literally almost staring me in the face.

He sheathes himself and then he gets on the bed and pulls us together so we're face to face and close. His hands thread into my hair and his mouth meets mine. He kisses me for minutes, taking his time until I've forgotten I'm nervous. His hands trail down my chest, my breasts, my stomach and between my legs until he's rubbing my clit and trailing fingers through my wetness. Ant moves his fingers until they're entering me, in and out until I can feel the pressure building within me.

"I'm close," I gasp.

"Enjoy. We're in no hurry. Boss perks." He smiles against my lips.

Closing my eyes, I focus on the sensations until they spiral out of control and my body clenches around his digits as I buck against him. "Oh God. Oh fuck." I pant into his lips as he's captured my mouth in his, swallowing my moans.

And then he's pushing inside me. As I'm soaked for him and relaxed from orgasm, he's entering me, slowly. I feel the resistance, and he carries on kissing me until with a short burning flash of pain, I know that barrier between us is gone. It hurts slightly as he continues to move within me, but all I can think is that Ant is inside me, fucking me. It's everything I've wanted for months, and as lust begins to take me over once more, I begin moving against him.

He pulls back to look at me. "Okay?" He checks.

"Okay," I say back, leaning upwards to get his mouth on mine once more. His movements within me get a little harder and a little faster and I raise myself against him to feel him deeper inside me. His mouth moves off mine and he rests his head near my ear, his breathing hard. He groans with pleasure as he continues to thrust.

"Fuck, I can't get enough." Ant increases the tempo, moving within me and grasping my arse cheeks. My own pleasure starts to build again and I meet him at every thrust until it's wild and animalistic as we smash our bodies together chasing release.

I feel him tighten and then with a huge, "fuucccck," Ant comes, taking me over with him. My pussy greedily tightens around his cock, not wanting to let him go or lose the sensations of him being inside me. He collapses over me, his head to the side as we fight to get our breath back.

The room is largely silent, only our breathing can be heard. His arms are wrapped around me and I feel safe, loved, and content. It might be a fleeting moment in time, but right now I close my eyes and take it all in. Recording every sensation of touch. The smell of his wood-based aftershave. The noise of our breathing.

The moans we emitted. All so if I'm struggling, I can sit and visualise these moments.

"Is it okay if I take a shower?" I ask Ant after a few minutes.

He rises up, his elbow pressing into the pillow and his chin resting in his hand. "You can take a shower later," he says and he starts kissing me all over again.

I sleep for a while after and when I wake it's early evening. "You grab a shower and I'll order us some food. Chinese okay?" he asks.

I nod and pad out of bed.

"There are large fluffy towels in the en suite, but I'm afraid there are only male toiletries." Stupidly, that makes me happy. Does that mean he doesn't bring women home? Could I actually be *his* first too? Not his first rodeo; it's way apparent that Ant has had plenty of practice, but the first woman in his bed? I won't ask. I'd look like an idiot.

The shower is invigorating and I luxuriate in the warmth, feeling the slight soreness between my thighs and smiling a smug smirk to myself. My heart is asking what this all means while my mind knows a life of disappointment and rejection and slows down the excited beat.

And then the bathroom door opens.

"Hey," I say nervously, my arms down by my sides. Ant holds his hand over a sensor and the glass doors of the large shower open. He's not wearing a stitch of clothing.

"The food's ordered. It'll be an hour. So as I need a

shower too, I thought I'd come dirty you up before we get clean."

He drops to his knees and pushes my legs apart and his tongue darts out to lick between my thighs. I can do this. I can be in the shower with him, as long as he's distracted from my bare inner arms.

Ant's focus is on one place only as he has me clutching at his hair as I scream his name into the water running over me and then my back is against the cool tiles as he pushes into me, taking what he needs from my body.

"I suppose we should get clean now. I'm starting to wish I'd never ordered that fucking Chinese and just concentrated on eating you all night." He kisses up my body, my heart thundering in my chest as my panic begins to get the better of me. He bites my ear and goose bumps skitter up my arms.

He grabs his shower gel and begins to soap up a sponge. He runs it from my ear down and soaps my chest. "I found a new favourite way to shower," he says. All is fine until he tells me to raise my arms.

"I can take it from here. You don't need to see my armpits." I hold my hand out for the sponge.

He shakes his head. "I need to see and kiss every single inch of you, Lola Hawley."

"I'd like to just get showered quickly now if that's okay?" I try. "That Chinese must be arriving any minute."

"What's going on, Lola?" Ant stops and looks me over, his brows pulled together in concern before he tips up my chin. "I'm used to the faces of people who hide secrets and they never win against me, little P."

Sighing, I raise my arms above my head.

"There are some things you can't clean away." I state as his mouth gapes in shock and a gasp escapes him as he sees the scars of my left inner arm and the fresh cut.

His eyes harden the longer he stares at my scars and my stomach drops. Have I just ruined everything?

CHAPTER TEN

Ant

My head spins as I stare at the faint scars on Lola's arms.

Fuck. Fuck.

Reality comes crashing down on me and regret floods my body faster than I can control.

I shouldn't have brought her here. I shouldn't have done what I did, taken what I did.

My eyes pause on each little scar until I see the most recent one.

My stomach damn near falls into my feet.

This isn't an old issue. She's not wearing the scars of her past, of her previous pain. This is very much real and I sure as shit haven't just helped.

She's a fucking kid. No, not just a kid; one who has

been through hell. I should be helping her, much like I should be trying to help my daughter.

I'm already failing Ellie. I have since the day she was born, and now I'm doing the exact same with Lola.

"Fuck," I roar into the silent shower stall. My hands find my soaked hair and I tug until it hurts.

I need to do the right thing. I need to stop being such a selfish bastard.

When my vision clears, I find Lola curled into the corner of the shower with her arms wrapped around her trembling body.

She's so small. So vulnerable. And I just took advantage of that in my need to push away my fucked-up mind.

I'm no better than the men I rescued her from that day. I used her.

Her eyes widen in fear as I take a step back from her.

"Ant, please. Please don't do this," she begs, her voice quaking and making my heart ache.

"I'm sorry, Lola. I shouldn't have brought you here. I should have... I shouldn't have..."

"Fucked me?" she helpfully adds.

I look away, unable to see the pain I'm causing her that's clear as day in her eyes. "I shouldn't have taken that from you."

"You didn't take, Ant. I gave it to you willingly."

"That's not the point. You're a fucking kid, Lola. What I did... it was wrong."

I turn my back on her and swipe a towel from the rail.

"I'm not a kid," she screams behind me.

Every muscle in my body burns for me to turn around and take away the hurt I just caused, but I can't. Not when I'm right.

"I need you to leave."

I push through the door and march straight out of the bedroom. The twisted sheets taunt me, reminding me of what happened here not so long ago.

My cock stirs as the memories of just how good she felt as I pushed inside her hit me.

After reaching my home office door, I step through before closing it behind me. The click of the lock sounds like a fucking gunshot ringing out through the flat and seals my fate.

Regret fills me as I fall down into my chair and rest my head back, but the second I close my eyes all I can see are those scars.

Her life is so fucking bad that she physically hurts herself and here I am dragging her to my flat and taking her virginity without so much of a second thought because I'm too fucking angry at the world right now to see straight.

Resting my elbows on the edge of the desk, I drop my head into my hands as my mind spins out of control.

This isn't my first dealing with someone who has an obsession with a knife and the images of what that led to fill my mind.

The hospital bed, the drips, the hours of staring at a

lifeless body knowing that there was a chance that she didn't even want to be alive, yet she was, and at some point she was going to open her eyes and realise that she failed herself, just like everyone else around her had over the years.

Movement outside the door pulls me from my dark memories. Her footsteps pause in the hallway. She's no reason to know which room I disappeared to, but I swear she stops right outside.

My fists clench with my need to go and open the door and pull her into my arms. But I can't. I want more.

I might be able to lie to her, but I can't lie to myself.

If I feel her body in my arms again then my restraint is going to snap and she doesn't want that. She's already had enough arseholes in her life. The last thing she needs is me locking her up to ensure she's safe. My limbs burn with the need to protect her, only this time it's not from other men, it's from herself. But I know all too well that others can't force you to change your ways, your bad habits, that's got to come from within. And by the look of that fresh cut on her arm, she's not in that place.

I don't breathe out the air I was unknowingly holding until the sound of her footsteps continue. Within seconds, the front door opens before the strength of the slam makes the floor beneath me vibrate.

"Argh," I cry out, my palm connecting with the solid wood of my desk with a painful slap.

Pushing the chair out behind me, it wheels off into the room as I head in the opposite direction.

The bedroom is exactly as it was when I walked through not so long ago. The only things missing are Lola's clothes that I had strewn around the place. But the moment I walk in, the reminder that she was here hits my nose.

Without thinking, I strip the bed. I can't have the scent of my mistakes surrounding me all night.

With fresh sheets on the bed, I fall down on the edge and drag my trousers from the floor to find my phone.

I unlock it and pull up a number that I've not called for entirely too long.

"Well, hello stranger," I say, a smile immediately appearing on my face as the sound of her voice fills my ears.

"Well, fuck me, is a miracle occurring or are you really on the line?"

"Hey, I'm sorry it's been so long. Things have been hectic."

"When aren't they?"

"You've got me there. So how are things?" I ask, falling back on the bed as I listen to my oldest friend chat away to me about her life. Most of it is total bullshit, but like always, she seems to know exactly what it is I need despite her not having a clue where my head is at.

I hang up when the buzzer sounds out to tell me the Chinese I ordered is here. I'm tempted to ignore it and let the delivery guy eat it, but as my stomach grumbles, I know I'd only regret it, and fuck knows that I've already got enough of those for one day.

How empty and quiet my flat is has never been more obvious than when I lay in bed later that night staring at the ceiling thinking about how differently this night could have gone.

If I hadn't freaked out then would she still be here? Or would she have regretted sleeping with her boss on only her second day?

My mind drifts to Ellie and what led to me dragging Lola out of the office like a man possessed. She was in the fucking toilets blowing the lead singer of Hendon Street. My fucking daughter.

"Jesus." I mutter, thinking of all the many ways I failed her. I know that there wasn't a lot I could have done back then. I was a fucking kid myself. I like to think that I did what I could, but seeing her now, I fear that it was nowhere near enough.

"No," I cry, looking into her dark eyes. Whenever she gets that look on her face, I know something bad is about to happen. I scramble from the makeshift bed she makes me sleep on which really is no more than a few towels on the hard floor.

"Come here, my baby boy." She holds her hand out for me and my stomach churns.

I don't do as I'm told. The second I take a step back, her face drops and I know that I've just made it worse for myself.

For some reason, she seems to like it when I'm scared. It makes her enjoy this so much more.

I should just do as she says, it would make it easier. But I can't. I don't want her touching me. I don't want to go to her willingly.

She stalks toward me wearing nothing more than a scrap of see-through lace. It's the kind of thing she always wears when we're home alone. She tells me it makes her comfortable. I can't help but think it must make her cold.

I know for a fact that all it does is make me want to run. Run as fast as I can. But just like before when I tried, I know she'll always find me.

"Let's try this again, shall we? Come here, baby boy."

Once she's close enough, she reaches for my wrist and pulls me into her body.

"That's better. Are you cold, baby?" She runs her hands down my bare back. Goose bumps erupt, but it's not because I'm cold, or even because it tickles; it's with disgust. I don't want her touching me. Yet she never stops, and if I beg for her to do so, she only touches me more.

"Mummy's feeling lonely, and you know I don't like to be lonely."

I swallow the scream that wants to rip from my lips because I know it's pointless. No one ever hears. No one ever rescues me.

She takes my wrists in both her hands and guides them exactly where she wants them.

"NO," I cry, sitting up. My chest heaves as I try to drag in the air I need. I blink a few times, my room becoming clear and I sag back against the headboard in relief.

It was just a dream. A fucking nightmare more like.

My skin is covered in a layer of sweat as the images that would have continued in my sleep play out in my mind regardless.

I did everything I was meant to in order to get rid of her, to be free of her threats. But they never left. They reduced as the years went on, but then just like the ghost that I wish she was, she reappeared and dropped the bombshell that she'd been hiding all these years.

That beautiful little baby that I did everything to protect. She's mine.

I should have known. I should have figured it out. I wasn't a stupid kid, but I was so fucking desperate that I never even put two and two together. Fuck, I had no clue about any of that, and for one good reason. She never allowed me.

At some point I must have fallen back to sleep, because the next thing I know the sun is streaming in through the still open curtains. Thankfully, the rest of my night was less painful, although even now, the images from my recurring dream cling to my mind. Not that they ever really leave.

Sadly, the new day doesn't bring any clarity.

When I roll onto my back, my phone jabs into my side.

Pulling it free, I find William's number and hit call.

"You're being outwitted by a fucking kid, man," I bark into the phone the second he answers. "We keep you on board because you're meant to be the best, but you can't find an eighteen-year-old."

"She's a fucking ghost, Ant. It's like she doesn't exist."

Pfft, no. The ghost is the bitch who gave birth to her. The one who haunts me no matter what I do.

I shake thoughts of her out of my head and sit up, focusing on the most pressing issue.

"She was at the office yesterday, offering her services to our clients it seems. She used a security pass to get in. I left Jack to figure out the rest. I need her fucking found, man."

"I know, I know. I'm doing my best. She might be young, but she seems to know how to hide in plain sight."

"Figure it the fuck out. I need her here. I need to know she's safe." I end the call and throw myself back in the bed.

I failed her all those years ago. Like fuck am I going to do it again now I know she's mine to protect.

That thought leads me to someone else who needs looking after, but I don't have the mental capacity to think about her as well. It's bad enough that I'm going to have to walk into the office and see her.

I don't normally give two fucks about bumping into women I've fucked, but usually they're well away from the office, old enough to know better and just... different.

I've never truly cared about any of the women from my past. Vivian is the closest thing I've ever had to a relationship, but all that consists of is a phone call and a repeat performance when one of us needs to forget life for an hour or two. I don't care about her, not really. I walk out after doing whatever she asks of me without thinking twice about her.

But that's easier, because my mind doesn't replay sex with Vivian over and over whereas Lola... always seems to be in the periphery.

CHAPTER ELEVEN

Lola

I'm reeling. One minute I'm in heaven, the next in hell. It's the same pattern my life has been lived in. Hope, then despair. A cycle I can't pedal away from. When truly bared to Ant, not in giving him my 'cherry' but in the total naked flesh with my soul bared on the outside of my body, his reaction was to push me away.

He called me a kid and put me at the same level as his daughter. A teenager who gives blow jobs in toilets and walks around dressed as the hooker I believe she is.

I need a bar, a shitload of booze, and then I'm going to get off my face. So firstly, I need something more than a bag of bud.

Walking down from Ant's apartment, I phone Johnny.

"This is a surprise, Jade, baby. You can't need any more yet, so are you after something else? Like my body?" He laughs.

"I need something stronger. Some E's or something. And I need them now. Name your price to get them here to me. I'll be in a bar called..." I look around me. "The Office". I snigger at the name. *I'll be late, I'm at the office.* Very clever.

He names his price and I walk across the street and into the bar where I order a double vodka and find a place near the door.

It's only half an hour before Johnny is walking through the door of the bar, smiling at me.

"Happy birthday," he says, kissing me on both cheeks, and passing me a card. We both know it's not my birthday. I pull him in for a hug and slip my payment in his back pocket. "Sorry I can't stay," he says, and he leaves me to it.

I make my way to the bathroom where I discard the card and put the little plastic sachet containing the small pills into the back pocket of my bag. I'm not taking anything here. I'll wait until I'm home and my mum's asleep. For now, I'm content to drink myself into oblivion and I don't even care how I get home.

Ordering two more double vodkas, I find a table in a corner and make myself comfortable. I can see outside and I people watch until the chair in front of me is pulled out and one of my vodkas is picked up.

"What the fuck do you—?" I stop, looking in the eyes of Ellie. She plonks herself into the seat opposite me.

"What's with the drinking? I was watching you earlier and you looked happy as you walked into the apartment with Daddy. Did he not buy you the pony you wanted?" she spits out.

"I'm not in the mood for guessing games, so what the fuck are you talking about?" I reply.

"The fact that somehow I was put in foster care, but he kept you. Clearly looked after you given the nice clothes you're wearing and the fact your hair is blow-dried, silky perfection."

Kept me? Oh God. She thinks I'm his *daughter* too.

"Ellie, I'm not his daughter. Your dad is my boss. I'm an accountancy intern at B.A.D. Also, my sister is married to one of his best friends."

"Oh," she says, swallowing down the vodka. She narrows her gaze at me. "So are you going to ring him then and tell him where I am?"

"I've left his apartment, come into a bar, and I'm trying to make my blood 100% proof so do you think I'm about to fucking ring him?" I put my glass down. "Do you want another or are you going to take off again? I don't think you've stayed in the same spot longer than five minutes so should I be honoured?"

She grins. "I like you. You've got sass. I'll be here when you get back, as long as that dickhead Daddy has watching me doesn't show."

Nodding, I return to the bar.

As I'm waiting to be served I think about the fact that I should be phoning Ant to tell him his daughter is here with me, but I don't want to communicate with the man who just abandoned me. I huff. Huh, seems he's good at abandoning people. My eyes run over the girl at the table. It's funny, she's only a few years younger than me, and yet I see her as a girl and me a woman. Yet no one in this bar and certainly not Ant differentiates between us about our age. They'll all be judging her for what she's wearing.

Ellie's make up is thick and maybe an attempt to look older, certainly to look sexy. She has jean shorts on, fishnet tights, ankle boots and a black vest top that shows a red bra underneath. I'm still in my suit from the office. Luckily my blouse only tore at the bottom which is tucked into my skirt.

"So what were you doing in my dad's apartment? Taking down notes?" She smirks as I place our drinks down on the table.

"What do you want, Ellie?" I sit back in my chair. "You've followed me in here. Why?"

"I want to know a bit more about him without having to speak to him... yet. I'm not ready. If that guy hadn't turned up and I hadn't robbed his phone... I wouldn't have even known."

"What guy?" I ask wanting her to carry on talking.

"I was having some trouble and a guy stepped in. Well dressed, salt and pepper hair even though he didn't look that old. Proper silver fox. Anyway, I stole his phone and when I read his messages I found out why he was there. To find me. I'm nothing if not resourceful, so I decided to come and see why Ant was sending an investigator to find me. And then I discover he might be my dad."

"Must have been a shock?"

"Just a bit. Anyway we need to do DNA. Though he's probably changed his mind now... It wasn't exactly an emotional reunion when I walked into his office. I don't think Daddy expected his daughter to be a whore turning tricks in alleyways."

Wow. She was what she looked like.

"So where have you been all these years and how'd you end up...?"

"Being a prostitute?" She rolls her eyes about the fact I can't say the word out loud. "I was fostered, then adopted, and they were cunts. Long story short. I make money how I can. Selling my body isn't my career but it gets me by when I've not stolen enough. So when I realised my dad might be a billionaire you can see why I hot footed it to say hi."

"Money's not everything."

"Said by someone who has some clearly."

"Look, you get shit life of the year right now, but my life's been no picnic." Alcohol is loosening my tongue. "I don't know who my dad is either. Could be a guy who I know was a really decent man, or could be the guy who..." I trail off. I can't say what he did to me. The words won't come out. Fuck, I need more. Maybe it's time to smoke a joint?

"So is my dad a good man?"

"I don't really know him," I say honestly. "He stepped up when I needed him, but he's also someone who can make you feel like shit. Your dad and the others who run B.A.D. They're ruthless and take no prisoners. If he wants to find you, he will. You might have managed to escape him so far, but you'll not outrun him much longer." I remember something. "How'd you get in the building today?"

"I pinched your sister's swipe card as I walked past. Surprised she's not reported it missing."

I laugh. "She's on her honeymoon."

"Ooh, I'm good for a week or two then."

"Two."

Her eyebrow rises at that. "You're not gonna rat me out?"

"Nope. Your dad can handle his own business. I'm keeping well out of his personal life. Strictly business from now on."

"Oh dear." Ellie tilts her head at me.

"What?"

"You have it bad. Do you have a crush on your boss...?"

"Lola. My name's Lola."

"If my dad's spy walks in right now it won't look like you're keeping out of his personal life."

I take a large slug of my drink. "Right now, I don't give a shit. Now, anything else you want to know, because I'm not planning on being able to speak soon."

She smiles. "I'll buy the next round."

The room is spinning and Ellie is talking, but I want her to be quiet. I didn't come into this bar to meet Ellie. I came here to get drunk and to run through everything that happened today with me and Ant, from beginning to end. I want to get in bed and pretend he didn't turn away from me. How the fuck am I supposed to turn up at the office tomorrow and act as if none of this ever happened? Especially when his office reminds me of him pushing his fingers inside me.

"Looks like it's time you went to bed," Ellie says. "Where do you live?"

"I'm going to phone for my driver. Do you want taking anywhere?"

She laughs. "No thanks. All I wanted was to find out more about Anthony. Maybe I'll let him catch me next time. We'll see."

I stab the number in my phone and arrange my transport. I've drunk far too much. I can barely put one foot in front of the other one. Ellie walks outside with me. "Here, pass me your bag while you get in. I'll be getting your keys out for you, so you can go straight inside when you get home."

I pass her my bag. She opens the zip, rummages inside and throws me my keys. "Thanks," I say... To fresh air. She's done another runner, and this time it's with my belongings. And I'm too pissed to do anything about it.

Getting the driver to take me home, I head straight for bed, incapable of doing anything until the morning.

———

When I open my eyes my head thuds, sharp pain in my temples making me wince. What the fuck did I do?" It all comes back to me slowly: Ant's rejection, seeing Ellie, her stealing my bag. Oh fuck, I had weed and E's in that bag as well as money and my credit cards.

Dragging myself out of bed, I need coffee and the home telephone to start to sort this shit out.

The coffee brews and I splash my face with cold water at the kitchen sink. My mum had an early shift and already left. How did I get so pissed? I know I had a lot of shots but to hardly remember the night... I realise then that Ellie must have been pouring her drinks into my glass when I wasn't looking, because she certainly was still in control of her faculties when she robbed me.

A loud banging at my apartment door has me nearly banging my head on the ceiling. Walking down the hall, I get to the intercom and press.

"Yes?"

"Lola. It's Jack. I need you to let me in, *now!*"

I press the door release and watch as the door pushes open and a harassed looking Jack steps through.

"You need to come with me. Get dressed and no delay."

"What's going on?" I ask her. "Only I need some time. My bag was stolen last night."

"Lola," Jackie says solemnly. "Ellie is in the hospital after an overdose. The drugs she took were mixed with PMA. She was in possession of your handbag when she was found. I need you to come with me and tell me everything, because you might be able to offer some clue as to where she was going and where she might have got this bad batch from."

My face pales and I start to panic, my breath hard to come by. "They were mine," I tell her. "They were mine."

CHAPTER TWELVE

Ant

I'm walking into my bedroom after only hanging up the phone to William less than ten minutes ago when his name lights up my screen once more.

He'd better have some fucking news for me.

"Yes," I bark.

"She's in the hospital."

My heart sinks and my hand trembles.

"Where?"

He rattles off the name of the one she's been admitted to as I scramble around to find some clothes.

"This is your fucking fault," I shout at him as I hang up. If he'd found her properly when he was meant to, I'd have had her safe by now.

I pull on the discarded jogging bottoms and t-shirt that were on the chair in the corner of the room and run my fingers through my hair. It'll have to do.

I pocket my phone and rush from the flat.

I didn't give William a chance to tell me why she was there or to even explain what is wrong with her.

My hands tremble as I wrap my fingers around the wheel and my heart pounds so hard that it feels like it's banging against my fucking ribcage. I probably shouldn't be driving right now but like fuck am I stopping.

I fly out of the underground garage and speed across the city until I abandon my car in a space outside the hospital. I don't bother sorting a ticket, I'll just pay the fine later when I know what's going on and know if my daughter is dead or alive.

My vision is blurred with panic as I race to the reception. There are people standing around, but I don't see any of them.

"I'm looking for Ellie... err..."

"Thomas. Ellie Thomas," a familiar voice says from behind me. "It's okay. I can take you."

I follow William over to the lift and watch as he presses his finger on the button for the fourth floor.

"What's going on?"

"She's overdosed."

"What?" I bark, not believing what I'm hearing.

"She had some pills that were laced with something that caused her to have a seizure. Thankfully someone called for an ambulance just in time."

"Fucking hell." I rub my hand over my face, scratching at my rough jaw.

So not only is my newly acquired daughter a fucking hooker it seems, but a drug addict too.

William guides me towards the ward where they are treating Ellie.

"I'll wait out here," he says as we approach the reception desk.

"Hey, I'm...um... Ellie Thomas' ...father?" It's not meant to come out like a question, but I can't help it. It sounds so weird passing my lips.

I'm a fucking father. Seeing as the girl in question is eighteen, you'd think I'd have had a chance to get used to it by now.

"Of course, please follow me."

The kind looking nurse leads me over to a room that has four beds in it. One belongs to Ellie right now but the other three are strangers.

"I want her moved," I state. "I want her in a single room."

"Oh, I'm sorry, sir. There aren't any available right now."

I smile at her, but it's anything but pleasant. She visibly shudders, the exact reaction I was hoping for.

"Then I think you should probably go and look again."

"Oh... um... I'll be right back."

She runs off faster than her short legs have probably moved in years and I'm left with my daughter, still having no clue as to what's really happened.

I sit myself down beside her and study her sleeping face.

She looks much younger than she did standing in my office the other day, although she's still sporting the evidence of the attack she endured along with yesterday's make up that's all over her face.

Only two minutes later, two different nurses walk in.

"Good morning, sir. We're just going to move Ellie now. If you'd like to grab her few belongings from the cabinet you may follow us to her new location."

After thanking them in a much politer fashion than I spoke to the previous nurse, I follow them out of the room.

It's not until they have her settled in her new single room that the older of the two turns to me.

"We have police in reception waiting to speak with you about Ellie's incident. They would like to talk to you as soon as possible."

"Is... is she okay?" I ask, looking down at my still sleeping daughter.

"She's going to be fine. They had to give her something to lower her blood pressure and her temperature. There should be no lasting damage. The toxicology report showed the presence of PMA in the batch. The police will be able to tell you more, I'm sure."

"Okay, thank you. I'll be out momentarily."

She nods and smiles at me before checking Ellie over once again and leaving us alone.

"What happened to you, kiddo?" Reaching out, I gently brush my thumb over her soft cheek.

She moans in her sleep and leans into my touch slightly. The move damn near makes my heart shatter.

I know I need to take a DNA test to have it confirmed, but deep down, I already know that she's the baby I tried so hard to save all those years ago.

I thought her dark eyes drew me in just because she was a helpless baby. I had no idea that the connection we shared was stronger than that. If I'd had any clue, then I wouldn't have allowed us to be separated like we were. I thought that she'd end up in a loving family with incredible parents. There are loads of those out there who are desperate for a beautiful baby, who'd love and care for her like she was their own. As it is though, I fear the opposite may have happened and that her life hadn't been all that different from my own.

I'm pretty sure I'll forever hate myself for letting her go that day.

"I'll be back in a little bit," I tell her, not that I think she can hear me.

Exactly as the nurse said, the police are waiting for me when I turn the corner into reception.

"Anthony Warren," I say, holding my hand out.

"Good morning, Mr Warren. Shall we?" one of them says, gesturing to an empty room beside him.

They don't bother with any pleasantries. Instead, the other copper places a familiar handbag on the coffee table between us.

"Do you happen to recognise this bag?"

I narrow my eyes at it, trying to place it. "Uh..."

"Let me help you out. It belongs to a Jade Hawley. We believe she supplied your daughter with the drugs."

"Jade Haw..." Then it dawns.

"Motherfucker," I bark, pushing to stand so that I can move.

Anger like I've never felt before races through my veins as I pull at my hair.

Lola did this? Lola gave my daughter spiked drugs?

The entire room spins as I try to get my thoughts together.

No, this can't be right.

Lola's not a dealer. She can't be.

I think of the scars on her arms and I realise that I don't even know the girl I'm trying so hard to defend.

I kicked her out last night. She clearly wanted revenge.

My teeth grind. I'm going to fucking kill her.

I stare at the two cops in front of me. I need this out of their hands. I can deal with Lola in a much better way than them.

"I need to make some calls. I'll get you the information you need on where that shit came from. Leave it with me," I state.

They nod. Getting a main supplier is a far better result for them after all.

After getting a phone number from them, I march from the room and out into the corridor where William still is.

"Is everything okay?" he asks when he spots me.

I hold my hand up and press my phone to my ear.

"Jack, I need a favour," I demand the second she answers.

She listens to everything I say before agreeing and telling me that she'll sort it all.

"Yeah, she's going to be fine. You can go. I'll call you if I need you," I tell William.

"Are you sure?"

"Yeah, Jack's on her way."

He nods once before pushing from the wall he's leaning against and disappearing down the empty corridor.

I ring Reggie, our solicitor next. I need him to fix it, so the dealer goes down, but Lola is left out of it. He reassures me he'll sort it.

I make my way back to Ellie but I'm unable to sit beside her. Every muscle in my body is tense as I wait for Jack to arrive with what I hope is a very apprehensive Lola.

She might have witnessed me rescue her. She might think I'm the good one. But she's about to witness another side of me. One that not many people get to see, but one that's desperate to get retribution. She didn't just fuck Ellie over last night by supplying her with those drugs, she fucked us all. And the last place anyone wants to be is on our shit list. Anna's sister or not, Lola Hawley is fucked.

It's almost an hour before the door opens and the familiar click of her stilettos fills the room.

Jack appears around the corner, dressed as usual in

a sharp suit, her hair styled to perfection and her make-up flawless. The woman behind her however, looks very much the opposite.

Lola has huge dark rings around her red, tear-filled eyes, her skin is pale, and she's trembling as she stands with her arms wrapped around herself.

"Thank you, Jack. Do you mind?" I stand and gesture to my seat. "I've got some business to attend to."

She tips her chin in acceptance and moves past me. But not before she places her hand on my forearm and squeezes in support.

"She's okay," I whisper for only her to hear. "Please excuse us. We may be some time."

Marching over to a terrified looking Lola, I grasp the back of her neck and push her from the room.

I walk us both to the same room I had my little meeting with the police in and push her inside with enough force that she crashes onto the sofa while I close the door and flick the lock.

"A- Ant, w- what are you doing?"

I spin and pin her with a look that has her scrambling to stand up.

Walking over, I once again wrap my hand around her neck, but from the front this time and I use it to push her back against the wall.

I squeeze lightly as a warning and her eyes widen in horror.

"I suggest you start talking. And it better be the truth or so help me God."

"I- I- I..." she stutters, pissing me off.

"Talk."

"I- I didn't do anything," she whimpers, her eyes full of tears.

"Bullshit. My daughter was found with your handbag, your drugs. How?"

She stares at me for a moment, something unreadable passing through her eyes.

"Are you that desperate for me that you'd fuck my daughter over for revenge?"

"Don't be so stupid," she finally spits out.

"Have you known where she's been this whole time?"

When she refuses to answer, my fingers tighten, but this time she doesn't react. If anything, her eyes dare me to push her further.

"Tell me why."

She lifts her chin in defiance and keeps her lips pressed together.

"Defying me will only make this worse, Lola. I'll just assume you did this on purpose."

She shrugs. "As you wish."

I take the zip of her hoodie between my fingers and pull it down, exposing her lace covered breasts.

"You won't give me what I need, then I'll make sure you don't get yours."

"Do your worst. I can assure you that it won't be as bad as what I've endured before."

Her chest heaves as I stare down at her breasts, her nipples are already hard beneath.

Slipping my fingers beneath the lace, I pinch one.

She fights her reaction, but I don't miss the hitch in her breathing.

"You like a bit of pain, don't you, Lola?"

She once again stares at the other side of the room. Taking her chin in my grasp, I force her to look at me.

"I can bring you pain. I can bring you more than you can handle, but I can also bring you pleasure. Only you get to decide."

My hand slides down her stomach and straight into her leggings. The second I part her, her wetness coats my fingers.

"You're already enjoying this too much."

A smirk plays on her lips before a squeal escapes when I quickly spin her around.

"Hands on the wall."

She immediately does as she's told and I pull her arse back so she's almost bent in half.

In seconds, I have her leggings and knickers around her ankles.

Releasing my cock, I waste no time in finding her entrance and thrusting inside her.

The second her heat engulfs me, something within me settles and for the first time since I locked eyes on her, the room seems to stop spinning.

She moans in pleasure as I pull out slowly.

"This isn't for you, Lola. But tell me why, and I'll let you come."

"Fuck you, Ant. Argh," she cries as I fill her to the hilt before fucking her hard and fast until tingles race down my spine and my balls draw up.

CHAPTER THIRTEEN

Lola

The journey to the hospital was agonisingly tense. While I'd spent so much of my own life in pain, I would never wish it on anyone else, and Ellie had already experienced a turbulent life. Now she was in hospital after taking an overdose of my pills.

The thought of them being a bad batch makes me sick to my stomach. If I'd have taken any of them last night myself in my room, would I even be here today? It was a stupid move and I vow that I'll never contact Johnny again. Just like that I sever my contact with that old life.

Jack sits alongside me talking business. She doesn't say much to me at all. Just says I have questions to answer at the hospital. I'm probably going to be arrested. My new career will be over. I survived the incidents with Tommy to sabotage my own life. He'll be laughing in Hell.

I walk into the hospital, and follow Jack until we come face to face with Ant. His eyes blaze with venom and he demands that we go somewhere to talk.

And then he immediately accuses me of giving Ellie drugs. He actually believes I would do that? Next, he asks me if I've always known where she was?

And as much as part of me wants to give him all the answers, another part of me thinks he can go screw himself. If he thinks I could be so evil and deceitful then I'd hate to disappoint him. But I forget that Ant has much more experience of manipulation than I do.

The next thing I know his cock is thrusting inside me and as he fucks me with what feels almost like hate, I feel his balls draw up. He withdraws and I feel spurts of hot cum against my arse. He leaves me feeling soiled and dirty and I suppose I deserve it. I almost killed someone.

No one told her to steal your handbag. My mind fights back.

"All I want to know right now is who your supplier is," he says to my back. I can feel his release dripping off me. There are tissues on the coffee table, but he's not reaching to get any.

I give him Johnny's name. While I hate the fact I'm revealing the identity of the brother of someone I called a friend, he could have more of that batch.

I turn around. "Johnny is from my old life. If you can manage to leave him out of it, if he was tricked..."

His jaw tightens. "He's a fucking drug dealer and he gave you drugs that could have killed my daughter."

Not you, just 'my daughter'.

I nod.

"I'm going to make sure your involvement is swept under the carpet. Not for you, but for B.A.D. and for your sister."

"Thank you."

"Oh don't thank me." His eyes narrow. "I intend to make you pay for what you've done."

Now he reaches over and throws the tissue box in my direction. "Clean yourself up. I've done with you for now."

He walks out of the room, leaving me at a total loss for what my next move is. Do I need to follow him to Ellie's room? Do I go home? Go to work? It's not long before I hear the clip of heels and realise Jack's been sent back to deal with me.

I slump down in a seat. "She followed me into a bar, Jack, and she stole my bag."

"I expected as much. She's a very mixed up girl."

"She could have died."

Jack shrugs. "Did you tell Ellie to steal your bag and take your pills?"

"No."

"There you go then. The woman is eighteen years old. She's streetwise. She knows the score."

"He hates me."

"Ant has just found out he's a father and before he's had a chance to even confirm it, she's almost lost her life. The man must be wondering which way is up. So right now, whatever mood you get from him, suck it up, because you did see Ellie yesterday and you didn't tell him and that is on you."

We're silent for a minute or so. "Do you want a hot drink or anything? I'm going to grab a coffee," Jack asks.

"I could really use a coffee. Then I'll go home. Would you get someone to box up my few belongings I left on my desk, or shall I call Rachel?"

"You need to ask Ant whether or not he still wants you to work."

"The answer is obvious, surely?"

She smile-huffs. "Not with any of us, Lola."

"Are you going to tell Ant that she stole my bag?" I say quietly as she reaches the door.

"No. You are," she replies as she walks out of the door. "Let's go."

I must be a sucker for punishment because I do as she bids and I follow her out of the room and to a drinks machine near to the lift area. Then she takes me to a waiting room. "Wait here, while I take this drink to Ant and see if there's been any more news."

While she's gone I sit wringing my hands. I'm no longer sure coffee was a good idea as I'm shaking, but I pick my mug up and take a sip anyway. Funny how my hangover dropped away as soon as a feeling of horror took me over. Closing my eyes, I thank God that Ellie lived, because if she hadn't, I'm not sure I could carry on myself.

It's not Jack who returns to the waiting room, it's Ant.

"How is she?" I ask him.

"She can come home because I've booked a private nurse to keep an eye on her when I can't be there. I've just booked you a driver. Go home and pack some belongings because you're fucking staying with me."

"What?"

"You're the reason she needs looking after right now. So do as you're fucking told and get some clothes and shit, and check your belongings to make sure no more of your drugs accompany you." He passes me a key. "She'll be going in the guest room, so you'll have to put your stuff in my room."

"I'll take the sofa."

"You'll do exactly what I fucking say," he yells. "You're in no position right now to dictate anything to me. You're going to help me with Ellie, so that she doesn't do another runner and to make up for the fact you gave my daughter drugs."

"I didn't give her drugs; she fucking stole them."

"They shouldn't have been there for her to steal."

"Oh my god," I rant. "Like I bet no illegal substances have ever passed your lips."

"They haven't actually. Scotch is my poison of choice."

"Saint fucking Anthony," I scoff. "Well, it's doubtful your daughter is quite so pure. Did they do a pregnancy test and run a screening for STDs while they were at it?"

"Ellie's had some tests done and she'll be getting a full work up. I want to know my daughter is healthy."

"And then you're going to what? Keep her in your apartment like a prisoner? Sounds like a plan."

"I don't know what to do, okay?" he yells again. "There's no fucking instruction book that came with her. I've no experience of a happy family life to know what the fuck I'm supposed to do. All I know is I have to try."

I look at the floor.

He walks over to me and tilts my chin up. "So you need to help me. You're almost the same age. You can try and be a friend, see if you have anything in common."

I feel like he just stabbed me in the heart. He wants me to be a friend to Ellie? Because I'm nearly the same age?

"Then I guess I need to share her room then maybe, you know like college dorms. Bit strange being your daughter's friend and then sharing a bed with her father."

He doesn't reply. He just starts to walk away from me. "I'm going back to Ellie. I'll see you at my apartment."

Then he's through the door and gone.

I do what he asks and pack some things. I pack more than I think I'll need as Ellie was a similar size to me and she might need some clothes. I also pack a few magazines I haven't got around to reading.

How the fuck I'm going to explain to my mum why I'm living with my boss remains to be seen. In the end when I phone her, I tell her about Ellie and just that he's asked for my help. I also tell her I'm in a guest room too. "You be careful not to get overinvolved," she warns me. "I know he did a good thing for you, but it doesn't mean you owe him anything. If you feel in any danger, you come straight home."

"Yes, Mum. I will." Huh, if I feel in danger it's more likely to be from my proximity to Ant than to his daughter.

Before I leave, I shower to wipe away any traces of Ant from my body. I'm still confused as to what our earlier fuck meant. Was it my punishment that I didn't come and he did? Was it hate sex, to get out his frustrations about Ellie?

The guy appears to be all kinds of screwed up. From a person I'd thought was my saviour, now I'm not sure if I actually went out of the frying pan into the fire.

I'm worried he's going to make me burn.

When I let myself into Ant's apartment, I leave my case in the hall, walk through and sit on the sofa. Getting bored, I get up and fix myself a drink, grab one of the magazines from my case and try my best to concentrate on it.

When Ant finally comes through the door it's with a nurse, two men in builders attire and a tired and drawn looking Ellie.

"That's the room," he says to the men.

"I can't believe you are putting security outside the door," Ellie huffs. "I told you I'm too fucking tired to go anywhere." Walking forward, she looks at me. "Your drugs are shit," she says, stalking past me and flopping onto the sofa.

Ant chats to the nurse. Apparently, she's being put up in a nearby hotel and will be monitoring Ellie frequently, particularly her mental state.

"I'm not crazy," Ellie yells from the sofa. "I just thought I'd have a party for one, but the molly was bad. I need a more reputable supplier." She gives me a narrow-eyed look.

"You stole my property. Serves you fucking right. Shame they don't still pump stomachs out. That'd teach you to take what's not yours." I've had enough of listening to her shit now. I turn around and find the nurse is looking at me aghast.

"I think if we want Ellie to be comfortable and to get better we need to be a little calmer," she says with derision.

"Yes, so why don't you get me a glass of water and massage my feet or something?" Ellie says. "Daddy says you're here to help look after me, so..." She makes shooing motions. "Go start."

Even though I shouldn't want another drink after all the events that followed my last bout, I have a feeling I'm going to crave liquor a lot in the coming days.

"I brought some clothes over if you want to get changed." I try to smooth over the waters.

"Oh that's okay. Daddy is organising a personal shopper for me to get me a whole new wardrobe." She smirks and inside I feel sick. Ant is being played and he's too busy worrying about Ellie to see it.

CHAPTER FOURTEEN

Ant

I knew she'd be here, but still, walking into my flat to find Lola making herself comfortable on the sofa did weird things to me.

I was fucking furious with her. It may be true that Ellie stole her bag; it seems that my daughter is less than innocent in so many ways, but Lola still spent time with her and didn't tell me.

Lola knew I was looking for her, that I was damn near desperate to get my hands on her and find out the truth, yet she failed to give me the heads up.

She betrayed me. It's that simple.

She pushes to stand as we all join her, and I delight in the fact she looks like a rabbit caught in headlights. Good.

I hope she realises that earlier was just a taste of what she's going to get for going against me.

I keep my eyes on her as Ellie drops down on the sofa and I give the nurse some instructions.

I don't want her staying here and getting too involved in my life, so I've set her up in a room at the hotel down the street, but I'd be stupid not to have someone watching Ellie. Not only is she a flight risk, but she's a fucking drug addict it seems. She also has the DNA kit in her bag that we both need before we get too comfortable.

The atmosphere becomes heavy and I worry I might have made a huge mistake, especially when conversation starts.

With a hard look at Lola and then Ellie, I spin on my heels and march from the room.

The sound of my bedroom door slamming rattles through the flat, giving everyone else inside a clear idea of the kind of mood I'm in right now.

That release I had with Lola in the hospital barely took the edge off of how I'm feeling right now.

Falling down on the bed, I drop my head into my hands.

Any rational, sane man would send Lola home and no longer look at her. So why does the thought of doing just that make my chest ache?

I shouldn't have any kind of interest in her. She's too young for me. She's more suited to being Ellie's friend like I suggested earlier than having any kind of relationship with me besides being my employee, but she calls to me.

Maybe it's the broken parts inside both of us. The secrets we both hold but won't share. Maybe hiding like we do gives us some kind of fucked-up bond.

Knowing that I need to get out of this house and away from both of them for a little while, I pull out my phone and open my contacts.

My intention is to call Vivian. I know it's barely been hours since my last visit, but Hell, if I couldn't use her brand of distraction right now. It's either that or I use someone closer.

My grip on the phone becomes almost painful as I try to force myself to call Vivian. She'd let me do anything, take whatever I needed to get out of my own head, but the temptation just isn't there. Sadly, said temptation is currently sitting on my sofa giving my daughter some sass.

I don't get to dwell on my decision because my phone starts vibrating in my hand.

Looking down, I find Rachel's name staring up at me.

Frustration tightens my muscles. I told her that I was uncontactable today.

"Yes," I bark, putting my phone to my ear.

"I'm so sorry, Ant. But there is a lady here who is adamant she won't leave without seeing you."

My blood runs cold. I don't need Rachel to tell me who it is. I know.

"I'll be right there."

I hang the phone up, stand and walk from the room without thinking. If I think, I'm likely to send a fucking hit man straight to my office to put an end to the situation, but I can't do that until I get some answers. I might wish the cunt dead on a daily basis, but it seems she's given me something that belongs to both of us and I need the truth. Then, I'll do what I need to do to get her out of my life once and for all.

I probably should have figured out a way to do it back then before I even considered putting her away for what she did. I was young and naive back then. Now though, there's a good chance that she'll underestimate what I'm capable of.

All eyes turn on me as I return to the living room.

"You will not leave, either of you," I snap, my eyes drifting between the two of them.

Ellie looks exhausted with her head on a cushion, so right now, I'm not too concerned about her making a run for it. Lola though, she's got fire burning in her eyes.

I hold her stare. "You will be here when I get back. We've got unfinished business." She squirms in her seat, hopefully remembering earlier and getting more and more frustrated about her lack of release.

Oh you've experienced nothing yet, little P.

I raise my eyes waiting for her to respond but she never does. She just holds my stare.

I nod, glancing at the nurse who just looks fucking confused by the whole situation and turn to leave.

I really don't want to do this, but this day is already screwed up enough, I may as well load more on.

"What the hell are you doing here?" Deacon barks as I make my way down the corridor toward my office.

"I've got business to attend to."

"But Jack said—"

"Jack needs to keep her fucking mouth shut."

"Jesus, man. You need to get laid. All your grannies booked up?"

"Fuck you," I spit causing his lips to curl at the edges. Mia makes him too fucking happy. It's sickening.

Pushing past him, I continue towards my office, where the fucking ghost of my past is waiting for me.

"If you need anything, man. You know where we are."

I don't respond, I don't need to. He knows I won't call. They all do. They're used to me dealing with my own shit alone. They hate it— none more so than Tyler who's desperate to get inside my head and try to fix all the fucked-up. Sadly, there's way more of it up there than anyone realises.

"I'm so, so—"

"Don't," I snap at Rachel who looks at me with concerned eyes.

"How is she?"

"She's going to be fine, thank you." I quickly rattle

off a few things I need her to do for me, including organising Ellie some clothes and other belongings seeing as she was taken into hospital with just the clothes on her back and refuses to give me an address for where she lives. I fear that might be because she doesn't actually have anywhere, but I'll push for that information later.

I pause at my office door with my hand on the cool metal handle.

I know she's inside. Even without seeing her, my stomach turns over. Suddenly, I'm no longer Anthony Warren, CEO of B.A.D. Inc, successful accountant with more money than he knows what to do with. I'm a little boy who's been abused within an inch of his life and terrified for what comes next.

Locking that vulnerability down, I find the anger. The anger that's been festering inside me since the first time she touched me.

Pushing through, I slam the door back behind me.

"What the fuck do you think you're doing?" I bellow. I'm not sure if I mean about her being here or the fact she's currently sitting quite comfortably drinking my scotch.

"Ah, here he is. I thought you weren't going to come for me. But we both know you always do."

My stomach turns.

"What do you want?"

The last time I was forced to see her, she attempted to blackmail me out of money as she explained to me about my daughter.

I had no fucking idea that baby was mine, but there was no fucking way on this earth that I was giving her any money to get the information I needed.

She might think that she could get a nice payday out of me, but I didn't get where I am by being naive and stupid.

"Come and sit down, have a drink with your mother."

"You're not my fucking mother," I spit, already feeling myself spiralling out of control.

Coming here was a really bad idea. If I get out without wrapping my hands around her neck it'll be a fucking miracle.

"What do you want?" I repeat, hoping she'll get to the point.

"I have some information I think you might be interested in."

"Oh yeah," I say, sounding bored. "What's it going to cost me this time?" I ask, remembering the huge figure she asked for previously.

"Oh, Anthony, what must you think of me?"

I bite down on the inside of my lips to stop myself from being honest. How she's not still locked up behind bars for the things she did fucking astounds me. She might have served what they thought was an appropriate sentence, but she got off fucking lightly if you ask me.

"What do you want?" I ask again, already fed up of this bullshit.

"She's in trouble, Anthony." My eyes widen

slightly. She probably thinks it's with concern but she hasn't a fucking clue.

"Right?" I ask on a sigh.

"Don't you want to help her? She's your daughter."

"Is she though? All I've got to go on is your word, and I hate to break this to you but you're an untrustworthy cunt."

She gasps, although she can't deny that my words are true.

"She owes some bad people a lot of money."

How convenient, I think to myself.

"She needs your help." Ain't that the fucking truth.

"And you need to crawl back into the hole you disappeared into all those years ago. How many times do I need to tell you this? I do not care." It's one big fat lie. I care more than I probably should for the broken girl who's currently in my flat but there's no fucking way I'm going to allow *her* to see that.

She clearly still thinks that Ellie is out there somewhere doing fuck knows what instead of being safe with me and I'll allow her to think that as long as possible.

"She's your daughter, Anthony. These guys, they're... they're going to kill her. And if they don't, the drugs will."

"Are you about done?"

"Anthony, please. We need to help her."

"No. What you need to do is fuck off. I don't need you or your bullshit in my life." Reaching down, I wrap my fingers around her upper arm and pull.

"Ouch," she complains when I grip too tightly.

"Get the fuck out of my office." I throw her through the doorway once I have it open. She stumbles away before landing on her arse. Bending down on my haunches, I stare into her now scared eyes. "You need to watch your back. I'm no longer the boy you remember and you're playing with fire because you're no match for the man I now am."

She swallows nervously before scrambling away from me, and then she runs from the office.

Rachel watches me, but she doesn't say anything as I march back into my office and launch the bottle of scotch she'd been drinking from at the wall.

My fists clench and my teeth grind as my need to let it all out consumes me.

There's only one person I need right now.

She's all wrong in so many ways but she needs to pay for her actions and she's about to learn that I'm not the nice guy she had me pinned as when I rescued her all those weeks ago.

CHAPTER FIFTEEN

Lola

Ant has gone off to sort out some urgent business. The nurse has left, and now it's just me, Ellie, and a security guy stationed outside the door. I'm a grown woman. I should just get up and walk out of the door, threaten to call the police for holding me here against my will. But is it against my will, or in some sick, fucked-up way am I exactly where I want to be?

Because Anthony clearly wants to punish me for my actions, and I want him to. He can give me what I need, without drugs, without blades. He can punish me and free me at the same time. And it's that which keeps me here in his apartment. The darkness that lives in my body swirls for attention. He's been gone minutes, but I already need him back. He can take out his frustrations on me because he doesn't know what I did, what they made me do, and there's nothing he can do to me that I wouldn't feel I deserved.

"What's going on with you and my daddy? Are you his fuck toy?" Ellie asks. It's clear to see now that I was played last night. She wanted the money from my handbag and had no interest in me at all. But what did I expect? I know nothing about her.

"Let's talk about something much more interesting. Like who Ellie Thomas is and what her current game plan consists of, shall we?" I pour myself a glass of water as Ant has had the place cleared of alcohol and anything else that could be hazardous to his current roommates.

Ellie's face darkens. "Who I am? I'll tell you who I am. He fucking abandoned me. Him and my mother. I was fostered, adopted, abused. While he's sat making millions, I've done tricks so I can eat. So forgive me if I'm a bit fucking bitter about things. He owes me. And yet I can see in his clueless head he thinks that sending out for some clean clothes and a mobile phone is somehow going to make the past erase itself. As soon as I have what he owes me, I'm out of here. Far, far away where no one knows me. I'll start again and I'll leave them all behind."

I scoff at her naivety.

"You can't escape ghosts, Ellie. If anyone knows that, I do."

"Huh, yeah, it looks like you've had a hard life."

Standing in front of her, I pull off my jacket and I start to open my blouse.

"What the fuck are you doing? I don't swing that way, bitch. Although maybe for the right price I can be persuaded."

I show her my scarred flesh.

"Lesson number one, Ellie. Don't take everyone at face value. You know nothing about my past, or about how I struggle to put one foot in front of the other one every single day." I put my blouse back on and refasten it. "You stole my oblivion last night. Though I only wanted some time out, not to die, so I guess I should thank you."

"I don't need a father," she says to me.

I sit down on the sofa at the side of her.

"I told you last night, that I have my own daddy issues, though you probably weren't listening."

"Oh?"

"The man who I grew up with believing was my father was an evil, malicious cunt. I found out he might not have been my father after all and the man that could have been... I never had chance to know him."

My mind wants to take me back, soak me in horror, but I won't let it. The ants are back though, trying to consume me and this time I have no way of dealing with them. My hand reaches for my inner arm. If I can just feel the pain, it can help bring me back. I can't go there.

Blood. So much blood.

A flash of steel.

Forgiveness in a broken face.

It's all dark as I'm consumed by my waking nightmare.

———

When I next come to, there are voices. So many voices.

"Lola. Lola! Can you hear me?" I'm dreaming, because Ant is here again to rescue me. I need him more than I need air.

I open my eyes and his face is near mine, his eyes wide, his hands around my shoulders shaking me.

"Wh- what...?"

"You've had some kind of panic attack. I've sent for the nurse. Ellie says one minute you were okay and the next you were screaming and then you passed out."

I see Ellie behind Ant. "You jealous of the attention I was getting?"

That brings a smile to my lips. "Y- yeah, you're an attention seeking bitch. It was my turn."

"I'll get you a fresh water now you're back with us." She walks off towards the kitchen area.

"What happened?" Ant has me sitting up on the sofa and takes the space next to me. His body is near enough to mine that I can feel the heat from his thigh. I need his touch, so I move myself a fraction nearer, so my thigh is against his.

"I had a flashback. I just need to sleep now, if that's okay?"

"I've sent for food. We all eat first and then you can sleep."

I nod my head. "I'm not very hungry."

"I've sent for sandwiches, soups, pizza. Just eat what you can. It's been a long day and we all need some rest." He turns to Ellie. "I get that you're probably not very fucking happy that I want to keep you here, but can you please just stay tonight at least? Let us all have some fucking rest?"

"Sure, but only because she's clearly a delicate flower." She passes me the water.

"Thanks."

"To be honest, it's not much of an ask to request I stay in a comfy bed with an en suite. Beats a hospital bed or a floor in someone's squat." The buzzer sounds at the door. "I'm off to my room. Tell Florence Nightingale I'm fine but she can check me if she likes."

"She will be checking you," Ant says, "so you might as well answer the door."

"Jesus, you'll be asking me to clean the apartment next." She stomps towards the door.

The nurse checks me over and satisfied she goes to Ellie's room. The food arrives and once the nurse has left, Ellie comes out, fills a tray with food and drink and disappears into her room.

"Do you think she'll really stay the night?" I ask Ant.

"She can't get past the door anyway if she does try anything, but she's exhausted even though she's been trying to fight it. I think she'll sleep. Tomorrow though is another matter."

"Did you get your urgent stuff sorted at the office?"

"I don't want to talk about work, or about Ellie. Right now, I want to go to bed."

My core flutters. I can't help myself.

"Shall I sleep out here?" I double check.

"I already told you that you'll be sharing my bed. My plan was to punish you for what you did to my daughter, but again, it can wait. Go and sleep. I'll be through shortly. I can't wait for this day to be done with."

Getting up, I walk into his room, but I have no intention of going straight to sleep. He wants to punish me, and I need it. I need the pain.

In his room I strip out of all my clothes. He's seen my scars now, so I feel no pressure to hide them. Going through his drawers I take out what I need and I place it under the pillow. Then I pull my silk robe around myself and I wait.

When he walks into the room, his eyes widen as he sees me sat up in the middle of his bed.

"I thought you'd be asleep by now."

I pull at the tie of my robe and open it. Then I get to my knees and pull the leather belt out from under the pillow.

"You said you'd punish me..."

He gasps, and I see his Adam's apple bob up and down as he swallows.

"I need it. I need the pain."

Crawling to the end of the bed, I sit on my knees, hold out the belt and place my head down, closing my eyes.

It feels like time stands still. I hear the clock ticking from his bedside table. And then the belt runs through my hand as he takes it from me.

"I'm not a good man," he says.

I don't reply. I keep my head down and await instruction.

He pulls me up from the bed and takes off the rest of my robe. It floats to the ground. I don't move as I hear him lower his zip and his own clothes begin to hit the floor.

"Get on all fours on the bed," he instructs. "I want your arse high in the air." I scramble onto the bed. This is all new to me. It's only days since he took my virginity, but it's not taken me long to realise that I have a new way of dealing with my inner turmoil.

I hear a sharp intake of breath. "If you have any fantasies that I'm going to give you tiny strokes and then love you, then I suggest you crawl into bed and go to sleep like I asked you to do," he says tersely. "Because just like most women in my life, you don't do as you're told and I feel a great need to punish you for that, Lola."

I stay where I am.

"Fuck."

The sound of leather whooshing through the air is the only sound in the room before pain hits my arse cheek and the resounding thwack from it echoes around the room. I flinch. It hurts like a bitch, but my body is screaming for more.

Punish me.

Hurt me.

Let me feel the pain.

His hand strokes over the burn. "What a beautiful mark. Are you sorry? Are you sorry for what you did to me, bitch?"

Thwack.

I gasp.

"Permission to speak, Lola. Are you sorry?"

"Yes." I hiss as he hits me a third time.

His hands move to between my legs and his fingers run through my wetness.

"Do you want me, Lola?"

"Yes."

"I won't be gentle."

The belt abandoned, his dick pushes between my thighs and his hand grasps my hair.

"You all need to learn your place," he growls out while he thrusts harder and harder inside me. My scalp hurts as he pulls hard at my hair, but inside me all I can think is that I need this.

Pleasure.

Pain.

Oblivion.

His hand comes to my neck and squeezes, taking me somewhere outside myself as I float into something else entirely to what I've ever known.

And then he's holding my hips and riding me so

hard my pussy burns, until he yells he's about to come and as he pinches my clit hard between his thumb and finger I convulse around him, feeling like I'm shattering completely and I carry on floating away into a place of peace.

Ant crawls behind me on the bed, pulls me in towards him and I fall asleep in his arms.

The next morning, I wake up when I hear cursing and shoot up in bed hearing Ant yelling from the bathroom.

Getting out of bed, I walk in and find him with angry tears running down his face, the bathroom in a state of destruction.

"What's wrong?"

"I hurt you. You let me. I'm fucked-up, Lola. You need to get away from me. Go on, get out," he yells.

Walking over, I drop my hands to my sides until my naked body is just an inch away from him.

"You hurt me. I let you. I'm fucked-up, Ant. You need to get away from me." I throw his words back at him. Then I walk over to the sink and place my hands on it.

"Your choice, Ant. Leave the room and I'll get my things and go." I wait with bated breath for his next move.

CHAPTER SIXTEEN

Ant

"Your choice, Ant. Leave the room and I'll get my things and go."

Her ultimatum plays over and over in my head as I stare at her. She rests her palms on the basin and hangs her head between her shoulders as she waits for me to make my decision.

Finding her like that last night was the last thing I expected. But then she asked me to... *Fuck.* I lift my hands to my hair, tugging on the long strands until it hurts.

My eyes run down her back until I find the bright red welts on her arse. Never in my life have I cared about the marks I've left on a woman. The benefit of being with older women is that I'm confident that they know what they want, they've had experience and they know what they can handle. But Lola. Fuck, I only took her virginity the other day, she's no idea what she needs. Yet one look at that belt and all I could think of was marking her, punishing her.

I know my intention was to come back here yesterday and teach her a lesson, but I had no plans to actually hurt her.

"Lola, I—" I start but my words are soon cut off when she turns to face me, placing her haunted eyes on me.

There's something so dark within them it terrifies me. I liked to think I knew what she went through when she was taken, but I'm starting to think it could be worse than I allowed myself to believe.

She's hiding some dark and twisted secrets within and I know that without letting them out, they're going to slowly kill her. She won't need the help of some questionable drugs when her darkness is eating her from the inside out.

"Decide, Ant." Her voice wobbles and her body visibly trembles as she holds my stare.

She looks so vulnerable, so weak, so desperate to be protected; to be looked after.

I make a snap decision, one that I could well regret but there's no way I can walk out of this room right now and leave her here.

I step up to her, slide my hand around the back of her neck until my fingers tangle in her hair and pull her to me.

Her naked breasts press against my equally bare chest and I crash my lips down on hers. My tongue pushes past her lips in its search for her own and she eagerly accepts it.

Running my hands down her back, I grip onto her thighs and lift her into my body.

My erection brushes against her core and her entire body shudders in my arms.

"Don't you dare change your mind," she mutters against my lips.

I still for a beat and she pulls back, her eyes wide.

"What I said last night stands, Lola. I'm not a good person. You need pain, I'll deliver it without question. You need to hurt, I'm capable of making that happen in a way you've never experienced before." A darkness I'm becoming used to passes across her face. "If you ask for anything, I'm telling you now that I will always deliver. Can you handle that?"

"I'll only ask if I need it."

I nod, my grip on her probably becoming painful.

"I need something from you."

She rears back slightly, shocked by my words.

"W- what could you possibly need from me?"

"Plenty. And eventually, I want it all. But I know that right now, you're not ready to give me everything, just like I'm not. There are things about my past that I might never talk of, and I'm aware that the same may go for you. But I need..." I hesitate because I've never needed anything from anyone in my life ever, and I'm not sure how I feel about being desperate for it all of a sudden.

Her eyes widen again as she gets impatient.

"I need you to stop hurting yourself, Lo. I need... If you need that... the pain. Use me. I'll give you anything you need."

She searches my eyes for a beat before nodding. "Okay," she whispers.

A smile twitches at the corner of my lips, but it never properly emerges because I fear she's only telling me what I want to hear.

I want to call her out on it, but I fear it's pointless. All I can do is ask and watch her.

Stopping her from saying anymore, I drop my lips to hers and carry her out of the en suite and back to the bed. I lower her down gently. I was rough on her last night and I need to show her that that's not all I'm capable of.

I crawl onto the bed, getting comfortable between her legs, but I don't stop kissing her. My hand runs down her leg and skims up over her waist until I find her breast. I palm it, pinching her nipple and making her arch from the bed.

"Ant," she moans quietly when I rip my lips from hers and begin kissing across her jaw and down her neck. "Fuck me, Ant. I need—"

"Shush. Let me take care of you."

My lips drop to her neck where I suck and nibble down the soft skin.

One of her hands runs up my back while the other

threads into my hair. She gently pushes lower and I chuckle against her. There's no way she's taking any control right now.

"Nice try."

I brush my lips over her shoulder before taking her arm and lifting it over her head, exposing the scars I know she's desperate to hide from me. I press my lips to the most recent scar and feel her body tremble beneath my touch.

With my lips still pressed against her, I look up at her. Her eyes are full of unshed tears as she stares back at me.

With our eyes connected, I lower my lips and kiss each and every scar that runs down her upper arm before moving to the side and sucking her nipple into my mouth.

"Oh God," she moans, arching once again. "Please, Ant. Please."

I smile around her.

"Fuck, I love it when you beg."

I give the other side the same treatment before kissing down her stomach, dipping my tongue into her navel and heading lower.

My palms engulf her thighs as I push them wider, exposing what I'm damn near desperate for.

I blow a stream of air across her pink folds and delight in watching her writhe with pleasure, despite the fact I've not actually touched her.

"Ant," she cries.

"Tell me what you want," I demand.

"You," she replies simply.

I chuckle at her. "Not that easy, baby. Tell me exactly what you want."

Our eyes hold as her cheeks heat. There's no point being embarrassed while I'm staring right at her pussy, but I kind of like it. Most of the women of my past never once got embarrassed about anything, no matter how taboo and kinky their desires were.

"I want your mouth. Your tongue."

"Better," I mutter, kissing up her thigh.

"I... I want you to make me come."

"Hmmm," I mumble as I lightly run my tongue over her lips.

"Ant." Her fingers dive into my hair and she pulls to try to get me closer.

"Shhhh."

"God," she moans as my breath caresses her.

Running my eyes up her stomach, I lock them onto hers before I close the final bit of space between us and press my tongue to her clit.

Her eyelids get heavy, but she must read the warning in my eyes because she never closes them.

My fingers grip onto her hips as I tease her. I lick, suck, and bite before plunging my tongue into her incredibly tight heat. My cock weeps to push inside of her again, but I need to wait. I want to prove to her that I can do more than rough, fast, and painful.

Releasing one hand, I push two fingers inside her, bending them so I can find her sweet spot.

"Fuck," she cries, thrashing about on the bed as it

begins to get too much, but I don't let up until she clamps down on me impossibly tightly and falls over the edge. Her eyes close in ecstasy.

She's so fucking sexy when she falls apart and I find I can't take my eyes off her as her previous blush expands from her cheeks, down her neck and across her chest.

"Fuck, you're so beautiful." I don't realise the words have fallen from my lips until her eyes open and find mine.

A small smile plays on her lips, and suddenly, I don't regret saying the words.

"Can you please fuck me now?" she asks, totally breaking the moment, although I'm not about to deny her what she wants.

Sitting back up between her thighs, I take myself in my hand and lean over her body so I can take her lips.

She moans when she tastes herself on me, but she doesn't so much as flinch as I push my tongue into her mouth. Instead, she sucks on it, much like I need her to do to my cock sometime soon.

Without thinking, I slide straight into her. She's so wet and ready for me that I fill her to the hilt with one quick thrust of my hips.

"Fuck. So fucking tight. So good," I groan against her lips as the sensations overtake my body.

Her nails scratch down my back until she's gripping onto my arse and trying to make me increase my speed.

I hold off for a few minutes but my restraint only

lasts so long before I sit up and lift her legs up over my shoulders so I can fuck her into her next release.

No sooner do her walls start rippling around me with her impending orgasm do my balls draw up.

I slide my hand up her body, pinching her nipples before I wrap it around her neck, my need for control getting the better of me.

If it's possible, her pussy gets even wetter as my fingers grip her before she begins to fall.

She calls out my name so loud I've no doubt it fills the entire flat, not just the room. Her release drags my own out of me with a low growl.

Falling down on top of her, we both fight to catch our breath.

"I really should get ready for work," I pant after a few seconds.

"Me too. My boss is a right cunt."

I can't help but bark out a laugh.

"I'm sure that's not the first time he's heard such a thing."

"Oh?" she says, turning to look at me when I fall to her side.

"You should hear the shit people talk in the staff room when we're not around," I admit without thinking.

"Wait... how do you hear.... You've fucking bugged it, haven't you?"

I shrug. I'm not going to deny the truth. "You wouldn't believe the number of snakes we've discovered because of it."

"I guess you don't need me as a man on the inside then to tell you all the gossip."

"We know everything that goes on in that building."

"Even down to your daughter turning tricks in the toilets?" I stiffen. "Fuck, sorry. I didn't think."

"It's fine, Lola. You're only speaking the truth."

Pushing off her, I sit myself against the headboard.

"What are your plans with her?" she asks.

"Wait for the DNA test results to come through and then take it from there. Heidi did the test on both of us last night and has assured me that it'll head to the lab first thing this morning. If she hangs around long enough for the results that is."

Lola grimaces. She clearly has about as much faith in Ellie sticking around as I do.

I want her here, of course I do. But I draw the line at forcing her to stay once I know she's fully recovered. I've been held against my will. I won't do the same to her.

"I need to shower and get to work," I tell her and I make my way back to the bathroom.

CHAPTER SEVENTEEN

Lola

While Ant's in the shower, I wrap a robe around myself and head to the main bathroom suite to have my own. Ellie's door is closed and I wonder if she's still sleeping. When I eventually leave the bathroom, wrapped in a towelling robe and with my hair in a turban, and head through to get a much needed coffee or juice, I find her laid on the sofa, eating a slice of toast, crumbs going everywhere.

"I thought you might still be asleep," I tell her.

"With the racket coming from your room?" She looks at me pointedly, and I feel my cheeks heat. "Oh God, don't get embarrassed on my account. I've turned tricks at the sides of others many a time."

I look around. I thought Ant would have been out of the shower by now.

"He already left," she informs me, and I can't help feel disappointment like a stone in my gut. Stupid, stupid woman. Did I imagine we'd head in together like some kind of happy couple? "He says to call a driver when you're ready and that the story is you've had a virus and now you're better."

Well that answered my question of whether or not I was still in a job.

After making my coffee, I take a seat at the island that separates the kitchen area from the living space. "So, what are his plans for you? Twenty-four-seven security detail?"

"Nope. Heidi last checked me over at seven am and declared me fit and well. My father said he hoped I'd stay here because he wants to spend some time with me this evening, but that if I take off, he'll just come looking for me again. He said I was an adult and he couldn't force me to stay." She shrugs. "So, I'll see how I feel. I can either stay in this luxury apartment and await delivery of clothes, shoes, bags and everything else my little heart desires, or I can run away and see if there's anyone else can give me five hundred quid for a blow job like the guy in the B.A.D. offices."

"Five hundred fucking quid?"

"Well, he didn't exactly give it to me, but you know, if he's gonna just leave his trousers around his ankles like that…"

"So you're staying in?" I change the subject fast.

Thank God the days of newspaper kiss and tell exposes are long over or she'd be posing in lingerie for the cameras while she spoke about how Demitri broke her heart.

"I make no promises," she says.

"I'll let Rachel know she might need to replace whatever you steal then," I retort.

Ellie's teeth grind. "I steal because I need to fucking eat. If I have enough for food then I won't need to steal. It's not something I do for kicks, I do it for survival."

"I'm sorry. That was uncalled for," I reply.

I rummage in my handbag for some paper and a pen and I scribble down a number. "Here, if you need me, ring it."

She doesn't make a move to take it, so with a sigh I drop it on the coffee table in front of her. "Right, I'm going to get ready and then I'm off to work."

"Don't actually need your itinerary," she snarks.

If she's trying to annoy me it won't work because all she's doing is reminding me of the times I spent with Anna before we were separated. Where we'd squabble like we hated each other one minute and share a duvet the next while we watched a movie.

Ellie has no experience of a proper relationship and is set on defence mode.

I don't take too long getting ready because I'd rather be near Ant than spending extra time trying to look good.

When I get to B.A.D. Inc and the accounts department, Rachel greets me. "Morning, Lola. There's a meeting this morning in Room three. It happens every Thursday morning at nine, so you've time for a coffee. It's just a round up of what's happening and is run by Marshall." Marshall was Ant's deputy manager.

"Okay, thanks."

"Hope you're feeling better," she says, with a smirk.

"Much thanks." I grin and I walk through to the office.

The blinds on Ant's office windows are down so I have no idea if he's in there deep in meetings or elsewhere. I've not been at my desk but a minute when Rob comes over.

"Hey, Lo. Good to see you back. Are you better now?"

"Yes. Thank you." I say, ignoring the fact he's shortened my name, despite knowing me just over a day in time spent together.

"Good. At first, I thought you'd been sacked. You know, after the whole *incident* the other day."

"I'm surprised I wasn't," I say with honesty. "But now I'm back, feeling better, and I'm going to keep my head down and learn the job, so where do you want me?" My mouth runs it out before my brain catches up.

Rob's eyes twinkle with amusement. "Gonna have to say Room three for the Operations Meeting on this occasion."

My morning passes quickly. Despite Rob's occasional flirty banter, we get on well, and I really am starting to enjoy the job. Keeping my attention on it had been easier than I thought as we were busy. If I'd thought being an intern meant light duties, I'd been mistaken. There'd still been no sign of Ant and I was starting to get withdrawals, even though it had only been hours since he'd sunk himself inside me.

I head down to the canteen for lunch where I see my new office colleagues laughing as they chat amongst each other. I wonder if I could become part of that, a true part of the team. Now seems a good a time as any to try, so I take a seat and when they mention a pub outing Friday night I agree to go.

Rob had his own work to do that afternoon and he felt I could be left with some basic inputting that had a failsafe, so I was left to my own devices. It felt good, like I was properly working, not playing at it.

Before long it's five pm and time for me to leave. I have to go back to Ant's to at least collect my things, and my heart and stomach fizzes with excitement at the thought of seeing him again, since I've barely seen him all day.

As I go to leave, Rachel stops me. "Can you go to Ant's office, only—"

"Sure," I say and I'm on my way before she can finish her sentence.

So when I knock and push open Ant's office door, I'm a little wrongfooted when Deacon King sits behind his desk.

"Lola, darling. Take a seat," he says. He's grinning, but it's like the Devil is sitting there offering me a spot by the fire.

Slowly, I walk towards the chair and sit down. "Will this take long? Only I need to be somewhere."

"Oh, Lola. I'm not about to torture you." I flinch at his words.

"Fuck, Lola. I'm a dick, okay. Did something like that...?"

"What do you want, Deacon?" I snap.

"I wondered if you knew what the fuck was going on with my friend. Only, I tried to ask him and all I get is that he's handling it. So do you know anything else about this kid that he's moved into his home before he even knows she's his?"

"I don't," I say honestly. "And if I did, I wouldn't discuss Ant's business unless he was in danger."

Deacon relaxes. "That's all I need to know. That he's not in danger. Not in any trouble." His steely blue eyes meet mine. "If things change, you come to me, you hear?" he warns. "Because I deal with danger, Lola. Head on. I make it disappear."

Chills run down my spine because his meaning is clear. I would never want to be on the receiving end of Deacon King's vengeance.

"It's good he has you. All of you." Is what I finally choose to say.

"We're his family. Where his own were useless cunts, and the people who fostered him fucked him over, we stick around whatever. I don't know why he

148

has you staying with him and I don't want to know, but if anything happens and you knew and didn't warn me... well, I won't care who you're related to."

"Message received and understood." I stand and walk over to the desk and fix him directly in the eye. "I wish I'd known you a long time ago," I say solemnly and then I turn on my heel and exit the office.

As I walk past Rachel she hurries from behind her desk. "You okay, Lola? I tried to tell you it was Mr King in there, but you disappeared so fast."

"I'm fine. I really do need to not be so eager to please." I make a joke of what I'd done. "It seems every day I manage to embarrass myself somehow."

"On my first day I walked around with my skirt tucked into my knickers," she explains. "Something tells me you'll settle in here and do just fine." She smiles. "Have a nice night. Ant's had a driver on standby to take you back to his apartment."

I blush slightly at her gaze on me and the curl of her lip.

"Good to hear you're coming out for drinks tomorrow. It's usually a good night. See you tomorrow, Lola."

I wish her a good night back and I wonder if Rachel might just turn out to be someone I can include in my tight circle, an actual new friend.

But my mind forgets everything as I reach the car waiting on standby, its rear door open. "I wondered if you were going to ever fucking leave. Get in," Ant says, and I hurry to climb in the back seat.

CHAPTER EIGHTEEN

Ant

The second she's in the car, I press my finger to the button to lift the privacy glass. The noise makes her look over and when her eyes come back to me they're dark and full of hunger.

"Come here." I pat my thigh and stretch my legs out.

"But..." She hesitates, trying to be a good girl but I already know that her panties are wet for me. It may have only been hours, but I can already read her body, and right now she's as desperate as I am.

"Don't make me come and get you." I raise a brow, getting impatient.

Immediately, she takes a step forward, hitching up

her skirt as she does. In seconds she's exactly where I wanted her, straddling my lap.

My hands go to her arse, pulling her down onto me as my lips claim hers.

Her hands run up my chest until her fingers play with the hair at the nape of my neck.

A low moan rumbles up her throat as I squeeze her arse tighter, grinding her down on me.

Pulling back from her lips, I look into her eyes.

"Rob wants to fuck you," I say, my voice flat as if unaffected by the words. It's not how I feel on the inside.

I've watched them both today. The way he smiles at her, how he reaches out for any excuse to touch her. He needs to watch his fucking back because no one gets to touch her but me.

Her gasp of surprise tells me she had no idea, and a small smile twitches at my lips at her naivety.

"No he doesn't," she argues, pissing me the fuck off.

"I wasn't suggesting it, Lola. It's a fact."

Her lips part, probably to attempt to rip me a new one, but wisely, she changes her mind.

"Make him back off before I'm left with no choice but to do it for you."

"You're aware that the only reason he's anywhere near me is because of you, right?"

"Error in judgement."

"Caveman," she mutters as I lean forward and brush my lips down the length of her neck.

"You love it. It makes you wet as fuck."

"Oh yeah?" I don't need to look at her to know her brow is going to be raised in challenge.

"You're really trying to tell me that you're not drenched right now? I don't give her a chance to respond, I'm already lifting the fabric of her dress higher and pushing my fingers inside her knickers. "Fuck, Lola," I groan when her heat surrounds my fingers.

"Ant," she cries, her head falling back as I push two fingers inside of her.

"Get my cock out."

The car moves from the traffic it had stopped in and I know that our time is running out, but I need her before we walk back into my flat to discover if Ellie is still there or not.

Leaving her today was a huge risk, but at the end of the day she's an adult and needs to make her own choices. Hell knows she has so far in life.

Lola rushes to undo my belt, her fingers running over the soft leather for a beat. I watch her face as she does.

"You want it again, don't you?"

"I think I want everything you're capable of, Ant," she admits quietly before biting down on her bottom lip.

My cock weeps at her words, dirty thoughts filling my head, images of all the ways I can satisfy her burning need for pain without reaching for a knife or a packet of pills.

"You might regret that. I've done some very, very bad things."

Her pussy clamps down on my fingers, her juices beginning to run down my hand, and it tells me just how much she really does want that side of me.

As her release creeps closer, I pull my fingers from inside her, much to her frustration. But in only seconds she's crying out once more as I pull her down onto my cock.

I fill her to the hilt in one movement before lifting her up once more and slamming her back down.

With one hand on her hip, I pull her wrap top open with the other and expose her breasts.

Pinching her nipples to the point of pain, she keeps up the pace as she fucks me.

Sweat glistens on our skin as we move. The small space around us is full of our moans of pleasure and smells of sex, all while the driver is blissfully unaware.

"Come, Lola. Come around my fucking cock," I demand as I surge up into her.

Her scream fills the car, probably alerting the driver now, but I'm far too lost to her body to give a single shit in this moment.

Her fingers grip onto my shoulders as her movements get more and more erratic.

I pinch down on one of her nipples, giving it a bit of a twist and the bolt of pain mixes with her pleasure and sends her over the edge.

The second she tightens down on my length, I follow her into orgasm.

"Well, that's one way to make use of the dead time on the way home," she says with a laugh as she climbs off and drops onto the seat beside me to right her clothing.

Only seconds later, we're pulling up in front of my building.

"Are you ever intending on allowing me to go home at any point?" she asks, looking out of the window.

"I'm not holding you hostage, Lola." Her body tenses at my words, but I refuse to shy away from everything she's hiding. She might not be aware of it right now, but I will get her secrets out of her one way or another.

"No. It's way more pleasurable than that." She looks over her shoulder and grins wickedly at me. Despite the fact I just pulled out of her, my cock swells to do it all over again.

"So what do you think?" I ask her as we make our way to the lift. She glances over at me curiously. "Is she still going to be here?"

"What time did everything you order for her arrive?"

"About two hours ago."

Lola blows out a slow breath and I nod.

"Yeah, that was my thought too."

"I don't think she's ready yet, Ant."

"You could very well be right. But what about you?" I ask, turning on her and standing so close that her breasts brush up against my chest.

"Wh- what about me?"

"I'm going to make you open up, little P." I brush my knuckles down her cheek and watch as she trembles before me.

"Good luck with that," she snaps and I can't help but smile slightly at her fire.

"What will it take to make you talk?"

She shrugs as the lift dings to announce our arrival on my floor. Silently, she follows me toward the front door and watches as I unlock it and step inside.

Clive, the security I hired, rushes to stand from his seat in the hallway. The second our eyes lock, I know.

"I'm sorry, Mr Warren. She wouldn't listen to reason."

My shoulders drop as Lola's hand wraps around mine.

I don't think I realised until that moment just how badly I wanted Ellie to give this a chance, to give me a chance.

"Thank you, Clive. It's what I expected. You can head off now, go and take your wife out for the night."

"Thank you, Mr Warren."

I nod at him as I walk us through to the living area.

I didn't need to be told that she's not here. I feel it.

Lola steps in front of me, runs her hand up my chest and wraps it around the back of my neck.

"I'm so sorry."

"I'd have been surprised if she stuck around."

"Just because you expected it; it doesn't mean it can't hurt."

I continue staring at the same spot on the wall I latched onto when I first stopped.

"Look at me," she demands, tugging on my neck slightly.

I blink a few times before looking down at her. She gasps at the look in my eyes, and so she should. The only thing I can think of right now is how to push all of this aside. Ellie, the bitch who gave birth to her and how she treated both of us, my past, hell my fucking future if my daughter refuses to let me help her. What fucking use am I if I can't even help my own flesh and blood?

"We should order dinner," I say after the longest silence.

"Oh... um, sure."

"What's with the hesitation, Lola?"

"Well, you wanted me here for Ellie and now she's..." She trails off, not wanting to say the words.

"You're not going anywhere."

"I thought I wasn't captive."

"Yeah, well, maybe I changed my mind."

Spinning on my heel, I march toward the kitchen, desperate for a huge glass of scotch but the second I pull the cupboard open, I remember clearing them all out to stop both Ellie and Lola from reaching for them.

"Fuck," I bark, lifting my hand to my hair and tugging. It's going to come out soon if I don't quit this shit.

"Ant?" Lola's soft voice drags me from my inner

turmoil and when I turn to look at her, I find her with a white envelope in her hand.

"Is that...?" I trail off.

"The results? I don't know, it was just on the table already opened."

Fucking Ellie. She already knows, yet she's run. That sure doesn't fill me with confidence.

"You need to read it." Lola holds her hand out for me.

"She's gone. Do we need any more evidence of the results?"

"It could still go either way."

"You do it."

"Are you sure?" I pin her with a look that has her reaching into the envelope and pulling the paper out from inside. She reads for a few seconds, her face serious as she focuses on it.

"She's yours," she whispers, making me take a step toward her. She glances up at me and holds my eyes. "She's yours, Ant. Ellie is your daughter."

It's like my entire world tilts on its axis with those simple words and I stumble back against the counter as my mind runs away with me.

She knows she's mine, yet she left anyway. What the fuck?

I don't hear her footsteps as she makes her way toward me.

"Ant?" she asks, concern filling her eyes as she approaches.

"I..." I have to clear my throat where it's clogged

with emotion that I don't want to show and fear I'm not able to hide.

Images of how Ellie came to be fills my mind and my fingers curl around the counter behind me, my knuckles turning white with the pressure.

I think about the way she treated Ellie from the day she was born, how she abandoned her, left her without food, without love, until I couldn't take it any longer.

I knew leaving with her while 'Mum' was preoccupied with one of her friends was wrong, but I couldn't take the screaming any more. Ellie was starving. I was too but I'd had plenty of experience with it by that point. But she was only a baby, she needed that food.

She was so light as I lifted her into my arms. She had none of the cute baby podge I'd seen and heard people talk about. She was just skin and bones, and as I walked away, I promised her I'd do anything to help her, to protect her.

I thought handing her over was the right thing to do. If I'd had any clue that we'd end up here eighteen years later, I never would have allowed us to be found. I'd have kept her because I know for sure that I'd have done a better job as a child looking after her than any adult she's dealt with has.

"Fuck," I roar, but Lola doesn't falter or even cower despite the fury that must be written all over my face right now.

"Ant, what do you need? Tell me what you need to make this better."

CHAPTER NINETEEN

Lola

"Ant, what do you need? Tell me what you need to make this better."

His head hangs down as his fingers grip the countertop so hard I can see his knuckles are white.

"I don't know what I need right now." He turns to me and I gasp, because he looks vulnerable and I've never seen Anthony Warren wear that look. His expression is haunted. It makes him look younger than his years as if I can see inside him to the boy he used to be.

"Can we try to look for her?" he asks. "I know we probably won't find her, but if we look around here and then where William tracked her down, then just maybe..."

I nod, although I doubt very much a search will be anything but fruitless. Ellie is a master at disappearing.

So only a few minutes after we walked through his apartment door, we exit it and go in search of the woman we now know for a fact is his daughter.

As I expected, we don't find her. My stomach is rumbling and so I make Ant stop at a takeaway for pizza and we take it back to his apartment. He rings a concierge and orders drinks seeing as he'd cleared the place of booze. He takes a quick shower while I warm up some plates. The drinks arrive: wine for me, scotch for him, and a bottle of water and two glasses for the table.

He walks out with a towel hung low on his hips and I find myself biting my bottom lip.

"Mmmm, that pizza sure smells good," he says taking a seat at the dining table. I slide into the seat across from him, and we make small talk about favourite and hated toppings while we take our fill of food.

As soon as he's wiped across his mouth with a napkin, my thoughts come out of my mouth. "Does Ellie know who her mother is? Might she be with her?"

Ant's face clouds over, his neck muscles cording. "I fucking doubt it. Though if she smells money she might have come looking. She'd take the clothing off Ellie's back would that cunt."

"Talk to me." I attempt to help him unburden some of his secrets.

"Oh, Lola. If I did tell you the whole sorry, sordid

tale, nothing good would come from it. There'd be no benefit to me from you knowing. In fact, the chances are you'd not look me in the eye, or your expression would be one of pity and I won't be pitied by you."

There's a pause. I swallow. "Do you... do you want to hurt me?" I ask him. "Like before? Would that help you?"

His plate flies off the table, smashing on the floor. "For fuck's sake, Lola," he yells. "Do you know how guilty I feel for doing that to you? For giving you pain? For marking your skin. It's a sickness I have. I'm a bad man. I have women I see and I do that to them. I punish them. You need to stay away from me."

"So what does it make me then that I enjoyed it?" I ask him. "Every smack of that belt, every frisson of pain. What if I told you, you didn't even go as dark as I craved, Ant? What does that make you feel?"

"Maybe you do need to see someone. Get some help," he grits out through clenched teeth,

I huff in disbelief. "Unbelievable. I want to explore who I am with you and you want me to see a shrink."

There's silence and I'm considering leaving when he speaks again.

"I know my reasons for what I do come from my past. It's not healthy and if you're doing the same then together we are a lethal and toxic combination."

I stand up. "I'm going to go home, Ant, and I'll see you tomorrow at the office."

"Why? Are you going to walk into your bathroom

with razor blades because I won't give you what you want?"

My eyes narrow. "That's a cheap shot and you know it. I know you're hurting about Ellie right now, but my body is my business. I'm not limited to blades. You said yourself you have women who let you hurt them. There'll be men who'll do the same for me."

I turn, ready to walk out of the door when he says something that gives me pause.

"I inflict pain and imagine it's the bitch who abused me. Is that who you really want in your bed?"

"I want to receive pain to punish me for what Tommy De Loughrey made me do. Is that who you want in yours?"

Dark, hooded eyes look me over. "We're a match made in hell, Lola. No good can come from this. I want to save you and hurt you and neither of those reasons are why a man should be with a woman."

"All I'm asking is for someone to meet me in Hell and let me rest there awhile, before it consumes me," I plead with him.

He stands up. "We're going out, Lola. Grab your bag. I'm going to get dressed." He sees the question on my lips. "I won't give you answers, you'll see for yourself when we get there."

He takes me to XCluSiv, the bar my brother-in-law recently took ownership of while his younger brother, Rex, worked his way through a drug misuse treatment programme. Ant leads me to the back of the club and nods to a security guy who opens a door to a set of stairs.

"Where are we going?"

"You'll see."

I follow him down the steps until we come to a reception area and a series of doors. As I look at some of them, the ones with plain glass, and I see what the couples inside them are doing, I gasp.

"What is this?"

"This is XS. The basement level only the privileged few know of." He talks to the receptionist and is handed a key. "Follow me."

I walk into the room behind him and find the space full of bondage gear and equipment. My hands trail across all the different whips, the paddles, and things that look like they belong in an operating theatre rather than a room where sex happens.

"We won't be staying, or playing tonight, Lola," Ant informs me. I just wanted to show you that there's a place we can go, where we can experiment, and maybe try to turn our anger into something more... personal."

"You bring me here and won't fuck me? That's a little like taking me to the playground and not letting me go on the swings." As I say it, I push the sex swing suspended from the ceiling.

"Well, I guess I could let you have a go on the swings, but that's your lot, young lady." He raises a brow and I smile. He locks the door and walks back towards me losing his clothes. I quickly strip out of mine until I'm naked in front of him.

Guiding me towards the swing, I have no idea what I'm supposed to do with it, so I let Ant guide my back into the support and my legs into the stirrups.

"Trust me and lean back," he directs.

As I lie back on the swing, he pulls me closer and I swing towards him. With his cock in his hand he pushes inside me and then he uses the swing to rock me back and forth against him. Once I get used to the motion, I concentrate on the feeling of him thrusting in and out of me.

He stops and I almost growl which makes him laugh. "We're going to try something else." He says and he has me lay on the swing on my front with him behind. My hands fasten around the frame and as he takes me from behind, I can push myself further onto his cock by using the frame to push off against. The room is silent except for groans and slaps of my sex meeting his cock.

"Pinch my clit," I demand as his pace increases and he does as I request, pinching hard until I'm coming hard around his cock. With a grunt he takes his own release. Once we catch our breath, he helps me free myself and get back on my feet.

"Thanks, Daddy, for letting me play," I say flippantly and then I place my hand over my mouth. I meant it as in the swings and playground, but could I have said anything dumber when he's currently looking for his daughter?

His horror is apparent even in the dimmed light. "I'm sorry, I'm sorry. It just, the playground, and—"

"Get dressed and then I do think it would be better if I took you home," he says, monotone.

"No," I shout. "I said I was sorry. It's too late for me to go home now. I'd disturb my mother."

Sighing, he nods his head. "Let's go," he commands and we get dressed and I follow him out of the room, back up the stairs and to the bar where he orders a bottle of scotch to go. The car journey back is completely silent and I feel like a chastised child.

Following him through the door, he throws his keys on the side in the hall. "I have a few things to deal with. You should probably take a shower and have an early night."

I'm being sent to my room now, but that's fine with me. I'll go. "I'll just grab a drink and then I'll be out of your hair."

I grab my glass and fill it to the brim with the leftover wine he had delivered earlier and then I enter the bedroom, leaving him sitting on the sofa, opening his laptop.

I fall back on the bed, and my eyes fill with tears. I am so damn confused. Ant Warren is not the man who I pictured in my dreams, the one who rescued me and who I'd put on a pedestal. Yet, he still speaks to my soul and when we're together in bed, I can't get enough. But I'm a mess and is it only some skewed notion that has me believing that by the use of a few sex toys he can find a better way for me to deal with my cravings to harm myself? I feel the ant sensation, feel their crawl. I drink the whole glass of wine and sit with my arms around myself rocking slightly on the bed. The feeling won't dissipate and inside my mind is saying *search the bathroom, look for something to help release the pain.*

I need to talk to Ant, to tell him how I'm feeling. He might be able to help me somehow. Opening the door, I pad down the hall towards the living room. He's on the phone. I'll need to wait until he finishes his call. I hope it's not long.

"It's so good to hear your voice. Thanks for listening. You have no idea how much I need you right now."

I freeze. He must be on the phone to one of his girlfriends. Oh my god, I'm so stupid. He told me he has women he fucks. I'm just one in a group of fucktoys. Slowly, and quietly, I back away from the living room and back towards Ant's bedroom.

I search the bathroom but there's nothing. He's cleared it of anything I could use. The only thing I can think of is the heat from the shower. Turning on the water, I put it to a high setting and stripping my clothes off, I step inside the cubicle. As my body becomes accustomed to the heat, I increase the temperature until it hurts. I dig my fingertips into my arm and do the best I can to break through my skin. As I see a small bead of blood, I sigh with satisfaction. When I feel the ants disappear, I get out of the shower, towel myself dry, dry my hair and then I crawl under the covers.

I'm spiralling out of control. I can feel it.

Tomorrow, I have work and then I have the evening out with the accounts department. Maybe it's what I need. An evening with new friends. An attempt at a new beginning.

Although how many attempts can you make before you give up?

CHAPTER TWENTY

Ant

By the time I make it to my bedroom, Lola is asleep in the middle of the bed. Part of me hoped she might wait up like the night before, but I knew she wouldn't.

I thought taking her to XS might be a good move. Showing her that what she craves isn't that unusual and that there are places we can go to really explore it, if she so wishes. I had no intentions on taking her while we were there, but it wasn't like I could ignore the desire that was darkening her eyes as she looked around the place. I just didn't expect for our night to end the way it did.

I'd hoped that maybe Ellie would have reappeared, but when I stuck my head in her room once we were back, I found it just as empty as before we went looking for her.

I expected it. That doesn't mean it didn't— doesn't — hurt that she took everything I offered her and ran at the first opportunity.

I understand it though. I've been in her position where your only concern is survival. I hate that my own flesh and blood is now experiencing it. I'd give everything I have to make it go away for her.

After stripping down, I crawl into bed beside Lola. My cock swells the second I feel her hot skin burning into mine. Unable to resist, I skim my hand over her waist and pull her body back into mine. Her scent fills my nose and my mouth waters. I can't deny that her presence doesn't make everything seem just that little better.

I lie there for hours wondering where Ellie might have gone; if she's in trouble, or if she's using everything I gave her as payment towards her debt.

I've no idea what time my body finally gives in, but I do know that the sun is starting to rise.

"Ant." Something shoves at my shoulder, but I ignore it. "Ant." My name is said a little more forcefully this time and it drags me from my slumber. "Ant, I think there's someone in your flat."

"What?" I bark, jumping from the bed and finding the boxers I left on the floor last night.

I'm almost at the door before I've pulled them up my legs.

"What the hell are you doing? You can't just go out there and confront them."

"Watch me," I snap over my shoulder as I drag the door open and storm down the hallway.

My fists are clenched ready to fight as I round the corner. Only the second my eyes lock on the person making themselves at home my entire body relaxes.

"What the fuck are you playing at?" I bark, storming over to where my daughter is happily making herself a coffee in the kitchen.

"Sorry, did you want one?" she asks, like yesterday didn't happen.

I ignore her question.

"I thought you'd left."

"I just had a few errands to run."

"And that required taking everything I bought for you, did it?"

"Yes, actually."

"What have you done with it?"

She shrugs, making something explode within me.

"I bought all that for you. Where is it?" I seethe.

"Don't worry, it's gone to a good home with someone who deserves it."

"*You* deserve it."

She shakes her head and looks away from me. Grabbing her mug from the machine, she goes to move past me. "No, I don't," she whispers.

My heart sinks that she thinks so little of herself.

Reaching out, I wrap my fingers around her forearm to stop her.

Her entire body freezes up at my contact, and when I look at her, her eyes are wide and full of fear.

I release her immediately.

"I'm not going to hurt you, Ellie," I say, taking a step back and holding my hands up. "All I've ever wanted is to protect you."

Her lips press into a thin line. "You've only just discovered I existed."

"That's not entirely true." Anger hardens her features as she registers my words. I rush to correct her before she gets the wrong idea. "I've only just discovered you're mine. I tried to protect you from the day you were born."

"How? I thought I was always in care." Her brows draw with confusion.

"Not for the first few months. I know you're probably going to hate me for this, but I can assure you, I only had your best intentions at heart, but I was the one who had you put in care."

"You what?" she roars, her anger beginning to bubble over.

"I thought it was for the best. I was a kid, Ellie. I had no idea how to look after you. I thought handing you over, handing us both over, would be better than staying with that cun... that woman."

"Do you have any idea what my life has been like?" her voice is menacingly quiet compared to her previous loud tone.

"I have an idea, yeah." Many times, I regretted putting myself back into the system, but I kept repeating that it was better than suffering her abuse and neglect. Yet there were days when I had to wonder if the saying, 'the better the devil you know' was true.

"If I knew, Ellie. If I had any idea that you were mine..." I shake my head. I want to tell her that I would have moved Heaven and Earth to ensure we stayed together. But I was a child, no one in their right mind would have listened to me. It wasn't until I was a few years older that I truly came to realise what *she'd* put me through. "I'm sorry, Ellie. I was so young."

"H- how old were you?"

I look away from her probing eyes. She deserves the truth, but I'm not sure I'm going to be able to say the words. No matter how much of a cunt your mother is, I'm sure no one wants to hear the things she did, the things she was capable of.

"When you were born... I was fifteen."

"Oh God." Her eyes are sad and it pulls at my heart. "And her..."

"Thirty-something." A shudder of disgust runs down my spine, goose bumps pricking my skin as I think of her.

She nods as if she understands the situation without me even having to say anything.

"I'm going to go to bed. I've been up all night."

"O- okay."

I stand aside and allow her to walk past me. Her

shoulders are slumped, the fight I've been used to seeing the past couple of days seems to have vanished.

She halts halfway to the hall and my eyes lift to what might have stopped her. Standing in her silk robe watching us is Lola.

After a beat, Ellie finds her footing once again and walks past her without saying a word, although I don't miss the look that passes between them.

Once Ellie has disappeared and her door is closed, Lola turns her eyes on me.

They narrow in question, but I'm nowhere near ready to answer any she has. She tried making me talk last night. She should know that I'm not going to take kindly to her asking again. I'm assuming she was standing there for some time listening, so she must have ideas forming in her head. She's not an idiot.

Ignoring the coffee I could really do with, I close the space between us.

"We need to get to work," I snap.

She opens her mouth to respond but must change her mind because I get to the bedroom without hearing her voice.

I shed my boxers and step into the shower.

Part of me wants her to join me. Hell knows, I could do with some tension relief right about now, but she never does and I know it's for the best. I'm barely holding onto my sanity right now and I'm terrified that I'm going to do something soon that's going to tip Lola over the edge.

By the time I emerge from the bathroom, she's slipping on her shoes and ready to go.

I nod at her, my words getting caught in my throat.

In only minutes, I have my suit— my armour— on and I'm ready to go.

Still, no words are said between us as I guide her out of the flat with my hand in the small of her back.

"Is she okay?" she finally asks once we're in the confines of my car and heading for the office.

I blow out a long breath. "I've no idea," I answer honestly.

"Maybe she needs to talk to someone," Lola muses.

"Like you've done?" I snap, regretting it the second she turns her narrowed eyes on me.

"Have you?" she asks, throwing it back at me.

"I've had someone over the years, yeah."

"Huh."

"What's that supposed to mean?"

"I'm just surprised. I didn't see you as a shrink kind of guy."

"There's a lot about me you don't know." As I say the words, I think of the person who does know.

Silence falls on the car as I make my way through the city before pulling up outside the B.A.D. offices.

Lola looks over at me when I don't make a move to get out.

"Aren't you coming in?" she asks, turning to look at me once she's gathered her bag.

"No."

"And here I was thinking you were keeping an eye on Rob."

If I were looking at her, I know she'd be rolling her eyes.

"Don't be mistaken, Lola. I have eyes and ears in every inch of that office."

"Ah, that's right. You record everyone without their knowledge."

"Enough," I bark, reaching over and wrapping my hand around her throat and pushing her back against the seat. "Do you really want to test my restraint right now, Lola?"

Her pupils dilate as she swallows, her neck rippling under my touch and I can't help my cock swelling as I watch desire consume her.

"N- no."

"Right answer. Now, you've got work to do and I've got a meeting to get to."

"O- okay. Will you be back later?"

"I don't know. There will be a car here to take you home."

"If it's all the same with you, I think I'd actually like to go to my own home."

"We'll see," I mutter, not liking the feeling her request drags up.

Releasing her, I sit back at the wheel, staring out at the office before us and waiting for her to get out.

"Who are you meeting?" she asks suspiciously.

"What's it to you?"

"Nothing." Without another word, she pushes from the seat and leaves the car.

The second the door is slammed shut behind her, regret fills me and my grip on the wheel turns my knuckles white.

She's only trying to help, but every time she looks at me, I fear she's going to see too deep. There's only one person who knows all about the darkness I hold within me, and that's where I'm going right now.

"It's me," I say into the buzzer when I turn up at her building. When I spoke to her on the phone last night, she assured me that she'd be here should I need her.

"Come on up," comes back down the line. Relief floods me that for the first time in quite a while, I can just be me. No secrets or keeping up pretences. She sees the real me, the broken boy of my past as well as the successful man I am right now.

Our connection goes back a long way, aside from Ellie and the cunt of a woman who birthed her, she's the only one who knows the truth.

"It's so good to see you," she says the second she opens her front door.

The second I'm inside, I engulf her in my arms, drop my nose to her hair and breathe out a huge sigh as the stress from the past few days starts to leave me.

CHAPTER TWENTY-ONE

Lola

Wow. Ellie came back. As I stand listening to Ant revealing some of his secrets to her, I'm amazed she's here. I really thought she'd taken everything and run and that Ant wouldn't see her again. She says her things went to someone who needed them. Looks like Ellie has a heart after all. It's just deep inside a body of hurt.

Rejection washes over me about the fact that Ant has just stood in front of her and admitted that he knew her as a baby and that he was fifteen when she was born. Fuck, that means he could have been fourteen or only just fifteen when the woman he said was thirty-something got pregnant. He calls her a cunt. He could have told me everything. I was here for him, but then again, I've told him nothing, so what do I expect in return.

My feelings for him are so confused. Do I like him or do I just see someone who mirrors my pain?

I'm pleased to get to the office. My mind is soon lost in accounts. The department is busy and Rob keeps my in-tray and Inbox loaded. He's been too busy himself to flirt with me today and I'm glad. I want to prove myself as an employee and I can't do that if my mentor is more interested in my appearance. Or maybe he was just being friendly and I misread his signals?

The more I think about it, the more I decide that I'm returning to my own home this evening. I'm going to go for the post-work drinks and then go spend the night at home, catch up with Mum, and try to get my head together a bit. It will give Ant and Ellie time to get to know each other one on one if she's sticking around.

In the late afternoon, my mobile phone rings and I'm ecstatic to see my sister's name on the display.

"Hey, Anna."

"Hey, Sis. Thought I'd give you a quick call and see how you're doing?"

"So you've actually come up for air?"

She laughs. "He can't make me any more pregnant than I already am, and I keep craving watermelon."

"Soon you'll look like you're carrying one!"

"True. So how are you? How's the job?"

I sit back in my chair. "I'm really enjoying it. The staff here are super friendly and I seem to be grasping what's expected of me. I think it was the right move."

"Told you so."

"Yeah, okay, smartypants. Thank you for the introduction. I'm hoping it leads to good things."

"Have you seen much of the boss? He's avoiding Tyler's calls mostly."

No way am I telling her the truth. "Ellie seems to be giving him the runaround. She's there one minute, gone the next. He's probably too busy to update Ty, and anyway, you're on your honeymoon and shouldn't be disturbed."

"Yeah, well, I'll be back a week on Monday to catch up on everything, but in the meantime if you get any juicy gossip about Ant text me."

"Hmm, did you actually ring to see how I was, or just for the gossip?"

"If it wasn't for the luxury and relaxation here, plus my super sexy husband, I'd be on a plane back with my ear to a glass against his office door."

I belly laugh this time and it feels so good. We may have had a strained relationship being apart at times growing up, but it's good to have my sister back and to be getting to know her.

She says goodbye and I sit for a while, happy to have spoken to her, but sad that I don't think I'll ever be able to tell her about the time with Tommy. It means there'll always be a barrier between us. But with a niece or nephew coming there's an opportunity for us to embrace a new chapter of our relationship. I decide that I must get her some baby things, a few cute clothing pieces and a cot toy. It's a time of celebration and something positive to focus on and God knows, our family needs some positives.

When the working day ends, I make my way to the ladies bathrooms where I find a couple of colleagues. We all freshen our lipstick and hair is scrunched and sprayed. A spritz of perfume and I'm done. I walk to the bar just down from B.A.D. with Rachel and a woman called Ava.

"So tell me, Lola, how's your first week been, apart from the days you were poorly?" Ava asks me.

"I've enjoyed it. Hopefully I've done a good enough job that they'll want to keep me on."

"I think Rob would protest if you didn't stay."

I can see Rachel has a small smirk on her lips.

"He's not my type. He's nice though, but I'd rather keep things professional."

Which is a word I wouldn't use for Rachel as she snorts and then pretends she almost swallowed a fly.

Luckily, we've reached the bar, so I buy the two other women a drink, making a point to ask Rachel if she's all right now.

Rachel points towards a large seating area that runs down one wall with a huge table in front of it. "There's our table. Let's go paint the town red."

A few drinks down us and some tapas style food and I'm enjoying the company and feeling more part of the team. Rachel and Ava are great fun and soon conversation turns to Ant.

"So what do you think of our boss, Lola?" Ava asks.

"He seems okay. I wouldn't like to get on his bad

side." Ava hadn't been there when I'd challenged his authority at the beginning of the week.

"Ooh I don't know," Ava says. "I could imagine it's quite enjoyable." She looks over at a barmaid. "But I'm too young, that's his type." She nods over to the woman. A woman with bobbed blonde hair who must be forty at least, if not heading towards fifty.

I'm trying my best to act cool, but I can't help look the woman over, wondering what she has that Ant wanted.

"He's dated her?" I ask.

"God, no. Ant dates no-one. But he came here once, as he sometimes does, and one of the guys caught him with his trousers down in a nearby alley. I seriously gave some thought to heavy sunbed use for a while to see if I could tempt him, but he doesn't bang anyone from the workplace."

"No?"

Ava's mouth has been loosened by the drink. "No. Deacon and Ty were always the ones who fucked the interns. It was like a competition who could get there first and believe me they queued up to try. Then they met Mia, and Anna."

"Is this a good time to remind you that Lola is Anna's sister?" Rachel elbows Ava.

"Oh fuck, yeah, sorry."

I shake her sorry away with my hands. "I know his history. As long as he's faithful to my sister, we're good."

"Well, anyway, then there's Jack and Oliver who

we believe have an on-again off-again relationship, and then Ant, who's the mystery man really. The most private one of them all, but he's been seen out with women and they are always old."

It hurts my heart to hear that his go-to woman is in her forties or fifties. Why is he bothering with me then? Also, I haven't been a one-night stand.

Rachel gets Ava chattering on about something else and I find I'm still looking at the bloody woman behind the bar. I want to scratch her eyes out. I'm pathetic, jealous of someone he was only with once, but it's like I want to question her. Ask her if he told her anything about himself, about his past.

Ava moves on and Rob comes to sit at my side. "Hey, you. Rachel said you were drinking gin, so here's another."

"You didn't need to do that but thank you," I tell him. "I'll get the next round in."

"Ava told me where you live. I'm only about ten minutes from you. We could share a cab home?" Rob asks.

Hmmm, how do you tell a colleague you have drivers take you everywhere? Maybe tonight I'll be normal and share a taxi with him.

"Oh, really? Yeah, okay, as long as you aren't slaughtered. I'm not cleaning up sick from the back of the car."

I feel eyes on me and look to see Ava winking. Seems she's not taking my words of not being interested as gospel.

As time passes, it's really difficult to extricate myself from Rob's conversation. In the end needing the bathroom means I can excuse myself to get up.

Walking across the bar, I once again look at the woman behind it. There could be any number of women in here Ant has slept with. If he doesn't usually do repeats, just how many conquests does he have?

An arm touches mine and I spin around to see an older woman with mid-length mousy brown hair staring at me. The front of her hair is peppered with grey as if she's not seen a hairdresser for a while. She looks a little the worse for wear and wobbles slightly on her feet.

Assuming she used me for balance I ask her if she's okay.

"I saw you getting into Anthony's car. Who are you to him?" She asks. *Oh fuck, is this one of his playthings?* She's the right age.

I move a step back from her and place my hands across my waist. "I work for him. Why?"

"Just checking, because he's mine," she tells me, her eyes narrowing as her voice fills with venom. "He's always been mine. So I just wanted to warn you that if you do try to fuck him, that it's me he'll be imagining when he's screaming in pleasure."

"I'm not fucking my boss," I lie. "But I find it very hard to believe what you're saying because I know he doesn't do repeats."

"I don't know who told you that, but it's not true.

I've had Anthony over and over. Only the other day he had me in his office."

As she's talking, I remember his phone call from the flat and I wonder if this is the woman he said he needed. And it all becomes clear. The reason he has so many one-night-stands is because there's obviously a woman he never got over. I'm so fucking stupid. Tears fill my eyes. My mother always said you shouldn't drink gin, Mother's Ruin, she called it. I rush away from the woman and into the bathroom. When I finally emerge, she's gone.

I'm going home now whether Rob wants to or not. Making my way back I tell him.

"That's fine with me. I never stay too long. I have a cat that needs feeding."

I let him tell me all about the cat and feign interest when my head is reeling from the woman who accosted me.

Rob keeps the conversation going on the ride home. I look at him from a romantic point of view. He's good looking and he's a nice person. He's making sure I'm home safe and that's the sign of a decent person. I bet he's reliable, not like Ant fucking Warren.

I sigh outwardly. He doesn't make my panties damp. They're bone dry. It's so not fucking fair. I want someone I can't have.

We pull up outside the apartments. "This is me," I tell him. "Thanks for sharing the taxi."

"Anytime. Now I know you're home safe," he says. There's a pause. And then I do something stupid. I lean forward, meaning to give Rob a peck on the cheek, but he misreads my signals and kisses me on the mouth.

I back away quickly. "Shit, Rob, I..."

"Oh God. I fucked up, didn't I? Seriously, Lola, just forget it. I've had a lot of beer. I'll see you Monday, okay?"

"I meant to do this." I lean over again and kiss his cheek softly. "I'm not saying no. I'm just saying I'm not ready for anything right now."

My gin-soaked body enjoyed his lips on mine, but all my mind screamed was that they didn't belong to Ant.

But Ant didn't belong to me.

He belonged to the woman in the bar.

Exiting the vehicle, I wave to Rob as he drives away and then I scream emptily into someone's hand and I hear Ant growl.

"You'd better fucking explain right now why your lips were on that punk, because I'm one car ride away from putting him in A&E."

His hand drops and he spins me around. His eyes are flashing with fury, a pulse tics in his cheek, and his hands are fisted at his sides.

"I'm fucking waiting, Lola," he grinds out.

CHAPTER TWENTY-TWO

Ant

She stares up at me with wide, terrified eyes, but even still, I'm unable to stop myself.

She let him kiss her.

Kiss her.

My fists clench with my need to go and find him and ensure he's unable to kiss anyone ever again, but that would mean leaving Lola, and she quite clearly needs me right now to teach her a lesson about who she belongs to.

I take a step towards her and she backs away until she hits the wall.

"Ant," she warns, her chest heaving almost as much as mine is right now.

I thought I'd got my head together somewhat after

my meeting this morning, but now it's just as fucked as ever.

Fuelled by my need for her, I press the front of my body against hers and just about manage to swallow the growl that threatens to rumble up my throat.

Our noses are a hair's width apart as I stare down into her eyes.

"Well?"

She tilts her chin in defiance. "I don't owe any kind of explanation to you."

Red hot fury explodes inside me. Without thinking my fingers wrap around her throat, squeezing lightly. Her eyes darken at my move and my cock twitches.

"Why was he kissing you?" I grate out, my voice low and menacing.

"Maybe because you weren't," she sasses. "Where have you been today, Ant? Who have you been with today?" Her brows rise in accusation which does nothing for my state of mind.

"Nothing to do with you," I spit.

"Exactly." She tilts her head to the side studying me. "So you weren't with one of your many older women?"

"What?" I bark.

"I know all about them. I even met one tonight, though I can't say I saw the attraction myself." My teeth grind at the thought of her meeting any of the women I use to unleash my need for revenge on.

"I told you, I inflict pain and imagine it's the bitch who abused me."

I can see her connecting the dots quicker than I'd like.

"Tell me," she all but begs.

"Fuck," I bark, doing the only thing I know to stop her questioning me.

My lips slam down on hers in a punishing, bruising kiss. Our tongues duel, and our teeth clash as I try to rid her of the suspicion that's already filling her.

No one needs to know about that part of my life. Especially someone who is already as broken as Lola. She has enough secrets weighing her down, she doesn't need the weight of mine on top of them as well.

Finding her thigh, I lift her legs around my waist, grinding my hard length against her core. Then I carry her around the corner into a dark alley.

"Ant," she moans, when I rip my lips from hers and begin kissing and sucking down her neck. "Why me? Why do you want me when you only date older women?"

"I don't date."

"Ah that's right. You don't do repeats, only with one."

The thought of her somehow bumping into Vivian has sweat glistening on my skin. Vivian could tell Lola all kinds of horror stories for the things I've done to her over the years. *But why would she?* A little voice in my head asks. Vivian keeps our activities as private as I do. She wouldn't be running her mouth off in a bar to one of my employees.

Lola's fingers thread into my hair as she tries to pull

me back to her lips and causes the thoughts to fall from my head, the only thing I can see as I take her lips once more is him attached to her.

She's mine.

Pushing her skirt up around her waist, I rip her knickers from her body and let them fall to the floor of the darkened alleyway we're making use of before lifting her against it and wrapping her legs around my waist.

I make quick work of undoing my trousers and releasing my straining cock.

"Tell me, Ant. Tell me what she did to you," she pleads.

"Stop, Lola. You need to fucking stop."

"Make. Me."

I surge up into her in one thrust making her gasp in surprise and thankfully forcing her to stop with the insistent questions.

My time is running out, I know that. With Ellie out in the open and everyone wondering who her mother is, my time in hiding is coming to an end faster than I can comprehend.

"Fuck," I grunt as her walls ripple around me. I've done all kinds of kinky shit over the years but none of it compares to vanilla with Lola. It's like her body was made for my pleasure.

"Anthony," she cries, her nails digging into my shoulders as she begins to lose herself to the sensations.

"Anyone could see us," I grate. "Anyone could walk

past night now and watch me fuck you. Watch me own you."

"Shit." Her head falls back against the wall, but she makes no move to end this. If anything, she just gets wetter.

"You're mine, Lola. Mine. No other fucker should be able to look at you, let alone kiss you."

"Oh God," she whimpers as her pussy clamps down on me. "Oh God."

Dropping my face to the crook of her neck, I sink my teeth into her soft skin. She screams out as the pain mixes with the pleasure and pushes her over the edge, followed a few seconds later by me.

I growl out as I release everything I have inside her.

Taking her chin in my hand, I tilt her head so she's no choice but to look at me. "You're mine, Lola. Mine."

"But it seems you're not mine because *she* was in your office only the other day."

I blink at her a few times. "I've not been with anyone else since we..." My heart starts to race as I think back over the past few days and who's been in my office. Hell, I've hardly been there so there's not much to think about.

"Lola," I say, dropping her legs to the ground and tucking myself away. "Who was the woman you were talking to tonight?" I try to keep my voice steady, but as her brows pull together in concern, I start to think I've failed.

She shrugs. "A woman in her fifties probably, brown hair, short-ish. You need to treat her to a root retouch. She's obviously in bed too much to book a hairdresser. I don't know anything else. I wasn't all that thrilled about having to talk to her. I certainly didn't want to memorise one of your playthings."

"Fuck," I roar, spinning away from her and pulling at my hair until all I can focus on is the pain. "What did she say to you? Tell me everything she said," I demand, turning my eyes on her.

She swallows nervously as we connect, before righting her clothing and pushing from the wall.

"I owe you nothing," she says, repeating her earlier words.

"Like hell you don't. This is about my fucked-up life, Lola. And if she is who I think she is then I need you as far away from her as possible."

"Then tell me who she is, make me understand." She grits out.

Taking her hand, I drag her from the alleyway and to my car that's parked a little down the street from her home.

"Get in," I demand, ripping the door open and pushing her forward.

I half expect her to refuse and turn back towards her own home, but after one more look in my eyes, she follows orders. I've no idea what she can read in me, and I think I'd rather not know.

The drive to my place is tense and silent. I know she wants answers and I also know that I've no chance in Hell of getting out of answering them. But if I have to touch on that time of my life then I'm not

ANGEL DEVLIN & TRACY LORRAINE

doing it in a dark fucking alley in the middle of the city.

The second we're in my flat, I march to the kitchen and pour out the remains of last night's bottle of scotch into a clean glass.

"What the hell is wrong with him?" Ellie asks behind me after I storm past her.

"Ellie, is there any chance you could give us some space?" Lola asks softly.

"Fucking hell, am I going to have to spend another night listening to you two fucking?"

"I bought you headphones. Use them," I bark without looking back.

"Right," she mutters before her footsteps get quieter and her bedroom door closes. I've still no idea what she did with everything I bought her, but to be honest, it's not been at the top of my priority list.

"Ant?" Lola's hand lands on my upper arm as my fingers wrap around the glass in my hand with such a tight grip, I expect it to shatter any moment.

"H- her name is Sharon."

Lola's fingers tighten on my arm and she tugs. She wants me to look at her, but there's no way I can right now.

I continue staring at my reflection in the window before me. But I don't see myself as the thirty-three-year-old man that I am now. All I see is the little boy she abused. The weak and helpless little boy who didn't know anything different to the way she treated me.

She told me she loved me. And I fucking believed her. I believed every word that came out of her mouth because I didn't have anyone else to listen to, who I thought cared about me.

I had no idea she was abusing every single bit of trust I had in her.

"She was... she was my foster mother."

Lola's gasp fills the silent space around us.

"And she's Ellie's mother?"

The glass in my hand goes flying across the room, shattering against the opposite wall.

I spin, needing to get away. I keep my eyes on the floor as I move past Lola, unable to look into her sympathetic eyes and see the pity that I know will fill them.

I don't look up until I get to the hallway, and when I do, I find Ellie watching me with tears running down her face.

"I'm so sorry," she whispers as I pass her, but I don't respond. I can't. I'm numb.

CHAPTER TWENTY-THREE

Lola

Ant walks out of the apartment and Ellie moves towards the door. I run and pull her back. "Leave him. He'll be back," I tell her, though really I've no idea what his plans are.

What I do know is after dropping that bombshell, he left me in his apartment with his daughter.

"L- Lola. My mum. She abused him. She was his mum. Okay, his foster mum, but..." She pales and I see her start to heave. I let go and she runs to the bathroom where she's sick down the toilet. I rub her back until she's finished and then I grab a tumbler of water and some tissue for her mouth.

"There's no wonder he didn't want me," Ellie says, her back against the cold tile of the bathroom wall now.

"He said he only just found out you were his. He's had private investigators looking for you and he's brought you into his home. That's not the actions of someone who doesn't want their kid to me."

"So you saw her. My mum?"

"Yeah, it would appear so." I think back to the drunk who grabbed me in the bar. "I don't know her, Ellie, but how can anyone who'd do that be a good person?"

"If she approached you then she's around. Does she know I'm here?" Ellie's eyes went wide. "I don't want to see her. Who wants that for a mum?"

Sighing, I sit down next to her on the bathroom floor. "I wish I could offer you answers, Ellie, but fuck, I don't know what to do with this information. Not at all." Then I realise I know someone who does. "Come on, let's go sit in the living room and wait for your dad. I need to make a few phone calls." I needed to text my mother to let her know I wasn't coming home tonight after all, and then I needed to get hold of Deacon. Because if anyone could help Ant, it was him.

I didn't want to disturb my sister on her honeymoon, but I didn't have Deacon's number. I sent her a text, but I wasn't surprised when a few minutes later my phone rang.

"Why do you want Deacon's number?"

"Just some business stuff."

"Bullshit, Lola. Now—" She didn't get to say anything else as the words, "I'll sort it," came her way and Tyler's gruff voice came down the line.

"There are five hours between you and me, Lola. Tell me what's going on, or I'll just come home anyway."

I sigh. "I met a woman tonight. Turns out it was Ant's foster mother..." I paused. "Ellie's mother."

There's silence for a moment. "Ellie's mother was Ant's foster mother? Did I just hear that right?"

"Yes. He just told me and then he walked out."

"Fuuuuuuuuccccck." The pain in Ty's voice is clear down the line. "He said his foster care experiences were rough. He told us about how he had to run away with a baby because of one experience. Oh God, that baby was Ellie wasn't it? Did he know and that's why he ran?"

"No. No. He didn't know she was his. Not until recently. She's been to his office. She told me. Sharon, he said her name was. Now, can I have Deacon's number?"

"I'll call him myself now, and then I'll text it you for future use. Keep me updated, Lola. I don't care what time it is, day or night, or that I'm on my honeymoon. That man is a brother to me in every way but biological. If he's cut, I bleed."

"Okay, Ty. I promise. Thanks for calling Deacon. Ant needs someone and I'm there to listen, but I don't know what to do."

"Why are you at his apartment anyway at this time of night?" Ty asks.

"I was just helping with Ellie. We're a similar age," I lie.

My sister's voice reappears down the line. But this time she sounds different. Like when she's about to get all bossy on my arse. "Ty's taken off. He's walking around the pool area ranting and pulling at his hair. I think the honeymoon's over," she says.

"No, Anna. No. That's why I wanted Deacon. And there's Jack and Oliver. We don't need you."

"Lola. I've been sat on my backside for days. Ty and I don't do still, not really. It's been amazing but I think we're both itching to come back anyway. I'm going to look at flights if Ty's in agreement, which looking at his face I think he will be."

"I spoiled your honeymoon," I wail.

"No you didn't. B.A.D. business came up, and that comes first. Now, Ty had you on speakerphone, so talk to me. What is it you're helping with in regard to Ellie?"

"Just keeping her company."

She sighs. "He shouldn't have gotten you involved in all of this. I mean you're just his accounts intern. I know he knows you from... before, but that should have made him realise you already had enough to deal with without involvement with a girl who is clearly going to have problems. Your job was supposed to be the fresh start, not a route to more drama."

"I'm a grown up, Anna. I'm fine. Listen, I'd better clear my line for in case Deacon calls."

She sighs. "Okay. Be careful though. I love you, Sis, and I worry about you,"

Ending the call, I close my eyes. I know she worries. So much she's suffocating.

Ellie is looking at me. "What's going on?"

"Sister lecture and Ty's calling Deacon. All we can do now is wait. So, lemonade?" I ask her.

She nods and I make us both a drink. Then I put on a television show neither of us really pay attention to, as we wait for the phone to ring or Ant to return.

"Tell me about your parents." Ellie's voice rings out in the empty apartment. "You said you didn't know who your father was."

While I don't really want to revisit my past, I feel Ellie needs an anchor right now. She needs to know that she's not on her own in the life of the fucked-up.

"The man I called Dad lived in New York. My mother is from London. He ran a magazine that was a rival to B.A.D. I didn't have much of a relationship with him other than when I was needed to look pretty at charity events and photo opportunities." I stare off into space.

"Then it all went weird. My sister had an accident and the next thing Mum has me on a plane back to London with her and we have different names and identities. Overnight, I go from rich to poor, and have to live in a neighbourhood where my accent kind of gives me away, so I have to pretend. Make up a story of why I'm there and try to fit in, except of course I don't.

"But my sister stays, and Mum tells me her and dad have separated and Anna is staying with our dad. So along with leaving my dad, and my whole new identity, my sister abandons me and my mum expects me to believe this is just a marriage separation that's turned toxic. Yet we can't do anything that might give our real identities away." I huff, raising a brow. "As time passed I heard her talking on the phone and I'd hear snippets, like that my sister was working for Dad and involved in his dodgy practices, although I know the truth now and it's not how it appeared and it's not pretty."

"So he lives in New York, but, what, you no longer see him?"

"He lived in New York. He's dead. He kidnapped me and didn't live to tell the tale." I stare at her. "I'm not telling you anymore about that. It's not my place and also I really, really, can't." I realise I'm scratching at my arms and stop myself.

"You were kidnapped by your own father? What, like for him to claim you back from your mum?"

"No, for him to do a DNA test to see whether or not he was my dad or whether I shared the same father as Anna."

"Oh fuck. And what were the results?"

"The results were I have no father at all. Both ended up dead."

"So you don't know? Was the test not done?"

"It was destroyed and there's no point to one now. It won't change my life in any way to know who my father is."

"But was the other guy a good guy?"

"Yeah, I believe so."

"So you could be his."

"Oh, Ellie," I say, with a sympathetic smile. "It won't make any difference to my life who my biological father is because Tommy destroyed me when he took me. My father could be the good man, but I am not a good daughter. Not a good daughter at all."

The memories want to take over, but I can't let them. Not now. "Talk to me, Ellie. Tell me anything about your own past. I need you to distract me. Please." I tug on her arm.

"Okay, okay. Well, all I knew from my foster information was that a young boy had turned up at a police station with me. From there I didn't know what had happened to the boy other than he'd also gone into the system. I don't remember anything about my earlier placements, but once I got to about eight years old, I ended up with two alcoholics. One fell down the stairs and died and I was moved on. From then none of them were anything good. They couldn't deal with my attitude, they wanted the money I brought them. One of them hit me so hard they broke my nose. So I was done. I slept on friends' floors until they all got sick of me, and then I started thieving and turning tricks so I could eat and here we are."

I manage a kind of snort-laugh. "What a pair."

"Yep."

"Where do you think he went?" I ask her.

She shrugs her shoulders. "Probably a bar. Maybe even the one where we went."

"Let's forget that evening ever happened, shall we? Anyway, are you planning on staying now? You came back."

"I live day to day, Lola. It's how I get by. How my few friends get by."

"Is that where the stuff went?"

"Yeah, they needed it more than I did."

"Ellie, I get that, but you can't take Ant's stuff and give it all away like that."

"Why not? He's a fucking billionaire. He can afford to bankroll a few bits of clothes."

"I'm sure he can. But why don't you try talking to him about it? Maybe there's a way to help people where you don't have to steal. There will be supportive charities. Perhaps somewhere down the line you can start one, to help people who ended up like you did."

"It's a lot easier to just take them my stuff though," she says, like the teenager she is.

"If you ever decide to do it, I'll help you."

She looks surprised at that. "Oh, okay, thanks."

The door opens and we both spin around expecting to see Ant, but instead Deacon stands in the doorway.

"You heard from him?" he bellows.

"Nothing."

"Fuck." He stomps over to the sofa and looks at Ellie. "Scotch, neat, kid. Thanks."

I want to burst out laughing when instead of telling him to fuck off, Ellie scrambles to her feet like she's in the Army and she strides towards the drinks cabinet. The Deacon King effect.

"There isn't any, sorry." She tells him.

"Oh yeah, he drank the last before he stormed off." I remember.

"Tell me everything you know so I can go find him, and then I can go find *her*." The way he says *her* sends a chill up my spine.

I reiterate my meeting with Sharon: what she looked like, which bar I'd seen her in, and he picks up his phone and gives the information to William.

"Go there now, will you? I'm on my way there too, but I'll check the nearby bars first. I've got a feeling though that he'll be there, the last place she was seen. I just hope he's not planning anything stupid."

He turns to Ellie. "Your mother's a cunt, but it's made up for by the fact your dad is the fucking salt of the earth. You want my advice, you stay by your dad's side and you'll be fine, kid."

And then he leaves as fast as he walked in.

CHAPTER TWENTY-FOUR

Ant

I was intending on going and locking myself in my bedroom, but my legs seemed to have other ideas, because before I knew what was happening, I was pulling the front door open and marching through it.

Everything around me was a blur as I stumbled out of the lift and onto the street. The cool air hit me, but I didn't notice. I was too lost.

I told her.

I told them.

Turning the corner, I bend over, resting my palm against the rough brick and retch.

The memories threaten to consume me, and I stand there like a fucking loser puking on the street.

I should be stronger than this. I'm a grown fucking man who runs a very successful company. People are fucking scared of me. Yet she still has the power to make me feel like a child and turn me into a shell of the person I really am.

After wiping my mouth with the back of my hand, I stand up and fall back against the wall.

My fists curl with my need to hurt someone.

Digging into my pocket, I pull my phone out and find my assistant's contact.

"What bar were you in tonight?" I bark down the line when she eventually answers.

"Waterside," she slurs down the line. "But we've already left if you were planning on joining us. Or... should I say, Lola's already left. She went home with... hiccup... Rob quite a while ago."

"Sober up, Rach," I demand before ending our call and pocketing my phone once again.

Images of that motherfucker putting his lips on what's mine flicker through my mind. And although it makes me want to hunt him down and show him exactly what I thought of the move, it's actually a welcome relief from the other images that have been in my head.

The bar is on the other side of town, but I'm in no mood to have anyone else's company, even if it is only that of a cab driver. So the second I push from the wall, I head in the direction of where she last was.

She accosted Lola. Which means she knows that Lola is something to me. There's no way it was a random meeting. That cunt is too conniving for that. I have a suspicion that she'll be waiting for me. Sharon will be expecting Lola to spill the details.

She's set this up, thinking she's really clever, but she's forgetting that I'm not that weak, naive little boy anymore. She's no longer playing this savage game with a child, but a man. A man who won't think twice about causing her just a little bit of the pain she caused me over the years.

It must be almost two hours later by the time I see the neon lights for the bar in the distance. I'm desperate for a drink. The lingering taste of my own vomit is making me want to throw up all over again, but the taste for revenge overpowers it.

I nod at the bouncer, hoping that he can't see the storm that's brewing behind my eyes and pull the door open when he gestures for me to do so.

I keep my head down as I walk to the bar and find a spot that gives me a view of the entire venue.

After ordering a scotch, I scour the room looking for the cunt who thought it would be a good idea to use Lola to get to me.

My frustration levels only grows when I don't see anyone vaguely familiar. That doesn't mean she's not here though. If she planned this, then she'll be waiting for me somewhere, ready to pounce when she thinks I least expect it.

"I'm ready, you motherfucker," I mutter to myself as I neck my third scotch that the barman is helpfully keeping refilled without me even having to ask.

When I eventually walk back out of those doors, the entire building spins around me and I've no idea how my legs actually carry me outside.

I fall almost face first into the cab that's idling at the curb and I must give him my address because the next thing I know, he's shouting at me and telling me to get out.

When I crack my eyes open and get them to focus, I find my building before me.

The lights still shine from the top floor and my heart constricts as I think about Lola. Surely after learning what she did tonight, she'll have left.

Why would anyone want me after learning the truth?

She ruined me for anyone else long ago.

"Mate, get the fuck out," the driver barks once again, dragging me from my nightmare and I reach for the door.

I miss the handle on the first attempt, but thankfully, I'm a little more successful on the second.

It could take me ten minutes, or it could take me three hours—I've no concept of time—but I eventually find myself at the front door.

I'm busy attempting to get the key in the lock, when the door I'm leaning on for support disappears from my shoulder and I go flying into the flat.

"Ant, fuck." Her soft, concerned voice shocks me. Why is she still here?

I roll onto my back as pain explodes in my shoulder from where I landed. In no time, she's right there, her hands on my rough cheeks and staring down into my eyes.

Concern is etched into every inch of her face.

"Are you okay?" she asks, breaking our contact to look over me.

"I've never been okay, Lola." My traitorous voice cracks at the end, but I've no control over it.

"Come on, let's get you to bed."

She does her best to pull me up, but she's barely got the strength.

"You're going to need to help at least a little."

"Humph," I grunt as I try to push myself up.

"Don't make me call Deacon back," she warns.

Deacon was here? Why?

I shake the thoughts from my head and focus on getting my feet to work.

The second I'm up, Lola tucks herself under my arm and attempts to lead me towards my bedroom. As we pass through the living room, I spot a blanket covered lump on the sofa.

"Ellie," I whisper, my heart aching for my girl. She's been through so much, the last thing she needs right now is me losing my head.

"She's okay, Ant. She's going to be okay."

I nod in agreement, although I'm not sure if I believe it.

Finally, we reach our destination and Lola allows me to fall down onto the edge of the bed. She helps pull the clothes from my body before pushing me to lie back with my head on the pillow.

My eyes remain open, watching her as she strips down to join me.

She's a fucking angel, yet the things she allows me to do to her...

Fuck, my cock stirs with the thoughts.

I shouldn't want to hurt her right now just as much as I want to protect her.

Her warm body climbs into bed beside me and she curls herself into my side with her head on my chest. I'm powerless but to pull her tighter to me.

"Why are you still here?" I don't realise I say the words out loud until she tenses and then replies.

"Where else would I be?"

"But... but what I admitted."

My voice cracks once again and emotion burns the back of my throat. I can't talk about this right now. If I do, I'll just break down and she'll think I'm even weaker than I'm sure she already does.

Her hand skims up my chest until she's cupping my cheek and looking up at me.

"Get some sleep, Ant. Everything will seem brighter in the morning."

She drops a sweet kiss to the corner of my lips before falling silent beside me.

When I wake the next morning, Lola is already dressed and placing a coffee down on my bedside table.

"Going somewhere?" I ask, my voice rough from my sleep.

"Yeah, I just need to shoot out. I shouldn't be long. How are you feeling?" she asks, brushing a lock of hair from my face.

"I've no idea," I admit, not moving.

"We should do something fun when I get back."

"Fun?" I ask with a laugh, making colour hit her cheeks.

"Forget it; it was a stupid idea."

"No, no." I reach out and take her hand. "Fun sounds good."

"Okay, well, you think of something and then when I'm back we'll do whatever it is."

She leans forward and places a kiss to my forehead.

I catch her behind the back of her neck and hold her so her nose is almost touching mine.

"Thank you for not running."

"Ant" she says with a sigh, her fresh, minty breath fanning my face, reminding me that mine probably smells like the back end of a donkey right now— it sure tastes like it. "None of this is on you. None of it is your fault." A small smile twitches at her lips. "Ellie is in her room. I think she'd really appreciate it if you talked to her. She's got a lot of gaps that need filling."

I nod, the dread at having to say some of the words Ellie deserves to hear feels like it's stuck in my throat, stopping me from speaking.

"I'll message when I'm on my way back."

With a kiss to the tip of my nose, she stands up.

A weird expression crosses her face for a beat, but it's gone before I can tell what it is.

"Okay. Thank you again."

"Stop apologising. Just spend some time with your daughter." With her words still lingering in the air, she turns and leaves.

I push myself so I'm sitting, and I drink the coffee she left before taking myself to the bathroom in the hope I can wash away the stench of last night's drinking and my raging hangover.

I don't feel all that much better when I step from the room dressed in a pair of joggers and a t-shirt, but at least I smell significantly fresher.

Coming to a stop outside Ellie's room, I pause for a few seconds to listen to her moving around inside.

Before I change my mind, I lift my hand to knock.

"Ellie, can I come in?"

After getting her agreement, I push the door open and step inside.

The room looks the same as it always has, but already, I can tell that she's making it hers. I fight the smile that wants to creep onto my face knowing that she wants to be here.

"Can I?" I gesture to the other side of the bed to where she's sitting.

"Sure."

Silence surrounds us for the longest time as we just sit side by side. But eventually, I know I need to fill the void.

"You were the cutest baby. I mean, I'd not really

seen many, but even still, I knew you were more beautiful than any other.

"The first time you looked up at me with your large dark eyes, I swear it was like I took a bat to the chest.

"I had no idea why I felt this huge need to protect you. I thought it was because you'd been born into the same hell I had to live in daily. I had no idea it ran deeper than that."

I blow out a slow breath.

"Your mother... she'd been abusing me for... longer than I even care to remember. I was so young and naive, and she kept me basically locked up so that I would remain that way.

"I had no idea that I could have had a hand in making you. I was a fucking kid. Yeah, I knew what she was doing to me, I knew it wasn't right, but it wasn't like I could do anything about it, tell anyone. She was the only person I saw, aside from the other men that would visit. I just assumed you were one of theirs.

"You were about four months old when I walked out of that house with you in my arms."

"Why?" she asks, startling me. I'd almost forgotten she was there, she's so silent.

"You were starving, Ellie. You were so thin, so frail. To start with you just cried, but at some point you must have realised that no food was coming because you just stopped. That was when I knew I had to do something. That sparkle in your eye from the first time I saw you was long gone.

"I could cope with being hungry, but I couldn't

watch her neglect you any longer. So while she was otherwise engaged one day, I wrapped you in the dirty sheet on my bed and I ran with you in my arms.

"Had I known... Fuck," I bark, my fingers gripping the sheets as anger surges through me. "If I had any clue you were mine, I never would have let them take you away from me. You were so helpless, suffering so much, all I wanted to do was look after you, but I had no idea how to. So all I could do was believe the social worker and hand you over believing that they'd place you with a lovely family and that you'd get the love you deserved."

"It didn't work out that way."

"Yeah, so I see."

Silence fills the room once more as we lose ourselves in memories of our terrible childhoods.

"I'm sorry," she says eventually, and I panic thinking she means she's going to leave. But when I turn to look at her, I know she's not.

She's got tears streaming down her cheeks, despite the fact she's not let out one sob. I know they're there; she's just fighting them.

"I'm sorry you had to endure that."

"Oh, Ellie, you've nothing to be sorry for."

Taking a risk, I reach out and pull her into me. She tenses for a beat before turning into my side. Her body trembles as she gives in to her tears.

"Never again, Ellie. I won't allow anyone to ever hurt you again." I drop my nose to her hair and breathe her in. "I'll kill anyone who even tries," I promise.

CHAPTER TWENTY-FIVE

Lola

I t's a sign of how off his game Ant is that he doesn't question where I'm going or what I'm doing this morning.

Last night William had called Deacon to say Ant was at the club, and Deacon had let him stay at a distance watching while he got as much information as he could together about Sharon.

And now we were going to deal with her.

I recall our conversation from the night before.

Deacon's voice came down the line. "Ant's on his way home. If you need me, call me."

"I will."

"Lola. I have something to ask you and it's a big ask, but I need your help."

"What is it?"

"I need to draw Sharon out of her cesspit. And to do that... I need you to be bait."

"I'll do it."

He barks a laugh down the line. "You don't know what I'm asking. I need you to think carefully about this. Given the situation you were in yourself not so long ago, are you strong enough to participate in my plans?"

"I can get Sharon to meet me. It's not a problem. I don't know how, but I presume you're going to set that up."

"Of course. But what do you think I'm going to do when I come along, Lola? She's been to jail, she's been warned to stay away from Ant over and over and yet she's still here, stalking you, and threatening him. Trying to extort him. If she gets to that girl, God knows what damage she could do and she's done enough already. Plus, I'm getting intel that she's advertising to do childcare."

"What?"

"People are idiots. They don't do the proper checks. She could hurt someone else, and I'm not prepared for that to happen. You need to know that when it comes to Ant, when it comes to any of them, I won't sit back and watch them get hurt. So do you really want to take part in this because it's not going to be pretty?"

"Yes."

My mind screams this is reckless, that it's fragile given recent circumstances, but the truth is I'm happy to be the bait to draw the bitch out. I'd sacrifice the last

*vestiges of my sanity in order to save Ant and Ellie from
any further harm.*

"*I'll be in touch,*" *he says, and he ends the call.*

I wake with a text notification hitting my phone. I
carefully extract myself from Ant and steal into the en
suite.

**She's making it too easy. She's watching the
apartment. Call me when you're ready to go
out. I have eyes on her to see if she follows
you or to see if she's waiting for either of
them.**

I text back saying I'll let him know when I set off
and then I quickly get ready, make a coffee for Ant, and
with another text to Deacon, I'm on my way out of the
apartment.

I have no real plans on where I'm going to go, so I
decide to walk for a few minutes and find a coffee shop.
My phone buzzes.

She's following you.

Finding a suitable place, I go inside, order a coffee
and sit down.

It isn't long before she joins me.

"Oh for fuck's sake, what do you want?" I ask
Sharon, acting surprised to have seen her.

"She's in there, isn't she? In that apartment." Sharon's

eyes look manic, darting around outside the coffee shop and then back to me. "That's why he's ignoring me. He has her anyway. She's my daughter, so what's to stop me going to see her? You need to pass him a message from me."

"What do you want to drink, Sharon?" I ask her. "And not a coffee or coke because you need to calm the fuck down, you're drawing attention to us."

"I'll have a cup of tea and a breakfast sandwich," she says. Standing up, I make my way to the counter. I want to text Deacon but she's watching my every move.

After a few minutes I take the seat opposite her.

"So why are you following me? What do you want? I've told you, I'm only his assistant."

"Bullshit. You stayed there all fucking night to have left so early this morning. He thinks I'm stupid, but it came to me in the early hours of this morning why he's been ignoring me, and why he's not paid me to be quiet. How long ago did he find her?"

"I'm presuming he's not paid you to be quiet because there's nothing you can say out loud that won't let people know you went to prison for abusing him."

Sharon laughs. "He doesn't want anyone knowing that happened to him. Ant likes to pretend it didn't happen. He doesn't want his business associates knowing he fucked his mummy and enjoyed it."

"Enjoyed it? You're sick in the head."

"Tell him he needs to come up with a deal large enough that I can leave him be. If he wants to play the dutiful father that's his call. But I'm going to create a huge scene if he doesn't contact me in the next twenty-four hours."

I sigh. "I'll message him now."

She smiles like the cat that got the cream. Her drink and food arrive and while she dives on them, I message Deacon and update him.

Tell her to come to his office at B.A.D.

Sharon finishes her food and wipes her mouth on a napkin. "You know, I wondered why he'd changed his type, gone from fucking older women in some attempt to mentally punish me; but I realise now. He's following my lead."

"What?" I push back from the table I'm so appalled at her words.

She looks triumphant. "Ant's clearly fucking you because you're some substitute version of our daughter. He doesn't want you. He wants her, and you're his way around that. Has he accidentally shouted out her name while fucking you?"

If we weren't in a coffee shop surrounded by the general public she'd be on the floor with a bruised cheek, but Sharon knows this and she taunts me, laughing.

"Ant says he'll meet you at his office now," I tell her. "He's not meeting you at the apartment because he wants to keep you away from her."

"I'm not interested in my daughter. I just want

money... and Anthony. He'll always be mine. I was his first. It's a special kind of love we share."

It's increasingly difficult not to smash her in the face with the coffee mug I've drunk from, but my hatred for this woman grows by the second, to the point where if we don't get out of here soon, I'll be in jail.

I flag down a cab to B.A.D. and when we arrive, I start to get out of the car.

"What are you doing?" she asks me.

"I'm taking you to him."

"We don't need you."

"Tough shit. You're not going in that building unaccompanied. If Ant asks me to move outside or go home I will, but I don't follow your orders."

She smiles like a Disney witch. "Such petulance. I bet he likes that. It's very... *teenage.*"

My stomach roils with disgust. I thought I'd hated people before, but this woman is taking things to a whole new level.

We check in with security who appear to have been appraised of our arrival to the point the guy says, "Mr Warren is waiting for you," when I know 'Mr Warren' has no idea any of this is happening.

She stands outside his office door and turns her head to me. "So, you're coming in? You can watch us if you like. You can hear how he screams my name and then... so endearing, he cries and curls into my side."

I knock on the door and get ready because when she sees Deacon she'll try and bolt I'm sure. Although she'll not get far.

I'm thrown when Ant calls, "Come in."

As I push the door open, she stalks on ahead and we come face to face with... Deacon? Huh?

Then I see the phone in his hand. I quickly lock the door behind us.

"I have everyone's greeting on here. You never know when you need such things. Hello, Sharon. I've heard such, well, terrible things about you. Take a seat and let's talk about how we're going to extract you from Ant and your daughter's life."

Seemingly unfazed, Sharon takes a seat at the front of the desk. "Shame he couldn't come see his mummy, but I have all the time in the world. Anyway as long as you have some money for me, we're good for now," she states.

Deacon laughs and it's so chilling I don't know how the furniture isn't layered with ice crystals.

"Sharon, Sharon, Sharon." He sits in his chair looking down at her. "When I said we're going to talk about how to extract you from their lives, I didn't mean with a financial package." He stands up and walks closer to her. "I'm a lover of fairy tales, you know? Since I met my future wife, I'm all for a happy ever after, and my favourite line now is, 'Ding dong, the witch is dead'."

"We're in a huge office. You can't do anything to me here. Too many witnesses," she says smugly.

"And that shows how much you underestimate me, Sharon. Because I. Don't. Give. A. Flying. Fuck." He draws out a gun and I swallow. This has the capacity to take me out of this room and someplace else and I cannot go there. Ant needs me. He was there for me. I need to be there for him.

Sharon's head pivots to the door looking for a way to escape, but I'm in her way. The reality of her situation dawns on her, her eyes widen, and she starts to panic and shake.

She squeals when the door behind me flies open and I swear my heart damn near stops.

When I turn, I find myself the sole focus of Ant's furious eyes.

CHAPTER TWENTY-SIX

Ant

I might not have been firing on all cylinders after the night before, but as I sat with Ellie filling in some of the holes of her past, a weird feeling settled over me as I realised Lola didn't offer up any information on where she was going and I could only assume there was a reason. She didn't want me to know.

I returned to my bedroom and set out searching for my phone. I eventually found it half tucked under the bed where it must have fallen when Lola helped to undress me last night.

I shake my head at myself. I took things too far last night. I shouldn't have put her in that position to have to look after me. I'm a grown fucking man, I should be able to handle myself. All these years on, my past shouldn't have the power to consume me like it did only hours ago.

It was dead—typical—so after locating my charger, I give it enough juice to turn on and immediately open my tracking app.

It shows that Ellie is in the flat and I smile that she clearly didn't hand over everything I gave her the other day. But then Lola's phone appears showing her at the office.

Why the fuck is she there on a Saturday?

My first thought is that she's meeting Rob. My muscles lock for a second. Surely, she's not that stupid, is she?

Dread settles in my stomach as I shove my feet into my shoes and head for the door. I call to Ellie that I'm heading out and in the blink of an eye I'm heading for the office.

As I'm driving, something she said to me when I got home last night comes back to me.

"Don't make me call Deacon back."

Why was Deacon at my flat last night? The few possibilities that float through my head have me pressing the accelerator harder.

My heart races and I park directly out the front on the double yellows and run through reception and directly into the lift.

I trust Deacon with my life; he'd never do anything to hurt me or Lola. But I also know that he would literally do anything to protect me and it's that thought that has me on the edge of panicking.

Lola knows, that means Deacon could know, and that means...

I race to my office knowing from the app that's where she is, and I assume he is too.

I blow out a breath as my trembling hand reaches for the handle.

I wait a second before pushing the door open with such force it flies back and collides with the wall.

Three sets of eyes turn on me but it's only one pair that I lock onto.

Lola's.

I watch as a shudder of fear runs through her.

I don't say anything, I don't need to. From the terrified look on her face I know she can already read my thoughts regarding this.

"I'm sorry," she mouths, but I dismiss her with a tilt of my chin to focus on the rest of this clusterfuck of a situation.

Deacon is standing before Sharon with a gun pointed at her.

"Thought it was time to take this scumbag off the earth. What do you say, Ant?"

"Son, please," Sharon begs, something I never, ever thought I'd see her do. "These people are crazy. Please, let me go."

"Shut up," I spit, desperately trying to get my thoughts straight.

"They kidnapped me, baby. Kidnapped me and stuck a gun in my face. They're fucking crazy."

Deacon scoffs. "We're the crazy ones. Pfft. So how old was your *baby* here when you forced yourself on him and made him a father long before he was ready to be?"

"Enough, Deac," I bark, not needing to listen to a rerun of my past. Being able to remember it is fucking bad enough, I don't need it read to me like a fucking bedtime story. "Give me that."

"Please, Anthony. I've only ever wanted the best for you, son."

"Enough," I roar, swiping the gun from Deacon and swinging until it collides with her temple knocking her out cold.

Her body slumps on the sofa as blood begins to trickle from the cut it caused.

Silence fills the room. All that can be heard is our combined heavy breathing as we all stare at the bitch who did everything in her power to ruin my life.

"What the fuck were you thinking?" My voice is low, and if I were speaking to anyone other than Deacon, possibly chilling, but that motherfucker doesn't care about my tone of voice.

"We were thinking that we'd do the world a favour and wipe this piece of shit from it."

"And you thought you had a right to do that?" I turn on Deacon.

"Yeah, I think I fucking do."

He stands toe to toe with me, not a slither of fear in his light blue eyes despite the situation.

"It's not your fucking call."

"She hurt—is hurting—you. It can be my call. Don't you want her fucking gone?"

Movement in the corner of the room catches my eye and I look to Lola who stands sheepishly chewing on her nails as she watches us.

I'm just about to tell her to leave when we're joined by another.

"Fancy you motherfuckers starting this party without me," Tyler announces, strolling in like it's a normal fucking day.

Anna and Jack trail behind him and go straight for Lola.

"Come on, Lo. Let's get you out of here."

"No," she cries, her eyes never once leaving me. "I'm not leaving him."

Her eyes beg for me to allow her to stay, but she's already been through enough. She doesn't need to witness whatever the hell is going to happen here. Sharon's not going to be walking out like I assume she walked in, that's for fucking sure.

"Do as you're told, Lola."

"Fuck you, Ant," she spits. "I did this for you, to help you."

"I don't need your help."

"No, you need a good fucking shrink," she shouts, but seemingly regrets it when my face contorts with anger.

"What I need is everyone out of my fucking business," I boom. I spent years keeping this under wraps and silently drowning in my own nightmares. Now it might as well be front page fucking news. All I need is Oliver to turn up and my entire fucking family will witness the fucking disaster that was my past.

I laugh to myself, much to everyone's shock. Of course Oliver already knows. This lot might be able to hide secrets like no other, but not within the five of us. It's why I've been the anomaly over the years. They've never broken me down to spill all. I know it's frustrated the fuck out of them, but just look what's happened once they discovered the truth.

"Let's go," Jack announces, and with Anna's help they all but drag Lola from the room before shutting the door behind them.

The sound of her screams and pleads fills my ears for long seconds before they either lock her in another office or get her in the lift, I've no idea.

"Now, are you going to end this bitch or do you need a real man to do it?" Tyler taunts.

"We're not killing her, not yet."

"Oh, do we get to torture her first?" The sick motherfucker actually rubs his hands together in pleasure at the thought.

"I don't know," I admit, falling down onto the unoccupied sofa in my office.

"You don't fucking know? The shit she did to you, Ant. To Ellie. Don't you want revenge?"

"Of course. I just didn't wake up this morning

thinking that this would be the day."

I lift my fingers to my temples, rubbing them, willing the fucking hangover to abate so I can think fucking clearly.

The bitch before me moans, her arm twitching.

"Well, you'd better make a fucking decision before the cunt wakes up."

I look from her, to my boys. I know they only want what's best for me right now, but to be quite honest, I've no idea what the best is.

"Have you got somewhere you can take her?"

Deacon's eyes widen while Tyler's glitter in delight. "Yeah, I was thinking the bottom of the fucking Thames, to be honest."

"Take her somewhere, tie her up, gag her, do what the fuck you want to her, just don't kill her while I decide the best thing to do."

They look at me like I've lost my fucking mind. To be fair, I might have. But that cunt of a woman is my daughter's mother whether I like it or not.

I refuse to take another choice away from Ellie. She's already lost too much in her young life.

"Let me know the address." Pushing from the sofa, I walk to the door and rip it open. I storm through, the silence of their shock behind me almost deafening as I try to decide where they will have taken Lola.

As I get closer to Jack's office, I know my instincts were right because I can hear Lola still shouting and screaming.

I march right up to the door and ram my shoulder into it, assuming correctly that Jack will have locked it.

"What the—" Jack barks as I barrel into the room and sweep Lola off her feet, throwing her over my shoulder and walking straight back out again.

"Anthony, put my sister down right now," Anna screams, running behind us.

"Pipe down, Mrs Ward. I'm not going to hurt her... much." Lola trembles in my hold. She understands my words and what she's got coming her way.

"You can't just walk out with her. She's my sister."

"Watch me," I bark, stalking into the lift and hitting the button for the garage.

The doors immediately start closing and when I turn, I just catch sight of a furious Anna standing before us.

Lowering Lola to her feet, my hand goes around her throat as I push her back into the wall with a crash.

"You lied to me," I seethe, my nose almost touching hers. "You fucking betrayed me."

My lips crash to hers in a bruising kiss as my fingers grip her harder than they should.

I don't release her until the lift alerts us that we've arrived. Releasing her neck, she gasps for breath.

"Ant," she pants, but when I lift her into my arms, her eyes are dark with desire, not fear.

Fuck this woman.

With her legs wrapped around my waist, her burning core pressing against my length, I walk us through the deserted car park and toward my car.

The only other cars here are that of the arseholes upstairs. I'm confident they're all preoccupied right now, but the thought of them coming down and catching us doing what I'm about to do doesn't faze me one bit.

It wouldn't be the first time we've all seen a little too much of each other that's for sure.

The second I'm at my car, I lay Lola out on the bonnet.

"Ant, what the fuck?"

"Shut up," I bellow, my hands going for her flimsy leggings.

The sound of the fabric ripping echoes through the silent garage. In seconds she's laid out before me bare from the waist down, her pussy glistening with her desire.

"You went behind my back today, Lola. And you're going to fucking pay for it."

"Please," she cries, knowing that her payment is going to come in the form of her favourite poison. Pleasure and pain.

Placing her feet on the bonnet, I push her knees as wide as they'll go.

"Hold them," I demand, reaching for my sweats and pushing them and my boxers down my hips, stepping out of them and freeing my almost painful length.

After sliding her down to exactly where I need her, I take myself in my hand and push inside her without any warning. Not that she needed it. She's wet, so fucking wet, and hot.

I roar in pleasure as her heat surrounds me before I begin a punishing rhythm of fucking her. Every security camera is probably trained on us right now, but I don't think about that, all I can think about is her and the things I want to do to her.

CHAPTER TWENTY-SEVEN

Lola

Ant's eyes and movements are wild and frenzied. He's punishing me but savouring me at the same time. I know he's screwed up, broken, and is struggling with which way is up right now, but we both have something in all this mess that we can reach for, an anchor, and that's us, together, panting and sweaty and taking our fill of desire.

"Harder," I demand even though every thrust is already being delivered with force. He grabs the back of my head, pulling my mouth to his, swallowing my moans. As he tenses ready to come, I give one final hip thrust. He yells out my name as he comes. A guttural roar that's all animal, primal. He's claiming me.

Pushing my top up, he pulls the cups of my bra down and bites on my breast making a mark, then he moves to the other. He heads to my neck, but I warn him. "No, not where anyone can see."

"You're fucking mine," he tells me, capturing a nipple in his mouth and biting on it.

"Fuuuucck."

He lifts me up and turns me around so I'm leaning over the car. Pulling my top over my head, he opens my bra and removes that as well, throwing them to the floor without a second glance.

Kneeing my thighs apart, his fingers brush between my legs. "So wet for me. Do you agree, Lola, that you did a bad thing today going behind my back? I think you need to be punished. Don't you?"

"Yes." I say, though it comes out more as a breathy moan. I wiggle my arse and I can hear his breath hitch. His hand comes down on my butt cheek hard, the slap echoing around the space.

"In future you tell me where you are going and what you are doing if it involves me." He brings his hand down on me again.

"In fact, in future you tell me where you're going anyway. Every. Single. Move. I want to know it. I own you, Lola. Do you understand that?"

I should tell him to go fuck himself, but my needy core wants his cock back inside me. His ownership of me, the thought of doing his every bidding is electrifying.

Slap.

"I asked you a question. Answer me."

"Yes."

"Yes, what?"

"Yes, I understand. Yes, you own me. Yes, I'll tell you where I am. Yes, I'll not go behind your back again."

His fingers run through my wetness and he brings his digits to my face. "Look at my fingers. Your cunt is dripping, Lola. Dripping for me. Do you want me again?"

"Yesssss," I beg.

"Today I'm going to fuck you raw, and when I've done that, I might just claim another one of your firsts." He runs a digit through my wetness and then I feel it pushing at my puckered hole.

"Please," I beg again.

He thrusts inside me once more. My breasts press against the coolness of the bonnet, my hands trying to steady me as Ant thrusts into me again and again and again. His fingers grip hard into my arse to a point where I think I'll have bruises, but I'm too delirious to care. When he pinches my clit, I explode to the point I'm seeing stars as I milk his cock for everything he gives me.

We keep doing this, fucking without taking precautions, and I don't even care. I'm walking on the wild side of life. Maybe I'll be devoured or maybe I'll find I should have lived here all along.

He pulls out of me and wipes us both with his boxer briefs before throwing them in the boot of the car. I pick up my clothes, looking around, knowing that the others could turn up down here at any moment.

Ant picks up my cues. "They'll know what we were doing. Security at the very least watched."

My cheeks flush as I look at my ruined clothes. My leggings and panties are ripped. My top is dirty from the floor and won't cover me enough.

"Too late to be embarrassed now. You didn't look coy when you were spread over my car begging for my cock."

"What the fuck am I going to do?" I look down at myself. "I can't go home looking like this."

"Personally, I wish you could walk around like that twenty-four-fucking-seven, but here." He hands me his shirt. "That'll keep you almost decent."

I slip it over my head. It hits at mid-thigh. There's still no disguising that I've been up to no good to end up halfway dressed, but it's an improvement on totally being exposed to the elements. Plus, it means Ant is going to be staying half-naked and that's one hell of a beautiful body I can stare at on the ride home.

"Anna is going to be doing her nut right now."

That brings a smirk to his face. "Yeah, I'll bet your sister has a ton of questions for you. Want to go back in?"

"No. Would you please drop me at home?" I ask him.

He looks disappointed for a moment, but then his face loses the slack expression and he nods. "Of course."

"You need to sort out what's happening with Sharon and talk to Ellie, and I want to see my mum. Make sure she's okay. Plus, there'll be no escaping my sister. I'd rather talk to her at home where I can lock myself in my bedroom if she pisses me off."

Ant walks over to me and pulls me against his body. I can feel the hard planes of his chest held tight against me. "Tonight, you come back to me," he orders, and I raise a brow. "I've told you. I own you, Lola. You agreed. So your place is in my bed."

I'm glad I'm going home so I can get my head around his words. I kind of thought they were sex play, but it seems it's more than that.

"What if I don't? What if I stay home?"

"Then I'll be paying your mother for a broken door and apologising for frightening her as I break into your place and carry you out of there."

Lowering his head, he bites the top of my earlobe.

"You."

Nip.

"Belong."

Lick.

"To."

Bite.

"Me."

I tilt my head to allow his tongue access as it trails

across my ear and then down my neck. I'm shivering under his touch, goose bumps appearing on my skin. He captures my mouth and bites down on my lip, before springing back away from me.

I feel his reignited interest against me before he moves.

"Get in the car and let me take you to see your mum. Otherwise, I'm going to lay you on the back seat of this car and fuck you over and over for the rest of the day."

I'm his. I do as he asks.

I've not been in the house fifteen minutes before Anna has used her key to more or less storm through the door.

I'm in my room as Mum isn't home.

"Lollllaaaaaa Hawley, get your arse out here now."

Instead, I push open my bedroom door and then retreat to where I was lying on my bed.

She walks in and looks at me. I know I have the most stupid expression on my face. Dreamy.

Plonking herself on the end of my bed, all she says is, "Spill."

I can't help but tease her. "About what?"

She puts her hand across her stomach. "Stress isn't good for the baby, so I think you should just confess all. I was away not even a week. You? Ant? Tell me!" Leaning over she shakes me just as she used to when we were smaller.

I giggle.

"There's just something there, and I can't explain it. We get each other." My dreamy expression is back. I can feel it.

"The security guy wouldn't let us leave. What the fuck were you doing?"

"The fuck." I wink.

"In the car park?"

"I'm not discussing the details with you. All I'm confessing is something is happening and it's too early to define it. But the broken parts of him fit to the broken parts of me, and somehow it makes good things."

Her lips downturn. "I wish you'd talk to me, Lo."

"I know," I tell her. "And maybe one day I'll be able to unlock that box, but not now."

It's the first time I've ever raised the possibility of talking about what happened to me and she nods her head and strokes down my hair.

"Whatever it is. You're my sister and I will always love you. No matter what." Her eyes meet mine. "The man was fucked-up and evil. I've tried to imagine what he did, what he made you do, and it tears me up inside because I want to help, but I trust you to talk to me when the time is right."

Emotions I've had locked up tight are bleeding out of me. One lone, stray tear runs down my face and using her thumb Anna wipes it away.

"It's your worst nightmare," I tell her. "It's my

nightmare. And I'm scared if I let it out, it'll destroy us all."

She clings to me then. Pulling me into her arms, holding me tight. She whispers near my ear. "My worst nightmare is my sister hurting to the point she can't live her life to its full potential."

I savour her arms around me and then slowly she moves away.

"Okay, I'm making coffee because I am so thirsty I might die, and then I'm coming right back here and I want more gossip about you and Ant, and to hear all about Ellie."

Just as she reaches the door, I call her back. "What happened to Sharon?"

She shrugs her shoulders. "Sometimes in a relationship you have to trust what the other one is doing even when you aren't privy to the details." With one last look at me she leaves the room.

If Ant kills Sharon... with what happened to me... can I accept that? Closing my eyes, all I can see is the two of us together: the looks, the caresses, the ownership and submission. I can help his demons see peace. He can bring light to the dark living inside me.

I realise I'm falling for him hard. So hard that if I'm not careful, as I fall, if he doesn't catch me, I'll break into tiny, splintered pieces I fear would be impossible to put back together.

When Anna returns with a drink for us both, I tell her the basics of everything that's been happening with

Ellie and how Sharon has been reappearing on the scene.

"Aren't you going to warn me away from Ant? Talk about the age gap, or the fact he has so much shit going down right now?" She is my bossy, big sister after all.

"When Tyler thought I was a corporate spy, he tied me naked to his office chair and left me there with the air con on. He also hate-fucked me thousands of miles up in the air as we flew back from New York. I married him, so I'm not in a position to judge anyone, sis."

My jaw needs picking up off the ground.

"If he's your future, then that's how it is. But just make sure he knows that if he hurts you, I know my hubby is real good at securing people to chairs and I'll be his worst nightmare."

We both burst out laughing. It feels good to be spending time with my sister this way. Opening up, enjoying her company.

When she leaves I feel content inside. Like a small spark of hope is flaring within me.

I eat tea with my mum and confess I've started to see Ant. After what feels like a million questions, she announces she's pleased for me. She still warns me about rushing into things when I phone for a driver to collect me and take me to Ant's. It's endearing, but no way can I stay away from him.

It's like there's an invisible rope tethering me and he's pulling it towards him.

Stepping out into the dark night, a car is idling at the curb. But there's no driver. He's in the car himself.

I run to it, run to him, and as I do his face lights up. There's no other word for it. The streetlamps warm glow has him looking like a fallen angel and as he leans forward and opens the door, I throw myself in and on him, my mouth on his.

No words are needed. My kiss says everything I want him to know.

CHAPTER TWENTY-EIGHT

Ant

I hold the car door open for Lola once I release her from our kiss.

I hate to admit it, but I really fucking needed to feel her lips on mine without the anger, the desperation, and confusion of a few hours ago.

I'd spent my time since dropping her off just driving around the city, trying to get my head on straight.

As I climb back into the driver's seat, I might feel a little calmer, but I'm just as torn about what to do about this whole situation as I was earlier.

The last thing I was expecting to have to deal with today was Deacon abducting my cunt of a foster mother and holding her at gunpoint.

I don't know why I'm surprised; we don't usually have a quiet day at B.A.D. I'm just usually not the one causing all the drama.

My knuckles turn white with the strength of my grip on the wheel as I head towards home and to the one person I really need to have a conversation with about what's happened today.

Ellie has shown me on more than one occasion over the past few days that she's more than capable of looking after herself, so I refuse to make any kind of decision about what happens to Sharon until I've spoken to her.

Should I be explaining to my eighteen-year-old daughter that my best friends are holding her mother against her will? No, probably not. But Ellie isn't just some average eighteen-year-old, and this isn't some normal, everyday issue.

This is fucked-up beyond belief just like every other part of our lives.

She deserves to know the truth if she wants to. She has every right to meet the bitch, and as much as I might hate the idea, I know it's a decision I can't make for her.

No words are said between us as we travel across the city, although I don't miss the concerned glances Lola sends my way. She wants to ask, I know she does, but she also knows that talking about this right now is the last thing I need.

"I- I just need to talk to Ellie."

"It's okay," she says reaching over and gently

squeezing my thigh in support as I pull up into the car park.

Bringing the car to a stop, I look over at her. How she's only twenty-two is beyond me. On most days I'd say she was the most mature out of the two of us. She sure knows how to keep me in line that's for damn sure.

I briefly wonder when I gave her the power to even do so, but I quickly realise that it happened the first time I brought her back here. Even to this day, I know doing that was wrong, but I was powerless to resist. And thank fuck I did, because I'm not sure I could do this now without her by my side.

Selfish? Hell yeah, especially after what she's been through. But fuck, I need her. I need her so fucking badly.

After blowing out a somewhat calming breath, I kill the engine and push the door open.

No time like the present to talk to my daughter about the possibility of us ending her mother's life.

Lola meets me at her side of the car and almost immediately threads her fingers through mine as we head toward the lift.

As the doors close behind us, I pull her into my arms. Tucking my head into the crook of her neck, I breathe her in, almost instantly feeling better about what's to come.

"Come on," she says after the lift has come to a stop and I've still not moved. "The sooner you talk to her about this, the sooner it can all be over." I glance at her as her face pales. She knows as well as I do that really this is only going to end one way.

"Ellie," I call the second we're inside the flat, knowing that Lola's words are right.

Her feet sound out seconds before she appears around the corner. I hadn't allowed myself to think about the possibility of her not being here. After our chat earlier, she'd given me the idea that she was here to stay, and I wanted to believe I was right.

"Is everything okay?" she asks, looking between the two of us. God only knows what she can read on our faces right now.

"Coffees?" Lola offers but she doesn't wait for our responses before she disappears into the kitchen area and starts crashing around.

"Come sit with me," I say, turning my eyes back on Ellie.

"What's going on?" she asks hesitantly.

I blow out a long breath, trying to form my words.

"I know where your mother is, and I've got a really important question to ask you."

"Riiight."

"Lola and a couple of guys from work picked her up earlier. They—"

"You mean kidnapped, right?"

"Uh..." I stare into her eyes. I hate the dark shadows I see in them, but they're the reminder I need that she can handle the truth here. I've just got to trust that she's already decided where her loyalties lie and that it's with me. "Yeah. I'm not going to sugar-coat this for you.

There's a very high chance that she won't be walking away from this. But I needed to give you the chance to see her, meet her, before you're unable to get another."

"Jesus," she mutters. "And I thought the life I left behind was dramatic."

I want to tell her that this kind of thing isn't an everyday occurrence for us, but then I think about Deacon's father, Lola's abduction and how that led to more losses of life, and I start to wonder if this kind of thing is becoming a little too normal for us. I really fucking hope not. Reggie is only going to be able to bail us out of the shit we get up to so many times, and we're all only going to be able to cover up so many dead bodies. A shudder runs down my spine at the thought.

"They were going to do it this afternoon, but I held them off... for you."

"Wow, and it's not even Christmas."

I sigh. "Ellie, I promise that if you're still here at Christmas then you'll get a fucking better present than this."

"Good to know. So what are we waiting for? Take me to the bitch."

"Are you sure you really want to do this?"

"Yes," she says standing, a determination in her eyes that I've not witnessed before.

She disappears off towards her room—I assume to get changed—as Lola appears with coffee.

"She really wants to do this, huh?" she asks, passing me a mug before sitting beside me.

"Seems that way."

"You think this is a good idea?"

"I've no idea. But it needs to be her call."

The heat of her hand covers mine. "You're going to be a really good dad, Ant."

I shrug. "Can't be any worse than her mother."

Lola's eyes widen at my terrible joke but neither of us can deny that it's true.

It must be twenty minutes later when Ellie reappears.

"Your coffee is in the kitchen, though it's probably cold by now," Lola says to her.

"Thank you." Ellie walks past us and towards the kitchen.

Dread sits heavy in my stomach, but I know that I need to go through with this. I have to trust that Ellie knows what she's doing and allow her to take the lead.

It's easier to think about that than what I want to happen to Sharon after all this.

She doesn't deserve to breathe the same air as us, I've known that for a long time. But can I kill her? I really don't know.

I hate her with a passion I can't even describe after everything she put both me, Ellie, and all the others through but there's some seriously damaged part of me that tells me I won't be able to do it.

"Right, let's get this shit show on the road, shall we?" Ellie announces as she re-joins us.

Lola and I place our mostly still full mugs on the coffee table and stand.

My blood runs cold as I take a step towards the

door. I guess it's fitting seeing as we're probably heading toward someone's funeral.

No one speaks as we head towards the car. I pull my phone out once I'm in the driver's seat and pull up the address that Ty gave me earlier. I've no fucking clue what it's for, I can only trust that he has a fucking clue what he's doing right now.

I plug the postcode into the GPS and give her a few seconds to find the location.

I glance to my girls. Both of them are lost in their own thoughts and staring out of the windows.

"Are you sure you want to do this?" I'm not sure which one I'm asking, both I guess. There's a good chance that something life changing for all of us is going to happen tonight and I'd hate for either of them to be doing this for the wrong reason.

"Yes," they both say simultaneously.

I nod and back out of the space.

Trying to push aside reality, I think about work as I drive. I mentally go through my to-do list for Monday, think about the meetings I need to have and plan at what point I'll be able to sneak Lola from the office so that I can bend her over my desk.

My cock swells at the thought of running my hands over her arse as she lays her top half over the dark mahogany of my desk.

Glancing over at her, I find her head resting back and her eyes shut. I've no idea if she's asleep or just resting but either way, I don't reach over for her like I'm desperate to do. She needs her rest.

Eventually the city starts to disappear behind us, and we pull into a deserted industrial estate.

The plate is eerie looking, which I guess is fitting. The sun is beginning to set and casting creepy shadows as we make our way towards the pointer on the GPS.

I pull up outside one of the huge warehouses and blow out a breath.

Looking back at Ellie, I find her staring forward with a totally unreadable expression on her face.

"You okay?" I ask quietly.

"Never better."

I nod at her before turning to Lola.

"Lola, we're here." She opens her eyes and looks straight at me. A small smile plays on her lips as she does so and it makes me feel a little lighter.

That all changes though when she turns and looks out of the window. Her entire face falls as all the colour drains out of it.

"What's wrong?"

Her body begins to visibly tremble before me.

Reaching out, I take her hand in mine.

"Lola? What is it?"

"N- nothing. It just reminds me of somewhere else." She can't hold my eyes as she says it, instead staring down at her feet.

"Lola?" I warn.

"It's nothing. Honestly. Let's go and do what we need to do."

I watch as she swallows down her apprehension and squares her shoulders.

Lifting my hand, I cup her cheek and turn her my way.

"Honestly, I'm fine. You need to do this," she says firmly.

She's right, I do. There's no turning back now.

This needs finishing.

CHAPTER TWENTY-NINE

Lola

I t's not the same place. I tell myself. It looks exactly like it, but there must be hundreds of abandoned and disused warehouses all over London.

Not the same.

Not the same.

Not the same.

I repeat it in my head as I follow Ant and Ellie into the building.

There's no sign of anyone as we walk in and I find a breath again. I hold onto it and keep it flowing: in and out, in and out. I need to be present for Ant and for Ellie.

I hear Tommy's maniacal laughter in my head and

force my fingernails into my palm. He's not here, he's dead, he can't hurt me anymore.

In the top corner of the room on a chair is Sharon. Tied, blindfolded and gagged, she stinks, mainly due to the urine soaking her clothes. I bend over as flashbacks assault me.

Tied up.

Bleeding.

No. No. No.

"Lola. You okay?" Ant is immediately at my side. *He needs you, Lola. Don't fuck this up for him. For them.*

I straighten.

"It was the smell," I lie. "I'm fine. Carry on."

"You sure?"

I nod.

He cuts the blindfold and then the gag off Sharon. She starts screaming while she tries to adjust to the fact she can see again, though the warehouse is dull with only a very small amount of light from some skylights.

She abused Ant and who knows how many other kids. This is not like what happened to me. This time she *is* the bad person. Evil incarnate. She deserves to be punished. As I tell myself this, I feel an inner strength seep through me. Watching Ellie, I walk over to her and take and squeeze her hand.

She steps forward. "Stop screaming, Mum. No one can hear you."

Sharon stops and looks at Ellie. I see the moment

she thinks she has a new bargaining chip, a flicker of calculation sweeps across her irises.

"Ellie, darling," she croaks. "I've been trying to find you." She nods her head at Ant. "He took you from me. Ran away. Said so many lies about me. You need to help me, please. I want to be a proper mum to you. We've wasted so much time."

Ellie looks at me for direction and I nod in reassurance. "Talk to her, Ellie, and then you and your dad can decide what to do next. Okay?"

She takes a step forward.

"Tell me about my birth, Mum, and about the time we did spend together before Ant took me away from you."

Sharon smiles. "Of course. Well, I'd not thought I could have children. It was why I fostered. But something happened between me and your father. Yes, he was young, but we had a connection, and things just happened. It was meant to be because a miracle occurred and I had you. It's not too late for us all to be one happy family. All you have to do is untie me."

"What really happened, Dad?" Ellie asks although she already knows.

"What really happened is this woman took me into her home and forced herself on me. Threatened that if I didn't sleep with her, she wouldn't feed the other two children she was fostering. I was fourteen years old, fifteen when she gave birth though I didn't know you were mine. Many men passed through your mum's life.

"Then when she had you, you were her leverage.

She'd miss giving you a bottle and let me hear your screams until I gave in and let her abuse me again.

"One day I couldn't take it anymore. I took you and your things, and I ran away. Thought I'd get us both a better life although it didn't quite turn out that way. But we couldn't have stayed.

"And Sharon was put in prison and on a sex offenders register, and yet here she is today, in front of us, lying about the abuse and harm she did to me and to other kids." Ant was now purple with rage, "and I can't be sure there aren't other children she's doing this to even now."

"It's lies," Sharon pleads. "All lies, Ellie. He's sick in the head. He's always had this weird obsession with me."

"Are you that stupid you don't realise my dad was able to get your police records? I've seen everything," Ellie says. "What happened to me after he left me with the social workers was unfortunate, but he did his best, whereas you... you just don't deserve to breathe."

Before I even have time to compute what is happening, Ellie has pulled out a kitchen knife—I recognise it from Ant's wooden block—and has plunged it through Sharon's neck. Blood spurts out everywhere coating Ellie, coating the floor, and the spray lands on my hand.

Lifting it towards my face, I remember the blood on my hands from *before*, and as Ellie pulls the knife back out and it clatters onto the floor, I see the glint of the steel and my mind is consumed by the past.

My 'father' pulls onto a winding lane and after a few minutes turns onto an abandoned industrial estate. There's no way I can walk or run back from here, but surely my own father won't hurt me? I mean he says he might not be my dad, but he can't prove that right now, can he?

Braking to a stop outside a building, he gets out. One of his henchmen, who'd taken the seat at the side of him, comes to my door and opens it. The other henchman who'd been sat next to me, making sure I didn't try anything stupid, moves his thigh and shoulder next to me, giving me a shove to follow the other one out.

As I step out of the car I look around.

"Don't think of doing anything dumb, Lola." My father nods his head. "Or Manny will have to persuade you otherwise." I turn to see the guy my dad called Manny has a pistol in his hand.

"Okay, let's go and play 'who's the daddy'." My father smirks. "We might not even need a test. We'll see."

He pushes open the door and I find his best friend Mark tied to a chair. His mouth is gagged and he's bound by his arms and legs. His eyes widen when he sees me being brought in.

My father walks up to him and rips the gag from his mouth.

"Let her go, Tommy. Don't do anything stupid. Do what you want with me, but don't do something you'll regret with your daughter." Mark's voice is pleading, desperate. What the fuck is my dad doing? He's lost it

completely. I should be looking for an exit, but I can't take my eyes away from Mark.

"That's just it though, isn't it?" My dad smacks Mark on the back of his head. "Am I her daddy, or are you?"

My head reels and I take a step backwards.

Dad smirks. "Are you shocked, Lo? Meet Mark, who I thought was my best friend, but who I found out had kept fucking my wife throughout our marriage and fathered Lucia."

He brings his arm back and then punches Mark in the nose. I hear the crack and blood spurts out, running down his face.

"Even when I discovered Lulu wasn't mine, I never for a moment suspected my friend since my schooldays would be her dad. No, it wasn't until she escaped herself that the truth was revealed to me. And now I need to find out if you're mine, or whether you're his bastard too."

He turns to Mark. "So? Is she yours?"

Mark tries to spit blood away from his mouth so he can reply. "I don't know. Lydia refused to do a test to determine the truth. Said it was too dangerous."

Dad's voice is chilling. "Lydia has been getting her own way for far too long. I think it's time she learned who's in charge and it's not her."

He turns to Manny and the other man and takes a small hammer from his inside pocket. "Okay, Lola, it's time to see what happens to people who cross your father. I'm sorry if it does turn out he was your daddy, but there's a lesson to be learned today and that's when your wife's a bitch, life's a bitch."

He proceeds to torture Mark slowly in front of me. They won't let me look away. If I try, one of them grabs hold of my head and forces me back.

At times, Mark begs for his life. He screams he loves me whether he's my father or not. He loves Lydia. He loves Lucia. He's punished for every word by the hammer and knives that are used on his body. Until his body gives in.

I see it all.

His mind goes first, the chemicals in his body send him into some kind of comatose state. He's alive, but not there. Just staring into space. Blood drips onto the floor, like some kind of ticking countdown to the end of his life.

Drip.

Drip.

Drip.

It pools around his chair like a port wine mark against a porcelain complexion.

Then they give me a knife.

"Dear, Lola. It's time to be a hero. Mark can continue to die slowly, or you can put an end to his suffering right now."

My eyes widen.

"Dad, don't do this. Phone an ambulance for fuck's sake. I'll say anything you want me to, just please save his life. He's suffered, look, for anything he did to you." I sob, looking at the man whose life is fading right in front of me.

My mum's true love.

My sister's father.

Maybe my father.

I belong to either the devil or this good man who took a backseat and kept an eye on us all.

"He dies by my hand or yours. Yours will be a less painful end," my father says.

Time passes by while I continue to beg and plead, and then Mark's eyes gain clarity. He focuses on me, and I read his intention. He's trying to find the strength to tell me that it's okay.

Swallowing, I take the knife from my father's hand. Tears stream down my face as I stumble towards Mark before I fall at my knees in front of him. Again, his eyes meet mine. I take his hand.

"I'm sorry. I'm so very sorry, and we love you," I tell him.

He squeezes my fingers, and then he loses focus again. Maybe he already passed. I'm not sure, but I know what I have to do anyway.

"Forgive me," I say as I stab the knife into his neck.

There's so much blood.

So very much. I'm slick with it.

I retch and vomit throughout the ordeal and then I'm dragged back into the car by my father's men and driven to a seedy hotel. No one on reception bats an eyelid as I'm bundled past and taken up in the lift despite the fact I'm covered in a blanket with bloodstains on my face. The last thing I see is the number 486 on the door.

They talk about getting Anna here.

They talk about her boss Tyler turning up instead, and my father boasts with how he's going to take over B.A.D.

I'm dragged into the shower to wash the blood from me, although it'll be forever imprinted into my skin.

I'm swabbed to find out my worth, and then my father tells me he'll catch up with me soon. He leaves the room to go meet whoever is turning up: my sister or Tyler Ward.

He leaves me with his two henchmen. They're warned not to fuck me... yet. I'm naked apart from my panties. They bind me to a chair and gag me. I can't move. I can only plead with my eyes, but I'm wasting my time. They touch my breasts, they feel between my legs, and I hate it because one of them, the one whose name I don't know, knows how to touch me right, and my body betrays me by getting wet. Manny leaves bored, but the nameless guy carries on coaxing me to come for him. He pulls my panties down my thighs and watches me as he fingers me, pushing inside. Tears fall down my cheek as I don't want to give him the satisfaction of my orgasm. I lie as still as I can, but I can do nothing as the guy puts his mouth to me and licks me there until I explode against his face.

Satisfied and smirking, he runs his fingers through my wetness once more and sucks on his digits. "Perfect, you taste like heaven," he says, taking out his cock and fisting it in his hand until he comes before wiping himself on a hotel towel. He pulls my pants back up and leaves.

And I am somewhere else, maybe the place Mark went to before he died, because I know I'm no longer in the room. My mind is in pieces, floating in the air, out of reach.

When the door opens again, it's the first sign there's still life in me as fear fills me that I'm about to be raped, tortured, or murdered, but instead a man tells me he's come to rescue me. He wraps me in a blanket and carries me. He takes me back to my mother and sister. He helps take care of me.

"Lola. Lola. Please, stop screaming please." Ant's voice is desperate. He's here, my saviour. He's here, come to rescue me again.

I realise where I am and what happened, and my mind just can't take it. "I need help, Ant, I need help. Please. I can't do this anymore." I beg him while I cling to him like he's the one last breath I have to take.

CHAPTER THIRTY

Ant

I stand with my mouth hanging open as Ellie lunges for Sharon with my kitchen knife in her hand.

I want to say something. I want to stop her. But I'm frozen in shock as she pushes the steel into the terrified woman's neck.

Sharon's eyes hold mine, but even in those last few seconds, I don't see any genuine apology for all the things she did to me and countless others. All I see is evil. She's the fucking worst of humanity and although I never expected it to be at Ellie's hand, I knew that this was how it needed to end.

She doesn't deserve to be on this Earth, walking the streets with us, being exposed to our children.

Everything happens in slow motion as the life drains from Sharon's face, when Ellie removes the knife from her and allows it to clatter to the floor.

She turns to me, fear filling her eyes. She came with a plan, that much is obvious, but I don't think she'd fully anticipated what it would be like. Hell, I just watched it and I'm not sure I still quite get my head around it.

Ellie is covered head to toe in Sharon's blood. She glances down, seeing it for the first time and her face goes ghostly white. I take a step for her when the most blood curdling scream I think I've ever heard rips from the woman beside me.

Both of our attention turns to Lola as she wraps her arms around herself and screams bloody murder. Her body trembles violently as she continues. Her eyes are locked on Sharon, but I don't think she's seeing her. They're dazed as if she's lost in a nightmare.

I move toward her, just as her legs give way. Catching her before she hits the floor, I lower us both to the ground.

Her cheeks are wet with tears as she shakes in my arms and continues to scream for a harrowing amount of time.

"Lola. Lola. Please, stop screaming please." I take her face in my hands, my thumbs wiping at her eyes to catch the incessant tears.

She sucks in a ragged breath while my heart thunders in my chest.

"I need help, Ant, I need help. Please. I can't do this anymore," she begs.

My brows pull together as I try to figure out what she's telling me. Her sad, empty eyes find mine once more and it hits me.

She's having a flashback.

"Please, Ant. Get me out of here. I... I can't. All I can see is him... W- what h- he made me do." She drags in another shaky breath and I pull her to me and stand with her in my arms. She clings to me like I'm going to save her, when really, I was the one to drag her into this mess with me. I'm just as guilty as those she's talking about.

Ripping my eyes from Lola, I look to my daughter who's standing still looking shell-shocked over what she did.

"We really should—" I start, although other than getting Lola out of here, I'm at a bit of a loss for what we should do right now. My kid is here too. I'm torn.

"Fucking hell, kid. That was some majestic shit you just pulled," Tyler announces as he and Deacon step from the shadows and look the three of us over. "You need to get her out of here," he adds, looking to Lola who's passed out in my arms.

No fucking shit.

"I know, but—"

"But nothing, we've got this, bro. Take your girl, make sure she's okay."

"Ellie?" I ask, looking at my daughter. I need to protect her, now possibly more than ever.

"Jack's on standby. We'll take her there. You join us when you're sorted. We got Ellie."

"Fuck," I bark, looking from Ty to my daughter.

I want to pull her into my arms and tell her that everything is going to be okay, but I can't. I've no idea if that's true and I refuse to lie to her.

Another of Lola's screams pierces the air. I hold her tighter.

"Are you going to be okay?" I ask Ellie.

She nods, glancing at Deacon and Tyler. "You trust these two?"

If the situation were different, I'd be amused by the shocked looks on both of their faces, but everything right now is too heavy to even think about laughing.

"Yeah. With my life, and yours. You've nothing to worry about."

"Okay, then go. Take her and get her sorted." I nod stepping away from the three of them and leaving the scene of devastation behind me.

"Dad," her one soft word has my body locking up tight. It's the first time she's called me it seriously and it threatens to rip my chest wide open.

"Yeah?" I turn back to her to find the blood that was covering her face being washed away by her tears.

"Please make sure she's okay. I... I need her."

"I will. I'll be back soon. Do exactly as they say." I narrow my eyes at her in warning, but I have a feeling she knows that right now would be a really bad time to start defying orders from any of us.

She nods and turns to Tyler and Deacon.

"You did good, kid," Tyler tells her, pulling her into his side. "But don't make a habit of it, yeah? That's a fucking big mess to clean up."

The sound of Ellie's laugher warms my quickly shattering heart as I make my way out of the warehouse.

I drop Lola into the passenger seat of my car and find that she's not passed out like I expected her to be, instead she's wide-eyed and staring into space.

"What do you need, baby?" I ask, studying her for a response, but none comes and I feel at a total loss.

There's only one place I go when I can't see a way through my own deranged life, so the second I drop down into the driver's seat, that's the address I put into my GPS.

"Everything is going to be okay, Lola," I assure her, hoping like fuck that it's not a barefaced lie.

Reaching over, I take her hand in mind and squeeze tightly.

Our journey across the city is fast. I break every speed limit and jump more lights than I think I even noticed but it still feels like years later when I pull up outside a familiar building.

I expect Lola to ask where we are, but she never does. She just stares ahead, and I wonder if she's even realised that we've stopped.

I soon find my answer when I pull her door open and reach in for her. She scrambles away from me as if I'm about to hurt her. The move guts me.

"Baby, it's okay. It's just me. I'm not going to hurt you. You're safe."

She looks at me, although I fear she doesn't actually see me. Whatever she does, though, has her relaxing enough for me to scoop her into my arms.

"Hey, it's me," I say into the buzzer the second it connects to the flat above us.

"Come on up." Her soft, calming voice works wonders even through the fuzzy speaker.

The door clicks and in seconds, I'm walking us inside and towards the lift.

"What the fuck?" Scarlett asks, her eyes wide when she opens the door and finds me clutching a limp Lola to my body, both of us speckled with Sharon's blood.

"Are you going to let us in?"

She immediately stands aside and allows me to carry Lola down to her living room.

"Do I even want to know?" Scarlett asks, her eyes frantically searching both of us, presumably for injuries.

"Probably not, but we're here now. I need your help, or more so, Lola needs your help."

"So this is her, I assume. The one who's stolen your—"

"Don't," I snap, afraid of what's going to follow. Whatever it is, Lola doesn't need to hear it right now. "I-I don't know what to do," I admit. "Shit went down tonight with Sharon." Scarlett gasps. She knows all about Deacon taking her, there's not a single thing about my life that Scarlett doesn't know about, Lola included. "I think it triggered something. She... she asked me for help and I've no idea how to do that. But you can." My eyes practically plead with her to take this on.

"Ant, I don't know if this is a good idea."

"Please, Scarlett. There's no one else I trust, and she won't talk to me. It's haunting her."

"What makes you think she'll talk to me? She doesn't know me," she asks, narrowing her eyes.

"Because you're a professional. Please, I need... I need her."

"Fucking hell, Ant." She drops onto the opposite sofa to us and runs her fingers through her hair. It's a move I remember well from when we were kids.

Scarlett and I first met when I was almost sixteen. I'd been dropped into yet another foster home and there she was. Looking like a fucking angel and a breath of fresh air after all the fuck-ups I'd been forced with since running away from Sharon.

We connected immediately. Until I met Deacon and the others at university a lot of years later, she was the only person I've ever considered as family. We might have been forced together, but now, she's just as much as my sister as Lola is to Anna.

"Let her sleep for now. I'll go and get a blanket. And then you can tell me all about it."

When I look down at Lola, I find her eyes shut and her breathing heavy. I can only hope that she finds some solace from all of this in her slumber.

Shifting her gently, I lay her down on the sofa before placing my lips to her forehead.

"Everything will be okay, baby."

I hear Scarlett walking back over, but I don't look up. Instead, I lift my hand to Lola's cheek and take her in. She's so fucking beautiful, yet so broken. My heart aches as I look at her and imagine what she's going though... what she went through at the hands of the man who could well have been her father.

"Here," Scarlett says softly, passing a blanket over.

"Thank you," I whisper, taking it from her and laying it over Lola.

"You want coffee?"

"I need something stronger than that after tonight."

"Go and wash up, I've got you covered."

With another look at Lola, I make my way to Scarlett's bathroom.

I stop at the sink and hang my head for a second. It's fucking pounding after the day I've had, but I push it aside. I'm not my biggest concern right now. I need to look after my girls before I even consider thinking about myself.

I wash my hands, before splashing my face and finally looking in the mirror.

Stress lines are etched into my features making me look older than I am. It's a harsh reminder once again that I'm not the man Lola deserves. But even after tonight and everything it's dragged up for her, I'm too fucking selfish to walk away.

I find Scarlett in her kitchen with her hip resting

against the counter and a bottle of scotch— my favourite— and two glasses behind her.

"Thank you," I all but sigh when I take in the sight.

"Anything, Ant. You know that."

Walking up to her, I pull her into my arms. For so many years, she was my only small piece of normal, the only light in my darkness. The only one who understood me.

"I'll do everything I can," she promises as she holds me just as tightly.

CHAPTER THIRTY-ONE

Lola

I wake up and wonder where I am. My eyes get used to the light. I'm on the sofa and Ant is asleep on the floor in front of me. Where the fuck am I? Oh, that's right. I vaguely remember being brought here and a woman's face.

Oh God, yesterday. I recall Ellie stabbing Sharon in the neck and then, fuck, I had a flashback. Was lost to the past. I swallow, my heart thudding. Please don't let it happen again. The sensation of maybe losing myself washes over me, the skitter of crawling over my skin. I realise I need to go to the bathroom, but also I need to see what's in the cabinets.

Sitting up slowly, I climb over Ant's gently snoring body and wander through the living room door and down the hall. I'm relieved to find the bathroom door ajar so that I'm not having to guess which door it is. After relieving myself, I start to open the mirrored cabinet, but there's nothing of any use to me.

"What are you looking for, Lola?" I startle and turn to see the woman I vaguely remember standing in the doorway.

"I- I..."

"There are no tablets, no razor blades, not anything you can use as a coping mechanism." She walks towards me and I take a step back.

"Lola. You might not remember me saying, so I'll start again. I'm Scarlett. Ant brought you here because I can help you. Really help you. I'm a trained psychologist."

The walls of the bathroom feel like they are closing in. Scarlett watches me as my eyes dart around and she moves away from the door and sits down on the closed lid of the toilet.

"You aren't in prison here. Neither am I taking you to a hospital. Not unless I can help it. I can do some work with you here."

Finally, I find some words. "I can't do this on my own anymore. Yesterday... Can you make it stop? Please, I beg you, make it stop."

I fall to my knees and begin crying and this virtual stranger puts her arms around me. I let her. She holds onto me while I let go of the feelings bottled up inside me.

"Yes, Lola. I can help you to make it stop," she says and I hold onto her words like they're a life-raft.

The bathroom clock tells me it's six am. Wow, that's a time I'm not used to seeing on a typical Sunday.

"If it's okay with you, Lola. I'd like for you to get a shower. You'll feel so much better after that. We're about the same size so I'll find out some clothes for you. You're a little slimmer than me, but I have belts. Then I want to do a preliminary evaluation. Just to see where we're at. I think you need a light prescription of something just to take the edge off everything.

"How do you know Ant?" I ask.

She pauses for a moment and then replies. "It's his story to tell, not mine. I'm sure he'll fill you in once he wakes up."

I nod, but my mind is already wondering if this is the woman he spoke to. The one who clearly means so much to him. He brought me to her for help. Has she helped him in the past?

"I would like to take a shower. Thank you."

"Let me get you some fresh towels and I have a spare toothbrush." She leaves the bathroom and I get to my feet and sit where Scarlett was sitting on the edge of the toilet seat until I hear her footsteps come back.

"How is Ellie?" Jesus, Ellie. She must be a mess.

"She's okay. She stayed with Jack."

I huff. "Jack must take in all the waif and strays. It's where I went after what happened to me..." My words trail off.

"Ant said she's someone who's been through a lot

herself, so she understands. But I think Ant needs to go and get Ellie, take her home, and start to provide the role of a reliable parent. I told him this last night, but he wouldn't leave you. He said while ever you needed him he'd be there." She frowns. "I know this is none of my business, but I think it would be good if you could stay here with me, at least today and tonight, and let Ant go and deal with his responsibilities before he ruins any chance he has of a relationship with his daughter, because if she can't rely on him to be there for her after such a traumatic event, then the girl will write him off, like the other people in her life."

What she says makes perfect sense. He shouldn't be here, he should be with Ellie.

"Yeah, he needs to be with Ellie. And, yes, please. If I could stay. I'll just tell my mum I'm staying with Ant. Thank you." I add, "because I know that if you can't help, I'm going to have to go into a facility. My mind can't process what happened to me anymore."

"Anthony said you'd told no one," Scarlett checks.

"That's right."

"So your mind is affecting you in other ways because you have to deal with the trauma that you experienced. It's not going to be an easy road, but telling me will help. I promise."

"And you won't tell Ant?"

"I won't tell anyone. It's your experience to share, if you choose to. But I want you to share it with me, slowly, and let me see how we can find a way forward for you. Okay?"

"Okay."

Scarlett passes me the towels and toothbrush. "As you've already seen, shower gel, shampoo etc *is* in the cabinets. Stay in as long as you want to. There's a guest bedroom behind the next door down. I'll put some clothes on the bed for you."

"Thank you, Scarlett. For helping me."

"Anytime," she says, and then she tells me something that surprises me, when really it shouldn't have surprised me at all. "I was a foster kid, like Ant, like Ellie. It's what drew me towards the field I'm in."

Then she closes the door behind her.

I wash every inch of my skin until the shower water no longer has blood or filth in it and then I start over and wash every inch of myself once more. I turn off the water, step out the cubicle and onto a bathmat, and reach for the large bath sheet, wrapping it around my body. I towel dry my hair on the hand towel, brush my teeth, and then I carefully and as quietly as I can in case Ant is still sleeping, open the door and head to the spare room.

A baggy shirt, a pair of jeans and a belt are on the bed. I put my underwear back on. None of this is ideal, but I have to work with what I have. I see my bag is on the dressing table in the room, and I reach in for my hairbrush. I look clean and tidy. It's a shame my inside doesn't match the outside.

"How are you?" Ants gruff voice comes through the open door as he pushes his way through and into the room, a steaming mug of coffee in his hand. "Thought you might be ready for this, or do you want a glass of water?"

I walk over to meet him. "No, coffee is good. I'm ready for coffee." I take the mug from his hand and Ant hovers, unsure how to proceed.

I sit on the edge of the bed and pat next to me. He sits beside me and takes a deep exhale.

"I'm going to stay with Scarlett for at least today," I tell him. "I trust that you brought me to someone who will look after me, and because of that, I'm asking you to leave."

He huffs. "Scarlett. Did she pressure you to send me away?"

"No, Ant. This is all me. I have demons I have to deal with, and you can't help me with them. You might want to, but you can't. But your daughter... she killed her mother yesterday, Ant." My voice rises. "What the fuck are you doing here?"

His eyes widen.

"Get the fuck out of this apartment and go to see to your daughter. She's not Jack's. She's yours. Go and be the father she needs. Your priorities are all wrong here."

He grabs my shoulders. "No, they are not, Lola. They aren't wrong at all. I'm damned if I do, and damned if I don't. You were a hundred times more broken than she was in the moment, so I made a judgement call and I'd do it again. Jack's as good as a sister to me and I feel I can let my daughter be with family while I have an emergency. You were unresponsive. Lost in a catatonic state. Do you have

274

any idea how fucking demented I was, wondering how best to help you? I did what I needed to do, so don't tell me I made a mistake, because I fucking didn't."

He tilts my chin up, forcing me to look at him. "I will go and see my daughter now and take care of her, because I know you're safe with Scarlett. But be warned. You leave here and I'll have you tailed, and then I'll come and get you and drag you back to either here or my apartment. I will *not* see you broken like that again, Lola. It almost damn killed me."

Tears run down his face. My beautiful saviour is weeping for me, like some kind of fallen angel. "I stood and watched my foster mother die and I felt no emotion at all, and then you broke and I broke with you."

I wipe the tears from his face, and he pushes his cheeks into my hand as I do so.

"You mean everything to me, Lola. I know it's been fast, but I'm fucking falling for you hard."

My hand drops away in shock. Leaning forward, he rests his forehead against mine. "We will find a way to happiness together, Lola. And if that means we have to be apart for a day or so while you heal, then that's okay. Because if I have my way, we'll have every day after."

He moves his head so that his lips meet mine. A delicate brush and then deeper, more pressing, urgent kisses, until he's telling me everything with his lips and tongue. When he breaks the kiss, I'm fighting for my next breath. That's what he does to me, this man; he takes my breath away.

"It's been fast, but there's no rush." Another sweep

of his lips over mine. "So do whatever you need to do to heal, and if you need me, you call. Okay?"

I nod. He stands up.

"Okay. I'm going to go be the fucking father Ellie needs now." He winks at me.

A smile curls my lips.

"That's what I like to see." He reaches down and touches his fingertips to my lips. "I hope I'll put many more smiles there." He looks at the mug still in my hand. "Drink that before it goes cold."

Then he's gone, out of the door. I hear him speak to Scarlett, but the words are mumbled, and then the door closes.

Scarlett comes to find me.

"We can start whenever you're ready. No rush at all. If you want to go back to sleep, or rest up with the TV for a while, that's cool."

"No, I'm ready to talk to someone about what happened to me," I state. "I need it out because it's eating me alive."

"Come on then." She holds out a hand and I take it, as she pulls me up off the end of the bed. "Let's head for my office."

"We have to leave?" I don't want to step outside these walls yet. I'm not ready.

"No, Lola. I have one here at the end of the hall. You are safe here with me. Okay? Remember that."

Nodding, I follow her down the hall.

CHAPTER THIRTY-TWO

Ant

Walking away from Scarlett's flat is probably one of the hardest things I've ever done. I thought waking up on her hard floor and finding Lola gone was bad, but it's nothing compared to this.

I look back at the door as I stand in the lift waiting to be taken away from here and my entire chest aches. I feel like I'm leaving my heart behind inside that flat.

Fucking hell, when did I turn into such a fucking pussy?

I know I'm doing the right thing. Watching Lola fall apart before my very eyes was terrifying. I knew it was coming, she'd kept everything bottled up for too long. My little Pandora was like a ticking time bomb just waiting to explode.

It's my fault it happened as it did. I shouldn't have taken her with us to that warehouse. She had no reason to go. It was just my selfishness that wanted her close to me for whatever was about to happen.

The image of Ellie stepping toward her mother and sliding that knife into her neck fills my mind once again, and the second the doors open, I march out, my legs carrying me faster than before.

Lola and Scarlett are right, I need to be with my daughter. She might try to show the world that she's grown up, that she's strong and unbreakable— just like someone else I know— but deep down, she is only eighteen and she just did something life changing.

I jump in my car and race across town. My heart pounds and my hands tremble as I get closer and I begin to admit to myself that Lola might have been right. Should I have been more concerned about Ellie yesterday? Should I have kept her with me and not sent her to Jack's? I just didn't want her to see what her actions did to Lola. I didn't want her to have that guilt on top of everything else she was probably feeling.

Pulling up to the barrier to allow me entry to the underground garage beneath Jack's building, I wait for it to lift and slam my hand down on the steering wheel in frustration.

"Finally," I mutter, my voice low and angry when it finally decides I'm allowed inside.

I make quick work of parking and getting out and in seconds I'm in yet another lift.

I don't even get to knock on the door. Jack knows I'm coming and is standing at her front door waiting for me.

"Well aren't you a sight for sore eyes."

"Where is she? Is she okay?"

"Good morning to you too."

Rolling my eyes at her, I step up to her and pull into a hug. She stiffens the second I touch her. This isn't the kind of thing we usually do, but I need her to know how much I appreciate what she's done.

"Thank you for taking her in at the last minute," I say, releasing her.

"Jesus, you getting sentimental in your old age?"

"Fuck off," I bark. "Where's my daughter?"

"On the sofa watching TV."

"Is she...?"

"She's fine, Ant. If I didn't know what had happened, I'd think it was just a usual babysitting gig."

"When the fuck do you ever babysit?"

She shrugs. "Last night apparently."

"I don't need fucking babysitting, I'm an adult," comes from inside the flat.

Jack's brow arches in amusement. "I kinda like her. I think she's got a bright future with us bunch of fuck-ups."

I can't help but laugh. It feels so fucking good after the past twenty-four hours.

Finally, Jack steps aside and I'm able to get a look at

Ellie for the first time since she took matters with Sharon into her own hands.

The second she sees me, she pushes from the sofa and runs over.

Much like Jack only moments ago, I tense as her arms wrap around my waist and hold tightly.

After a second, I somewhat come back to myself and return the gesture.

"Is Lola okay?" she asks, tilting her head up so her large dark eyes lock onto mine. My breath catches at the similarities I see to my own when I stare in a mirror. There really was no doubt this girl was mine.

"She will be. I've left her with a friend who just so happens to be the best psychologist in the city."

"That's good," she says, releasing me. "Because that was really scary."

"Yeah it was. I'm more concerned about you right now though."

Jack wanders through and makes herself scarce in the kitchen after offering us coffee.

"I'm fine," she says flippantly, falling back down onto the sofa.

"Ellie, you killed someone."

"I know, and she was a cunt who deserved it. Trust me, I'm not going to make a habit out of it. But she hurt you... in ways I'm sure you've barely scratched the surface of— she deserved it and more for what she did to both of us and all the others that came before and after."

I shake my head as I listen to her.

"What?" she asks almost shyly.

"You did that for me?"

She shrugs. "For all of us. It's time for a fresh start, don't you think?"

"I couldn't agree more."

Jack joins us with mugs and takes a seat on the other sofa. Her and Ellie lock eyes for a moment and something passes between them.

"W- what?" I ask, looking between the two of them. "Tell me she did as she was told," I beg Jack.

"Everything is good, Ant. Right, E?"

"Right." The smile on both their faces is suspicious as fuck, but I push it aside because they're both smiling and right now, that's what matters.

Conversation turns to mundane things that thankfully don't involve dead mothers, child abusers, or broken girlfriends. My thoughts falter on that last word. Is that what Lola is? Is she my... girlfriend? The word feels weird even in my thoughts. I've never had any relationship with a woman. It's just one of a list of many things that Sharon ruined for me. Until I found Lola, I didn't trust a woman outside of those I consider my family. But there was never a question with Lola; she was different to all the ones who came before, and not just because of her age.

Knowing the room has fallen silent around me, I look down to Ellie who's watching me with curiosity before glancing at Jack who's staring down at her phone with the widest smile on her face.

"You'd better not be sexting Ollie while we sit here," I bark, amusement filling my voice.

She looks up at me immediately, her eyes wide. I don't need to hear her words to know it's not him.

"Oh... um... no, I'm not."

I want to ask who it is, but I don't, seeing her happy is enough.

"It's been a long time since I've seen you smile like that."

Colour hits her cheeks at my words and she rips her eyes from mine. She opens her mouth to respond, but I cut her off.

"Shall we head home?" I ask Ellie.

"You still want me there?"

"I wouldn't allow you to be anywhere else. Come on, grab your stuff."

After finishing off her coffee, she heads toward Jack's bedrooms to collect up what little she has here.

"She's a really good kid, Ant."

"I'm starting to see that."

"Just keep a very close eye on her. That brave face she's putting on right now is going to slip at some point."

"Don't worry. She's going to be meeting Scarlett very soon. I'm not letting another of my girls break."

She smiles softly at me. "Your girls?"

"Yep. Lola's mine. Make sure every fucker in the office knows about it. Especially Rob."

She chuckles and shakes her head. "Fucking hell, not you too."

"It happens to the best— or should I say the worst— of us. Who knows, it might be your turn next?"

"I highly doubt that, Ant. You know how I like to do things."

"I have an idea," I say, pushing to stand when footsteps head back our way. "But you keep that shit locked up so tight most of us can only imagine."

"There's a very good reason," she whispers before joining me. "Thanks for last night," she says to Ellie as they share another secret look. The question about what they've been up to is right on the tip of my tongue, but Jack's recent words stop me. She's the master at secrets so if she doesn't want me to know then I won't. Ellie however...

"Jack's really nice, I like her," Ellie says once we're out of the car park and heading home.

"Oh yeah? So are you going to tell me the big secret now?"

She laughs. "It's hardly a big secret. She took me to a concert last night."

"She what?" I balk. "She was meant to be looking after you."

"And she did. It was a great distraction."

"What concert?"

"Hendon Street. She had backstage passes and everything. Look." She pulls the neck of her shirt down slightly to reveal a signature across the top of her breast.

My fingers grip the wheel. "That better be as far as that musician got, Ellie."

"Keep your hair on, old man, we had a great night." She winks at me and my teeth grind.

"I'm going to fucking kill her."

"Leave Jack out of it. It was exactly what I needed. Plus, she had a pretty good time herself."

"Oh yeah?"

"My lips are sealed."

I glance over at her, my mouth agape. "You can't leave it at that."

"I can and I will."

"Pain in the arse," I mutter.

"What have you done without me all these years?" she jokes, but it falls a little flat with me as I realise everything I've missed out on.

The rest of the journey is in silence. I wish I knew what she was thinking, what her plans are now she's found me, but I don't want to push too hard. As far as I can tell, she's never had a real home before, and I know just how hard it can be to suddenly attempt to settle into one.

"What do you fancy for lunch?" I ask

"Chinese?"

"Sure. Any dish requests?"

She rattles a couple off before telling me that she's going to shower. I place the order and then do the same. I need to more than ever after yesterday's events and then sleeping on Scarlett's floor.

My fingers inch to reach out to Lola to find out if she's doing okay as I pull my phone from my pocket and place it on the bedside table, but I know I can't. I need to leave Scarlett to do her thing and hopefully, once Lola is ready, she'll come back. I have to trust that she will because I'm not sure what I'll do if she doesn't.

Ellie is already out on the sofa when I emerge a while later. The doorbell rings and she jumps up to get our lunch.

We sit on the floor in front of the coffee table at her request and pop the tops of the containers.

"So what are your plans now?" I ask the question that's been eating at me all morning.

She shrugs. "I've no idea."

"A- are you... staying?" I hate the hesitation in my voice, but I can't deny that I'm afraid of what the answer might be. Now she's here, I'd like it to stay that way. At least until we've talked through her past and sorted out any issues that might be waiting to come and bite her in the arse. She's done with that life now; I'll make damn sure of it.

"Yeah, I'll stay. If you'll have me."

I laugh at her as she says it so casually, but I can see the fear in her eyes that I'm going to cast her aside like so many others have in the past.

"This is your home now, Ellie, whether you like it or not. Start thinking about your future, because I'm telling you now, it's going to look a lot different to your past.

She nods, shoving a forkful of noodles in her mouth. It's impossible to miss the tears that fill her eyes though.

When I climb into bed, I do one final thing I've

been meaning to do. Since I met Lola I've ignored Vivian's texts, but as much as we were just a convenience for each other, I want her to know I won't be contacting her again.

All it takes is once quick text.

I met someone.

The reply comes back quickly.

Happy for you. Oooh, that means I can add some fresh meat to my schedule ;)

I delete her contact information and messages and put that part of me to bed for good.

CHAPTER THIRTY-THREE

Lola

I end up staying with Scarlett for a whole week. Slowly, I confess what happened to me in that warehouse and she helps me process how it's not my fault and gives me help in ways I can work through the skin crawling feelings and flashbacks. But the main thing she encourages is that I tell my mum and sister. That by doing so, by not burying what happened, my mind and body can heal.

So on this Monday morning I sit waiting for them to arrive at Scarlett's. I'm so nervous. What if they reject me? What if they can no longer look at me? These are all questions I've discussed with Scarlett, but while she can tell me we can work through any possibilities, she can't tell me what their reactions will be.

Then after that, if all goes okay, I'm going to see Ant tonight, because it's been too long. We've spoken on the phone, but agreed this was for the best. I stayed with Scarlett, he spent time with Ellie to make sure she truly was okay. He took time off work.

I don't know what I'm going to do to explain my absence from work yet again. It's not the best start to a job, but as long as I'm starting to heal then I don't care.

Anna knows where I've been staying. Ant told her. She sent me a text to let me know she'd spoken with mum and that they loved me. My fingers tap against my knee. I wonder if they'll feel that way when I tell them what happened.

I jump as the buzzer goes. Scarlett squeezes my knee. "We stop at any point, okay?"

I nod.

My mum and Anna walk in and I greet them. They hug me and pleasantries are exchanged with Scarlett. She goes to make them a drink. I hate seeing the anguish on their faces, knowing I've yet to tell them my past which will just make everything worse.

And then it's time and I begin to tell them what happened to me in the warehouse. Tears are streaming down the three of our faces way before I get to the part where I have to say I killed Mark, but I carry on until it's done.

Mum and Anna's arms are around me.

"Lola, Lola, Lola, you are not responsible for his

death. You saved him from further torture," Mum says. "Tommy would have continued until he died anyway. It would have been a slow, painful death. You are not to blame, darling. Not to blame."

Scarlett lets us have some time and then she encourages me to tell the rest of my story, about the sexual assault.

"I'm so glad Diego's team killed them both, so I don't have to," Anna says.

Scarlett asks Mum and Anna if they would be willing to engage with her alongside me so that we can all work through what happened together as a family, and also have individual sessions because of what each of us went through at the hands of Tommy De Loughrey.

"One of the things you need to think about, Lola, is whether or not you want to pursue knowing who your father is, because although the DNA kit was destroyed, there are ways," Scarlett says. "I know you feel you're better off not knowing, but by doing that you're internalising things again. Your mind will torment you about potentially being Tommy's daughter. But it's your call."

"You should find out," Anna tells me.

"It's Lola's decision," Scarlett points out.

"Sorry. Yes, of course."

"I'll do it," I say. "You're right. I should find out and deal with it. No more sticking my head in the sand and not dealing with things head on. I just need to find out how, seeing as both of my potential fathers are dead."

Anna swallows. "Actually, Diego sent Tyler the DNA kit. He had it processed and the results put in an envelope and it placed in a safe. For in case you ever wanted to know."

I leap up from my seat. "And you didn't tell me this? This is my life. How can you keep stuff like this from me? Any more secrets I should know about?"

"We've all been keeping secrets, Lola. That's why we're here. You said you didn't want to know, so I didn't tell you. I thought you'd feel I was pressuring you to find out."

Scarlett makes us sit down and take a few moments. Then she makes us think about the other's point of view.

"The main points from this are about there not being any more secrets and you all actually talking to each other, and about Lola finding out the results."

We nod in agreement.

"So if you're ready today, Lola, then your sister can phone her husband and have the results brought here."

I take a deep breath. "I'm ready."

Anna phones Tyler and he says he will arrange for a courier to bring the envelope. In the meantime, we leave the office and Scarlett arranges lunch for us all, just light stuff like salads and sandwiches. Things we can pick at. We are warned not to speak of anything from earlier; that this is a break and topics should be as light as the lunch.

I can feel a headache starting, which doesn't surprise me after the unburdening and crying.

"You know, learning about Scarlett has been a revelation for Tyler and the others," Anna tells me. "Ant was the only one who wouldn't open up about his past beyond saying it was horrific. The others had no idea he had a sister figure."

"I thought she was a past love when I first discovered her," I confess. "I heard Ant talking to her from his apartment. Put two and two together and made five. Thought that was why he had women issues, due to a lost love."

"You two are really a couple then?" she asks.

"I don't know. I think so, but since we got together there's been so much upheaval and shit going on... I'm not sure we've had time to work out what we are. I'm looking forward to finding out." I smile but I know it doesn't reach my eyes. I'm scared that what brought Ant and I together was a desperation to fix ourselves and finding a way through the other one. I know I feel complete when I'm around him, but we need time for our relationship to properly develop. I also know another thing: the recklessness about not protecting myself has to stop.

I'd got my period and I was pleased. Scarlett and I had spoken at length about this and she felt there was an issue there about risk and maybe me and Ant internally hoping I'd get pregnant so we could both have 'fresh starts'. But she pointed out this wasn't the way. We had to make these decisions consciously. I'd talked to Ant over the phone and we agreed. We needed to date properly. Meals by candlelight. Walking hand in hand down the street.

It was all going to take time, but we had time. I still needed to find my own way. I'd decided I wanted to settle into a job, whether I went back to B.A.D. or got another post elsewhere. I would continue to live at my mums even if I stayed at Ant's sometimes because I needed the consistency of having that base and Ant needed time with Ellie. While I hoped for a happy ever after, we both had to take our time and settle for happy right now.

As lunch is almost over, I get an idea. I pull my sister to one side to discuss it and her eyes light up. "I think that's perfect. I'll help." Excitement sparks within me, and the small kernel of hope for my future is just what I need.

Back in the office, I open the envelope while everyone watches with bated breath. I bring out the sheet of paper inside and exhale deeply.

"Tommy's not my father. Not any chance of it."

"Oh thank God," Mum says as Anna leaps up to hug me.

It was the right choice to find out. I'm not the daughter of a monster, and while I'll have many issues to work through about my real dad, just knowing I'm not Tommy's has brought a relief I can't put into words.

I know I need to sit in this room with Mum. To discuss why she kept her lover from us. Why she chose not to find out who our real father was. I know it's wrapped up in the bastard that was Tommy De Loughrey, but it's time... no more secrets.

Well, apart from nice ones that lead to good things.

My mum and Anna leave and Scarlett talks to me for another hour before wrapping the session up. And then with appointments booked, and being reassured she's on the end of a phone call if needed, I pack up my things and get ready to see Ant. He's arranged for Ellie to stay at Jack's. Apparently the two of them have really hit it off and bonded over music. It's good Ellie has someone to go to outside of Ant. She'll be starting to see Scarlett from next week. Ant has been warned that Ellie isn't just going to suddenly turn into the perfect daughter. Like any of us are perfect anyway.

I shower, change, and say a final farewell and thanks to Scarlett, and then I'm on my way to Ant's apartment. I'm out of the car and rushing upstairs as fast as carrying my belongings allows me and then they are abandoned on the hallway as the door swings open as my feet reach the outside of his apartment.

His arms come around me and he sweeps me up. My legs wrap around him and his mouth crushes mine. He kicks the door shut behind him and I'm glad no one has access to this floor and can take off with my things. Then all my thoughts are gone as he throws me down onto the bed.

Rearing back, a wicked smirk is complemented by

mischief flashing in those eyes. "It's just you and me, babe, and these," he waves a huge box of condoms.

I giggle.

"Don't expect to get much sleep." He waggles his brows. "Because this has been the longest week of my goddamn life and I intend to make up for every lost minute."

His kisses come both fast and slow. Fast, devouring, intense one minute like he wants to consume me. Slow, teasing, almost painful as he trails his mouth down my body.

Clothes are discarded fast.

Teasing touches are slow.

His hand finds my centre and he strokes my clit, then trails his fingertips in my slick heat. I gasp and raise my hips, greedy for more. It's been too long, I need him in me.

"Please, Ant, fuck me. We can go slow afterwards. I need you." I plead.

"Thank fuck, cos I think I'm gonna explode at any moment," he pants. He stops to roll on a condom and then pushing my thighs apart and licking his lips as he takes in the sight of me bare and ready for him, he moves and pushes inside me.

"Fuck, this is everything." He swears and then we are lost to each other, awash with frenzy and need.

It's carnal and raw as we take what we crave from the other until we're breathless and sweaty, and screaming the other's name as we sail off the cliff together.

Ant gathers me into his arms.

"I know we're going slow, but you need to know this," he whispers into my ear. "I already know I love you, Lola Hawley."

I smile, turning around to face him and I tell him. "I already know I love you too, Anthony Warren."

It makes the surprise I have being made all the more perfect.

CHAPTER THIRTY-FOUR

Ant

It's been a little over two weeks since Lola left Scarlett's and although she was only with her a short time, and has a long journey ahead of her, the difference in her was astonishing. The moment I looked at her, I could see that the weight of her past was no longer pressing down on her shoulders. The secrets that used to cloud her eyes were no longer as dark.

I've loved discovering the fun-loving person that I always knew was hiding just beneath the surface.

It killed me to allow her to move back in with her mum, but I knew it was the right thing to do. We'd already rushed this thing between us too much, and I knew others were concerned about how fast things were moving but I was powerless to stop.

I'm still desperate for her to be in my bed every night and to wake up to her every morning. Although, I can't deny that it makes the nights and mornings she is here that much more exciting.

Ellie and I have managed to find ourselves some kind of routine. She still doesn't know what she wants to do, and that's fine by me for now. She's had her world turned upside down in more ways than one. I think the least I owe her is a little time to adjust. She's also been spending time with Scarlett, and I can see her slowly shedding her past life. I've no doubt that in time she'll figure out who she is now.

I sit back in my office chair and watch Lola through my windows. She can't see me as I've tinted the glass knowing that it drives her crazy, and equally, because everyone in the office is going to learn a little too quickly how obsessed with her I've become if all they see me do all day is watch our newest recruit, instead of doing any actual work.

A knock at my door drags me from my Lola stalking daze and I'm forced to look up to see who's decided to pay me a visit.

"Hey, man," I say when Tyler slips into the room.

"Busy?" he asks with a laugh when he sees my clear desk and dark computer screen.

"Yeah, rushed off my feet."

Movement from outside the office catches his eye and he looks out of the window.

"Fucking hell, don't tell me you were just watching her work."

I shrug, not willing to lie to him.

"You've turned into a right pussy. You know that, right?"

"Couldn't give a shit, Ty. Anyway, it's not like you'd be any different with Anna."

"Damn fucking straight. She's got these new curves with her pregnancy. I can't get e-fucking-nough. Plus, she's horny as fuck so that's always a bonus."

"Okay, sharing time is over," I say with a wince.

"You all set for Friday night?"

"Uh... yeah. We're just going out for dinner."

A suspicious smile appears on his face.

"Am I missing something?"

"Nah, man. I just thought you'd be nervous or some shit. Going on a date isn't exactly a normal thing for you."

"Is it for any of us? It's just dinner with my girl, why would I be nervous? It's not like I'm about to pop the... Fuck, is she expecting me to?" I ask in a panic.

"Nah, man. It's not like that. She's just got something planned is all."

I widen my eyes, sitting forward and resting my elbows on the desk before me.

"Which is..." I prompt, needing him to continue.

"Fuck," he barks. "I promised Anna I wouldn't say anything."

"Well you've already fucked that up so you may as well continue now."

"Ugh, fine."

He tells me all about Lola's plans and I immediately feel guilty for not even considering doing something for her.

"You're going to want to brainstorm ideas now, aren't you?" Ty grumbles.

"Nah, I already know."

"Sweet. Anyway, I'll leave you to it. I've got a meeting in the deputy fashion editors office."

"You mean you're going to bang your missus during work hours?"

"Well what do you do in meetings with your new intern?"

"Discuss important matters and her performance progress."

"Bullshit, do you. The only performance you care about is if your fucking her on your desk or your sofa." He throws a look over his shoulder to said sofa.

"You know that's your sister-in-law you're talking about."

"And?"

"Get the fuck out of here. I've got work to do."

Shaking his head, he pushes to stand and walks to the door.

"If Anna asks, I told you nothing, right?"

"You got it. Enjoy your meeting."

"Oh I fully intend to."

The second he's gone, I'm on the phone and booking an appointment for Friday afternoon. As soon as I've hung up, I tell Rachel to rearrange my afternoon appointments that day before calling Lola's internal number.

"Hello," she answers hesitantly, although I'm pretty sure she knows it's me when her eyes land on the glass separating us.

"I've got a problem," I admit, keeping my voice low and deep.

"Oh? I thought you had an assistant for those kinds of things."

"Hmm... this problem requires a different set of skills, and it's pretty time sensitive."

"How urgent are we talking? Only, my boss is a bit of an arsehole."

I manage to catch my splutter of shock. "Very urgent. Although, I have it on very good authority that your boss can be very flexible when needs be."

"Flexible?" she asks, a little too loud, causing heads to turn her way.

Noticing their attention, she pulls her eyes away from the windows.

"Although, right now, he's more interested in finding out just how flexible you are. What do you think? My desk? The sofa? The wall? Against the window?"

"Ant, everyone would see my arse," she gasps quietly.

"Exactly. Imagine how hot it would look from down below as I claimed what's mine."

"Oh God," she whimpers.

"I'm so fucking hard for you right now. Do you

BAIT

know how sexy you look while you're deep in thought? I've been watching you all morning."

I can't help but smile as she squirms in her seat.

"Anthony," she chastises. "I should be workin—"

"My cock. Now if you don't get in here in the next twenty seconds, I'll be forced to take matters into my own hands."

"How is this not taking matters into your own hands?"

"Do I need to come out there and throw you over my shoulder in front of everyone?"

"No, no. I'm coming."

"You fucking will be. Unless you don't hurry up and then I might not let you."

I can't help laughing as she stands from her chair so fast that the phone in her hand clatters to the floor.

She bends to pick it up, and knowing that I'm watching she ensures to flash me the stockings she's wearing under her skirt.

"You are in so much fucking trouble," I growl when she's got the phone in her hand and I know she'll hear me.

"Exactly where I like to be, Mr Warren. Now if you'll excuse me, I've got a very important meeting to get to."

I bark a laugh as she slams the phone on the base with a little too much force this time and strides towards my office.

She keeps her eyes locked on the glass, but despite

301

not being able to see me, her eyes seem to hold mine the entire way.

In seconds, she's pushing through my office door.

"I suggest you lock it." The click sounds out through the silent space.

Lola made it clear when she came back from Scarlett's that if she was to continue working here, then she wanted what was between us to remain separate from work. I agreed, because I wasn't about to let her leave, but I knew it was never going to work. Maybe if she was in a different department, but with her teasing me on the other side of the glass every fucking day there's no chance of me being able to think about anything else.

"Yes, sir," she sasses, making my cock jump in excitement.

"I think it's time we discussed your performance, don't you?" A smirk curls at my lips as I replay mine and Tyler's conversation from not so long ago.

"I've been trying my best, sir," she says, stalking toward me with her hips swaying. "But I'm sure I can make it up to you." Her fingers lift to the top button of her blouse and she pops it open revealing her full breasts beneath.

"Show me what you've got then, and I'll see if it's enough for me to keep you."

Her silk blouse hits the floor, leaving her in a fire-engine-red lace bra, black skirt and her sky-high heels.

"Oh, I think you'll be pleased with what I can do."

She lowers the zip on her skirt and allows it to pool at her feet.

My mouth goes dry at the sight before me. The tiny thong and garter belt matches the bra and her legs are encased in dark stockings.

Stepping out of her skirt, she continues forward.

"Anyone would think you came to work today with intentions of sleeping your way to the top."

"Trust me, sir. I came to work this morning with plenty of dirty intentions." She winks, biting down on her red bottom lip.

She stops before me and leans forward. I expect her to kiss me but she never does. She doesn't actually touch me. Instead, she pushes my chair back a little, throws her leg over mine and hops up onto my desk, placing her heels on my arm rests.

Reaching down, I palm my straining cock as I commit this image to my memory.

She rests back on her palms and allows me to take my fill.

"I've had such a stressful day," she says seductively. "I could really do with a little release."

"Fuck," I bark as she runs one hand down her stomach and over her mound. Pushing the lace aside, so I get a shot of what she's hiding beneath, she dips her fingers into her heat, moaning in delight as she does.

"Lola," I warn, my restraint on the edge of snapping.

"Oh, did you want to help?"

"I'm never going to get any work done with you

here," I mutter, pulling at my tie and undoing the first few buttons on my shirt.

"Maybe you should have considered that before employing me then."

"I think I might need to give you a promotion."

"Oh yeah?" she moans as she continues strumming herself.

"Sex slave has a certain ring to it, don't you think?"

"It sure has its benefits."

"Lola?" I say, my voice serious all of a sudden, making her look up at me with concern. "Your time in charge is over, baby." Pressing my hands to her thighs, I spread them as wide as they'll go and I dive for her pussy.

She screams as I eat her like I've not had a meal in weeks. She writhes on my desk, soaking it with her juices until I push her over the edge.

Then I flip her over, my palm connecting with her bare arse cheek so that it leaves a mark.

"Ant," she cries. My kinky bitch loves a little bit of pain with her pleasure, that's one thing about her that's not changed in the past few weeks.

Releasing my cock, I roll a condom down my length before pushing inside her.

A growl rumbles up my throat as her heat surrounds me. It's not quite the same with this barrier between us, but I'll put up with it for now. The time's coming where we can banish it again, I'll make fucking sure of it.

CHAPTER THIRTY-FIVE

Lola

I t's Friday night and I feel so nervous it's ridiculous. More like I imagine a bride on her wedding day would be, rather than someone going out on a date. I tell myself to calm down, but my heart is not listening to my head and keeps thudding through my chest.

For once, I completely embraced being the sister-in-law of a billionaire and I asked Tyler to hire me an Italian restaurant for the evening. I chose it based on reviews and the fact the interior was intimate. Tyler has reassured me that not only has he bought the restaurant for the night, but he's made sure anything that happens in the restaurant stays in the restaurant, and that staff know to leave us alone if required. My sister also told me that in one massive, elaborate and very Tyler gesture, he'd had a new sign temporarily replace the restaurant's real one, so it said *Lola's*. Billionaires!

I give myself one last look in the mirror. My hair has been styled into an elegant chignon, with a few jewelled pins here and there that glitter in the light. I'm wearing an emerald green dress with a slightly jewelled bodice and a swishy skirt perfect for dancing.

I triple check the box is in my handbag and then I'm ready for the driver. He takes me straight to the restaurant where I will be seated, waiting for Anthony to arrive. He thinks I'm calling for him, but I'm only sending a driver.

The owner of the restaurant, Alberto, a gentleman in his late sixties, greets me and air kisses me on both cheeks. I had talked to him by telephone and appraised him of my intentions.

"Everything is ready, mio caro. I know it is not a marriage proposal, but it is a proposal of sorts, so I hope all is to your satisfaction," he gestures as we walk around. To one corner is just one circular table and two chairs. The table is set with a neat white tablecloth and there are three small lanterns of different sizes casting an ambient glow.

The dance floor is surrounded by the flickering glow of LED candles that look so real. Thanks to Scarlett I know Ant's favourite dishes, and everything is set. All I need is the man himself. I take my seat and before long there he is.

A knock comes to the door of the restaurant and then I walk over and open it. My heart leaps as I see his handsome face, my smile mirrored right back from him. He's dressed in a smart, charcoal-grey suit that fits him to perfection. All I want to do is undress him, but that will have to wait; though as I see he wears just the most perfect amount of scruff on his chin, my core pools with desire imagining the chafe he could raze down my body.

He laughs. "Are you going to let me in then, or is the surprise that I have to wait outside all night?"

"Oops." I giggle and I step aside. Alberto now joins us and takes our first drinks orders.

"So, this is our first date, huh?" Anthony looks around him. "A restaurant to ourselves. I like your style."

I grin. "I didn't want anyone disturbing our date. Which reminds me. You need to turn your phone off. We have a history of dramatic happenings. This time it's about me and you and the rest of the world needs to take care of itself."

"Is that so?" He inches himself forward so his knees fit around my own.

"Yeah, that's so."

"I think I quite like you in control sometimes." He winks. "But just don't get used to it."

Drinks are dispensed. Dinner is served. The evening is amazing. The food is delightful and Ant and I, we just connect. I know it's early, but I also know he's my forever.

"Would you care to dance?" I ask him once the table has been cleared of food.

He nods and I walk over *to where I set up my iPod and playlist and select my song. I Only Have Eyes for You* by the Flamingos. Ant removes his jacket, putting it over the back of his chair, joins me and takes me in his arms, rocking me to the soul beat.

Lowering his mouth to my ear, he whispers. "If this is dating then I definitely want to do more of that with you."

I snuggle in closer, taking in the heat of his body and the smells of his aftershave. The time is almost upon me and then the evening just might come off as one of absolute perfection.

We dance to a couple more songs and then I break away saying I'm thirsty and would it be okay if we went and sat down. I lower the music to an ambient background level and we take our seats again.

"So, Mr Warren," I begin. "Do you remember that short time ago when I came for an interview with you and you called me little Pandora, saying I was full of secrets?"

His eyes darken and centre in on mine. "How could I forget?"

"Well, now I have none from you, Mr Warren, except this last one." I reach in my bag and bring out a long, slim, rectangular box.

"Although I want to date you and get to know you better, I want you to know that for me there is no one else, Anthony Warren. You're my forever." Opening the box, I reveal a Cartier watch that's cost me a month's salary. Lifting it out of the box, I turn it over. Engraved on the back it says.

Forever Yours

Lola xo

"It's stunning, like the woman who had this surprise prepared for me." Anthony says, as I help fasten the watch around his wrist. We hold hands across the table. I'm loving every minute of our time together, but I'm also ready for him to take me home now.

"Shall we get the bill?" Ant asks.

"Oh, there's no bill. I took care of that. Asked for a favour." I wink. "So if you pick up your jacket, we can go home now."

"I hope you mean we can go to my home?"

"That's exactly what I mean."

"Good, because I know you currently have two, but my casa is your casa." Going into his pocket he hands me a key. "It's not quite a watch, but this is for you. I can have it engraved if you like?"

I nudge him with my elbow. "It's fine as it is, and it's nice having the control this time. Being able to spoil my other half."

"Other half. I like that." Ant says threading his arm through mine as we walk through the door, after saying goodbye to Alberto and asking him to thank his staff.

As we get outside, Ant pulls me into his arms and kisses me in the street, right outside the door. "I want to remember this moment forever," he says. "The perfect woman, the perfect ambience, the perfect restaurant."

We break off and I smile. "It really has been, hasn't it? And look, did you notice, Tyler even had the restaurant's sign changed temporarily so it said Lola's. A touch extravagant, but I'll let him off."

Ant looks up at the sign. "Oh yeah. Except, Lola, that it's not temporary at all."

My brow creases. "What are you talking about?"

He laughs, looking very smug and self-satisfied, and he says. "I bought the restaurant, Lola. For you, for us. It's where our first date happened. I decided we should keep it."

My mouth drops open. "But I don't know how to run a restaurant. Do you? And what about Alberto?"

"Alberto wanted to retire. He was about to put the place on the market. I've bought it and Deacon's brother Scott is going to manage the place under the careful eye of his current boss, Jenson. It's all sorted." He looks back up at the sign. "I bought you a restaurant to show you, you are my forever," he says,

I punch him in the arm. "You are such a topper." I huff. "I get you a watch, you buy me a restaurant. Is this how it's going to be dating Mr Anthony Warren?"

"You betcha," he says. "Now let's go home where I might let you get your way for a bit in the bedroom, though I can't promise." He gives me that wink I adore so much.

"You're an insufferable smug billionaire, but you're

my insufferable smug billionaire and I love you," I tell him.

"And I love you, Mrs Insufferable Smug Billionaire eventually to be," he says. "Now get in the car, wench, I need to have my wicked way with you."

CHAPTER THIRTY-SIX

Ant

I didn't give Lola the key as a way to ask her to move in with me. I understood her need to have some space and to continue coming to terms with everything that happened to her along with our very fast moving relationship.

I'd spoken to Ellie before getting the extra copy made and she'd assured me that she had no problem with Lola having it. It felt weird asking someone else's permission to do something, but it was the right thing to do. I wanted Ellie to be a part of my life from now on and it was important that we moved forward as a team. She's an adult and capable of making her own decisions, so it's important to me that I treat her as such.

"Lola, Ellie," I call from the kitchen. "Dinner is ready."

I drop the final piece of chicken to the plate and pick it up to take through to the dining table as the two of them walk toward it.

They're both smiling at each other and continuing with whatever they were previously talking about. The sight of them both happy after everything they've been through makes my chest constrict.

"This smells incredible," Lola says, wrapping her arms around my waist once I've put the plates down.

Spinning in her arms, I kiss the tip of her nose. "Anything for my girls."

"Barf." Ellie makes a show of mock-gagging as she pulls her chair out. "Any chance you two could be less sweet. You make my teeth shiver."

"Oh, you're just jealous. I've not heard any mention of a boyfriend," I mock.

"Yeah, well, when you've spent your time hanging around with the arseholes I have, that would be considered a good thing."

She might be an adult, but still, the thought of her having a boyfriend sends a shiver down my spine.

"Then we'll need to introduce you to some good ones. There are some very eligible bachelors who work at B.A.D," Lola says much to my displeasure as she takes a seat.

"Lola," I warn. The thought of my daughter getting with the likes of me and the guys terrifies me. I already want to run anyone who she slept with to survive, out of town.

"What?" she asks. "I'm just saying that there's some real man-candy in that place."

"Do you want to lose your job?" I ask, deadly seriously.

"Anthony Warren, are you jealous?"

"No," I argue. "I just don't like the idea of you checking out the men I employ."

"I don't check them out, caveman. But I do have eyes."

Smacking her arse as punishment for her lip, I return to the kitchen for my plate and the wine in the chiller.

No sooner have we started eating does Lola's phone start blowing up.

"Who the hell is that?" I ask after the fourth time it's rung off.

"How should I know?" she sasses. "I'm sitting here with you."

"Go and look and find out if someone's died. It's putting me off my dinner."

"Sure thing, sir." She winks at me and my cock swells. Fuck, she knows I love it when she follows my orders.

I sit back and watch her arse sway and she walks toward the sofa.

"The lovesick puppy look is sickening, I hope you know that."

I flip Ellie off much to her shock if the fact she chokes on her dinner is anything to go by.

I hope Ellie does make some friends soon though, someone to get her out of the house every once in a while.

Keeping my eyes on Lola, I watch as she swipes the screen and puts it to her ear.

"Is that it?" she snaps, but I don't miss the amusement in her tone. "I was thinking Mum was hit by a bus or something." She falls silent as the other person, I'm assuming Anna, speaks before telling her she loves her and hanging up.

"What's wrong?"

She sighs. "Where's your phone?"

I pat my trousers, finding my pockets empty. "I've no idea. Why?"

"Tyler wants you and he thinks you're ignoring him."

"Ugh, he's such a petulant child at times. I'll find it and call him back after dinner."

For a seriously dysfunctional family, we have what could be considered an almost normal family meal. We talk about our days. Ellie tells us about the college courses she's been looking at online and the things she's considering for her future now all the options are open to her.

As I look between the two of them, I can easily say that I'm happier than I've ever been in my life.

These past two weeks might have been fucked-up

beyond belief, but out of it, I've found my place, my family, and for that, I'll forever be grateful.

Ellie offers to do the cleaning up once we've all finished and I head off in search of my phone.

"I can't find it. I must have left it at work."

"Use mine if you want to call him back."

"I should probably go and find it. Come with? We could stop for dessert somewhere after?"

"Is that an innuendo for something else?"

"It can be whatever you want it to be, Lo."

Her smile turns wicked as ideas form in her head. I can almost see her thinking about XS and all the things she wants to try.

Stepping up to her, I snake my arm around her waist, pressing us tightly together so she can feel what she does to me.

She gasps.

"I can practically read your thoughts, you know?"

"Oh yeah?"

"And I'm game." Her cheeks brighten with excitement as her eyes darken with desire.

"Ellie," I call, "We might be late."

"Whatever," comes back and we take that as our cue to leave.

I check the car and come up empty before we head to the office. I've been in back to back meetings all over the building today, it could be anywhere.

"Where was the last place you remember having it?" Lola asks from her seat behind my desk.

"My last meeting was with Jack, so I guess we try there."

"Sweet. Let's go." She runs her hand up my chest and wraps it around my neck when she stops in front of me. "I'm getting a little impatient. Turn your tracker on next time, so we don't waste valuable time we could be spending in other pursuits."

"Yeah, but sometimes I don't want people knowing where I am." I wink at her. "Especially if I'm seducing one of my interns in an unused room somewhere in the building."

I brush my lips over hers teasingly, but as she leans forward to deepen the kiss, I take a step back. "We'd better hurry then if you're that desperate for my cock."

I hold my hand for her and after growling her frustration, she slips hers inside it.

The entire top floor of the building is in silence. It's not very often that we're all home of an evening, but I guess it helps that three out of the five of us have someone to go home to now.

Jack's assistant and receptionist's desk are both empty, so assuming her office is too, I reach for the handle and swing the door wide open.

"Oh my god," Lola gasps as we both stare at the scene before us.

Jack is pressed up against her office wall, a guy I recognise as from Hendon Street has his hand around her neck. Other than that I can see his arse clenched as he's inside her. Ollie is standing behind them watching and scrambles to pull up his boxer briefs.

The three of them freeze at our intrusion.

"Oh fuck," Jack cries while Ollie stares at us with wide eyes and guilt written all over his face.

"Well it seems this place isn't empty after all," I mock, reaching for the door so that the three of them can have some privacy.

Just before I close it, I shout, "I've lost my phone, have you seen it?"

"Fuck off," Jack barks much to everyone's amusement.

"Well, I didn't see that coming," Lola mutters as we walk away with that image of what was happening burned into both our brains.

"Ant?"

"Yeah, baby?"

"Can we hurry up. I'm even hornier after seeing that show."

"It'll be my pleasure, literally."

Spinning her into my arms, I pull her close. "I'd do anything for you, baby. I love you." I drop my lips to hers and kiss her with everything I have.

The final duet PROVOKE and BREAK are coming 4[h] and 18th March 2021

Pre-order here

PROVOKE

BREAK

ALSO BY ANGEL & TRACY

Hot Daddy Series

Hot Daddy Sauce #1

Baby Daddy Rescue #2

The Daddy Dilemma #3

Single Daddy Seduction #4

Hot Daddy Package #5

B.A.D. Inc. Series

Torment #1

Ride #2

Bait #3

Provoke #4

Break #5

ABOUT ANGEL DEVLIN

Angel Devlin is the contemporary romance penname of paranormal/suspense writer, Andie M. Long. Check out Angel for stories as hot as her coffee.
She lives in Sheffield with her partner, son, and a gorgeous whippet called Bella.

Newsletter:
Sign up to Angel/Andie's newsletter here for her latest news and exclusive content.
http://www.subscribepage.com/f8v2u5

ABOUT TRACY LORRAINE

Tracy Lorraine is new adult and contemporary romance author. Tracy is in her thirties and lives in a cute Cotswold village in England with her husband, baby girl and lovable but slightly crazy springer spaniel. Having always been a bookaholic with her head stuck in her Kindle, Tracy decided to try her hand at a story idea she dreamt up and hasn't looked back since.

Be the first to find out about new releases and offers. Sign up to my newsletter here.

If you want to know what I'm up to and see teasers and snippets of what I'm working on, then you need to be in my Facebook group. Join Tracy's Angels here.

Keep up to date with Tracy's books at
www.tracylorraine.com

SOLD

ANGEL DEVLIN

Everything changes for realtor, Tiffany, with an anonymous email to her business account where the sender describes what he'd like to do to her in vivid detail.

Then she meets him at a viewing—Henry 'H' Carter, owner of Club S, where patrons bid for the stage. Soon the email is being lived out in the flesh. But after H asks her if she'd ever consider an extra male in the equation, she leaves.

Tiffany begins dating neighbor Brandon. However, she can't get thoughts of H and threesomes out of her mind, especially after she visits the club and sees one up close. Is Brandon going to be enough for her, or is fate about to offer her another option...

ONE-CLICK NOW

HATE YOU
TRACY LORRAINE

I loved to hate her...

She made it so easy. She was everything I wasn't—everything I didn't want to be.

A reminder that from the moment I was born, I was the outcast. The rebel.

I went against everything that was expected of me and created a life on my terms. I built my own empire, carved out my own destiny.

Then she shows up at my tattoo studio, representing everything I tried to escape. She expects to just fit in... like she ever could.

Tabitha Anderson.

The posh girl trying to prove everyone wrong... that she can be something else—someone else. She hates me because she knows I'm right.

Or so I think. Turns out this isn't the first time we've met, and our hate has history. *We* have history.

I might not have remembered, but I damn sure won't forget now. Won't forget how her smile is always directed at everyone but me.

If everything changes and she proves she does fit in, will it still be hate I'm feeling or something else entirely?

And if I'm wrong, then she's right where she belongs... with me.

ONE-CLICK NOW

28595529R00194